HIGHLANDER'S HEART

Called by a Highlander Book Three

MARIAH STONE

.

Stone
Publishing

GET A FREE MARIAH STONE BOOK!

Join Mariah's mailing list to be the first to know of new releases, free books, special prices, and other author giveaways.

freehistoricalromancebooks.com

ALSO BY MARIAH STONE

MARIAH'S TIME TRAVEL ROMANCE SERIES

- Called by a Highlander
- Called by a Viking
- Called by a Pirate
- Fated

MARIAH'S REGENCY ROMANCE SERIES

- Dukes and Secrets

VIEW ALL OF MARIAH'S BOOKS IN READING ORDER

Scan the QR code for the complete list of Mariah's ebooks, paperbacks, and audiobooks in reading order.

Goodbyes are only for those who love with their eyes. Because for those who love with heart and soul there is no such thing as separation.

— Rumi

PROLOGUE

Baghdad, Abbasid Caliphate, 1307

"Hey, Scot. Scot, wake up."

Ian opened his eyes and lifted his head, ignoring the ache in his old wounds. Moonlight fell on the dirt-packed floor through tiny vertical windows up by the ceiling. It was warm, even at night. Around him, other slaves wheezed peacefully on the benches by the walls. The air smelled of unwashed bodies, dry dirt, and the orange tree that grew outside the windows. Even after eleven years here, Ian missed the fresh air of the Highlands.

Abaeze, the slave from Africa, whose bench stood right next to Ian's, raised his head, his eyeballs glowing white in the darkness.

"Yes?" Ian whispered back. "What is it?"

They spoke Arabic, the common language here. Learning it when he'd arrived had been the difference between staying alive and dying.

Abaeze glanced around, sat up, then slithered soundlessly to

Ian, quick and efficient. A slender man even taller than Ian, he was as dark as the night, his hair a black cloud.

Abaeze crouched next to Ian's bench. "Abaeze hear a thing," he whispered, his accent thick. Since Abaeze had only arrived recently, his Arabic was limited, but he could get his point across. "You be careful today. You watch you."

A bad feeling settled in Ian's stomach. "For what? Something during the fight?"

The man nodded. "Abaeze sleep and see death. You watch you."

Fear gripped Ian's throat in its icy hand. With that final message, Abaeze left Ian and settled back on his bench. Soon, he wheezed rhythmically.

Ian lay on his back and stared at the lime-cured white ceiling.

Death.

Would it be so bad, to let it finally take him? What hope did he have with a life like this? He'd never see the Highlands or his family again.

He always asked this question before a fight. His opponent and he needed to kill the other to live, to continue giving their masters the bloody satisfaction of power. The entertainment. The rush of a bet.

And on and on.

Every fight he'd won since he'd been here meant he'd taken a life. Ian had lost count of how many he'd killed. He'd become famous. The red-haired unbreakable beast of the caliph—the Red Death, they called him. Or simply, the Scot. Because the caliph valued him as a rare find—no other Scotsman had been captured.

Thank God.

He'd fought Germans, Spanish, Indians, Turks, English, Africans, and many, many Arabs. It didn't matter what skin color they had, what language they spoke, if they had a family back home, mayhap children and a wife. They all fell from Ian's hand.

Because he wanted to live.

But maybe Abaeze had seen the time for him to welcome his own death. Was he ready?

Ian asked himself that question repeatedly during the sleepless night and again in the morning. The sun shone into the room, and slaves brought food. The men were let out into the inner yard to clean and sweep. He was still thinking about it during the midday meal.

Other slaves were afraid of him. Abaeze, being relatively new, was Ian's only friend. He'd had friends here before. They all were dead now.

The fights were always in the afternoon and towards the evening, when the sun had already started to set, to avoid the main heat. As always, Ian and the others were given armor first, then led into a windowless chamber full of weapons—scimitars, spears, and shields. There were two doors: one led to the courtyard where the caliph held the fights, the other—back into the small wing of the palace meant for slaves.

"You watch you," Abaeze repeated, taking a sword.

"You watch you, too," Ian said. "Thank you for the warning, friend."

The door to the courtyard opened, bright light blinding Ian in the darkness. They waited to see who'd be called first. But instead, many feet pounded against the dusty ground outside. Guards who stood lined along the walls shoved the first of the men standing closer to the courtyard door, yelling for everyone to get out.

Abaeze and Ian exchanged glances. "Looks like we fight many against many," Ian said. "I will have your back."

"And Abaeze fights for Scot."

They shook hands. Then the crowd pushed them forward, and they were out in the daylight. Bloodthirsty shouts and cries filled the air. Warriors beat their weapons against their shields. There weren't many spectators for these things, just the caliph and his rich, important subjects and their invited guests. They all sat up on the second-floor balconies—away from the warriors, away from the danger of slaves turning against their masters.

But the yard, which normally held only two fighters, swarmed with slaves. They stood in two groups, beating swords and spears against their shields, ready to launch at one another, just like in a battle.

This would be quick and bloody and deadly.

They set off and the audience bellowed.

Shields and swords clashed. Spears flew and pierced live flesh. Blood sprayed and bones cracked. Taken lives disappeared in swirling clouds of dust.

A dark-skinned giant launched at Ian with a hammer. Ian raised his shield, which met the man's blade with bone-crushing power. He stabbed, and Ian jumped back. His opponent's sword slashed empty air next to Ian's abdomen. Ian stabbed from under his shield and struck right below the man's chin, sinking the blade into his head.

The next blow came from behind, someone's sword scratching against Ian's armor. He whirled to see a quick, slender Arab. Ian fought him, but more came from all sides. They all must have decided to finish him. Someone slashed his shoulder, pain burning him. Another went for his neck, but Ian ducked. A third attacked from the left side, and Ian barely managed to hit him with his shield. He fought for a while, losing strength, being chased back. As soon as he fought one, two more appeared.

Abaeze managed to rescue him once, but soon he had to fight his own battle.

Death looked into Ian's eyes and invited him to come along.

Maybe it was for the better. He deserved death. God knew, he'd taken enough lives. But his body kept fighting, kept clinging to life.

And then everything changed.

Screams rang all around—from behind the walls of caliph's palace, from inside it. Everywhere. Giant rocks began falling on the buildings. Arrows flew and hit the ground and the men.

Ian's enemies stopped fighting him, ducking under their shields, running for their lives. The caliph and his guests disappeared inside the building.

"Abaeze! Abaeze!" Ian cried, looking around.

Men lay dead, crushed under the rocks, blood soaking dry dirt. There were men Ian had been sharing a room with. Black, white, brown bodies with gashes and wounds lay around the courtyard.

Something shielded the sun, and a shadow was cast over Ian. He glanced up, seeing a rock fly right at him.

This was it. The great, bloody death.

Out of the corner of his eye, he saw Abaeze leap towards him. They flew to the side, the rock hitting the place where Ian had just stood. Dirt and gravel showered down on them.

"Thank you," Ian mumbled.

They stood up. The buildings around them were crumbled, corners destroyed. People screamed in pain, some crushed under the rocks, some suffering spear and scimitar wounds. Rocks continued falling from the sky, no doubt shot by distant catapults. Then the arrows flew. Masters, guards, servants, and slaves were scattered on the ground, wounded or dead.

An arrow swooshed past Ian, and relief flooded him at the near miss. Then someone yelped. He turned and froze as an icy wave of horror washed through him.

Abaeze sprawled in the dirt, the arrow protruding from his chest.

"No!" Ian fell to his knees by his friend's side.

Abaeze gurgled blood and reached out for Ian's hand.

"You watch you," Abaeze murmured.

His eyes locked with Ian's, desperation in them.

"No." Tears burned Ian's eyes.

"I am finally free," Abaeze said. "Go, Scot. Go."

His eyes stilled, and Ian knew then that his friend would never be a slave again. He pulled him to his chest and hugged him.

Then he saw that the gates were still open. No guards. None alive, anyway. Another rock flew at him, and he rolled onto his side.

"I'll watch me," he whispered. "Thank you, my friend."

He rose to his feet and hurried towards the gates. Mayhap, the dreams of green-and-brown Highlands wouldn't be just dreams, after all.

Mayhap, he'd finally get a chance to go home.

But if he made it through the dangers on the way, would his clan take him back once they knew what kind of man he'd become?

CHAPTER 1

Inverlochy Castle, Scotland, July 2020

KATE ANDERSON STOOD IN FRONT OF THE RUINS OF AN ancient castle. This was the farthest she'd ever been from home, from New Jersey. Her whole life, she'd wanted to get away, and now that it happened, she wished her sister, Mandy, and her nephew, Jax, were with her.

Instead, by her side stood Logan Robertson, the man who would define her restaurant's and her family's future.

Kate's heart pounded. She tapped her palm against her hip to relieve the nervousness building up within her. She should just relax and enjoy the private excursion he'd taken her on. It wasn't like one wrong word from her would make him kick her off his chef training program.

The day was warm and lush with greenery. The air smelled of grass, wildflowers, and a barely noticeable whiff of river water. Cars whirred by somewhere in the distance from time to time.

"This is my favorite place in the neighborhood." Logan brushed his hand through his dyed blond hair. Funny. He'd appeared naturally blond on TV. "If only those walls could talk, aye?"

After three days of training in the TV studio, Kate was finally somewhat used to talking to an international star like she would to a regular human being. He was as charming and as pleasant to talk to as he seemed in his shows, especially with his soft Scottish burr.

"Oh yes." Kate didn't even have to look up that much—turned out he was only an inch taller than her. And from close-up, his forehead was too smooth to be natural, and the skin around his eyes was frozen. Did he get Botox treatments? "The walls would probably say 'thank God these people don't roast boars every day.'"

Logan laughed and shook his index finger at her playfully. "You're a funny lass. Keep that up when we film. People will love you. They will queue up at your restaurant to get a spot."

He'd given Kate a couple of looks that she thought might be flirtatious over the past couple of days. He always laughed at her jokes, which weren't as good as they were nervous. But she'd told herself she was reading too much into it.

"Hopefully they'll come for my food, not for my jokes," she said. "I'm okay with the first, but I can barely keep up with the second."

Logan shook his head once. "When I'm finished with your restaurant, you won't need to settle. You'll be famous, lass." He winked. "Shall I show you around?"

They walked through the ruined gate under the ancient walls into a green, sunlit courtyard with four crumbled towers that rose at its corners. Even looking at them, Kate still couldn't believe she was actually in Scotland.

"I'm so fortunate you picked Deli Luck," she said, her insides vibrating with excitement. "When my sister, Mandy, told me we won—"

"Your sister?" Logan glanced at her with curiosity. "They called your sister first?"

"Yes. She applied. I had no idea. If she'd told me from the beginning, I'd have locked her up in the storage room until she changed her mind. Never in my life would I have thought you'd pick us."

Kate was surprised Mandy had taken such initiative, considering the depression she struggled with sometimes kept her from getting out of bed at all.

He crossed his arms over his chest. "Aye, Deli Luck isn't exactly what we normally go for. It's too American. Too traditional. And that's where, I think, the problem lies. You're too safe with your burgers, spareribs, and fries, aren't you?"

Kate's neck burned and she looked down. She picked at a rock with the point of her boot and kicked it as they walked. Those had been her exact thoughts right from the beginning. It was her clients who had forced her to abandon the creative pot roast with a Thai coconut sauce, quinoa burgers, and spareribs masala. She'd wanted to combine unusual with traditional since the beginning. As the owner and the chef, she was ashamed to admit to him that the community had pressured her into changing her menu.

And now, bankruptcy threatened Deli Luck in about a month if nothing changed.

"That's what the market in Cape Haute, New Jersey, wants, Logan," she said. "They don't want anything different."

"True. But what you have is too familiar. That's why you're barely makin' ends meet. You need to find that fine line between old and new. That's where I come in. Dinna worry, lass. You're a family restaurant, right? Tell me how you started."

Kate put her hands in the pockets of her jeans, something she always did when she felt uncomfortable. Talking about her past hurt. She'd never even discussed their childhood with Mandy, let alone reveal things to a stranger.

"I never knew my dad. My mom died when I was eighteen.

To support my sister and myself, I worked in local restaurants. I cooked my whole life, and people love my food. After a couple of years, some locals loaned me money to open my own place. In a way, it's a community restaurant. I haven't repaid them all yet. That's where the biggest chunk of income is going to. Your show helping us with renovations and the whole new design of the menu and billboards and all that—that's going to be exactly what we need to save the restaurant from the bankruptcy."

Bankruptcy would mean losing the whole building—including the apartment where Kate, Mandy, and Jax lived. The three of them would be on the streets. Mandy wouldn't have her antidepressant meds and the therapy she needed to stay afloat. They wouldn't be able to send Jax to a decent school and make sure he got medical care if he needed it.

This show was Kate's last hope.

"A community-funded restaurant." He narrowed his eyes and studied her with curiosity. "Great story. But don't you feel like they own you?"

Kate chuckled, her cheeks heating up. "Of course they own me. Hence burgers, ribs, and fries."

He tilted his head back and laughed. "This is goin' to be a fabulous show. When they find out what I have planned—it's goin' to be a Boston Tea Party in New Jersey."

Kate hugged herself. She wanted to stand out, to be liked because she was different. Instead, she'd spent her whole life trying desperately to be liked because she fit in.

And look where it had gotten her.

She chuckled. "As long as Deli Luck turns out to be a new independent country afterward..."

He tilted his head back and laughed. When he looked at her again, his eyes became intense, taking her in as though he were peeling off her clothes. Kate chided herself for imagining a star like Logan would be interested in *her*.

"You're a bonnie lass, aren't you?" he mumbled and took a step towards her.

Kate tensed, physically making herself stay in place and not back away from him. She opened her mouth to make a joke out of it when his phone rang.

"I need to take this, lass." He lifted the phone to his ear and walked to the other side of the courtyard towards the big gate.

Kate exhaled, the tension in her muscles softening. She wasn't used to being treated kindly. And he had no reason to be nice to her other than to make a great show.

She looked around. What a beautiful, mysterious place this was. She agreed with Logan—if those stones could talk, they'd tell many stories. What would cooking in a medieval kitchen be like? What dishes did they make in the past? What spices and kitchenware did they use? Her stomach growled with hunger. Thank goodness she always packed food with her—the aftereffect of her childhood.

Kate was a hoarder. Well, not literally. Mainly, she hoarded food in her stomach and fat on her thighs. She never knew if she really was hungry or if she just felt panicked to stock up while food was available. Something she'd done ever since she was little.

Kate opened her bag and fetched one of the BLTs she'd made for her and for Logan. It was made with fresh ciabatta bread, crispy bacon she'd picked up at the local market yesterday, cherry tomatoes, and a touch of the truffle mayonnaise she'd bought in an artisan food shop in Edinburgh. Instead of simple lettuce, she used romaine salad. She settled on a rock baking in the sun, near a tower with a railing around the entrance. Turning her face to the sun, she closed her eyes and imagined sitting here many years ago when the castle wasn't ruined yet, back when it swarmed with people.

What sounds would there be? Would it smell like grilled meat? Like mud? Like horses?

"The wee bread ye have, lass, it looks delicious," a female voice said next to her.

Kate opened her eyes. A pretty young woman in a long dark-green cape with a hood stood by her side. Her hair was red and shone in the sun. She stared at Kate's sandwich as though it were the food of the gods.

"Uhm," Kate said. "Do you want some?"

Kate cooked food for a living, but she didn't remember anyone staring like that at what she prepared.

"Oh, may I?" the woman said. "Ye dinna mind?"

She had a much stronger Scottish accent than Logan, stronger than anyone Kate had ever met, in fact. Her voice sounded beautiful, melodic, almost like a song.

Kate held the sandwich out to her. "Help yourself. You aren't allergic to truffles, are you?"

The woman took the sandwich with both hands, a smile full of wonder on her lips. "What are truffles?"

"It's a delicious mushroom, well, a fungus..."

"Oh, I'm sure I'm nae allergic."

"There's also mayonnaise, so eggs and—"

But the woman had already bitten into the sandwich and was chewing. She rolled her eyes in ecstasy and was producing sounds that could only be associated with very good sex.

"Oh, sky and stars," she mumbled through a full mouth, "and kelpies unhinged, 'tis the best food I've ever had!"

Kate studied her, amazed. She had to give it to the woman, Kate rarely saw people so openly enjoying their food. She couldn't remember the last time anyone had given her a compliment like that. Was it because she was bored cooking the same stuff over and over? Or because she was actually a bad cook?

The woman continued her feast of one. Kate would have taken Logan's sandwich, but if he came back now, she wouldn't have anything for him. So better she was hungry than offend him and make him change his mind about the TV show. Deli Luck really needed this.

"Are ye a cook?" The woman sat down right on the grass and continued chewing.

"Yes. From the United States."

"Oh. Aye. I've met someone from there. Verra nice people. What is yer name, dearie?" She bit into the sandwich again.

"Kate. Yours?"

"Sìneag."

She said it as *Sheen-ak.*

"What a pretty name. I've never heard it before."

"That's because 'tis ancient. Like me." She giggled. "Is that man yer husband?"

"What? No! I just met him three days ago. He's a colleague, I suppose. Or a boss, rather."

"A boss? Like a master?"

Kate laughed. "Yes, in a very innocent way, I suppose he is."

Sìneag stared at Logan who was still speaking on the phone, his back turned to them.

"He likes ye, I can tell."

"I'm sure you're wrong. It's *Logan Robertson.*"

"Ye're saying it like I should ken who that is?"

"You don't?"

"Nae, I dinna. But I can tell ye this. He isna the man for ye."

"Well, duh. I could have told you that. He'd never go for someone like me."

"Someone like ye? He'd be lucky to have someone like ye, lass. But dinna fash, I ken a man just for ye."

Kate shook her head. "Thanks, but I'm not looking for a relationship. I need to get my restaurant back on its feet, and Logan is helping me. I have no room for men in my life. All spaces are occupied by my sister and my nephew back in Jersey."

"Oh, ye poor lass. I understand. Sìneag will help. Look, it was the year 1308 when Ian Cambel, a warrior long thought dead came back home. He'd been imprisoned and enslaved in Baghdad for several years with nae hope for freedom. But luck turned around and gave him a second chance. He became free and returned to the Highlands. But he was broken. Slavery made him believe he doesna deserve to be happy, to be loved. He was forever lonely after that."

Kate nodded, thoughtful. The story resonated somewhere deep in her heart. "Yes, some things break us and we can never heal."

"Aye, well. If two broken souls can connect through time, that might bring them both happiness, aye?"

"Through time?" Kate laughed. "That's romantic, I suppose. And impossible."

Sìneag pushed the last bite of the sandwich into her mouth and moaned. "What's impossible is that I havna tried this bread before. And traveling through the river of time is verra real. In fact, there's the rock this castle has been built upon, which is saturated with the powerful magic of time travel." She gestured behind them, where the ruined tower stood. "Mmmmm. Thank ye kindly for this treat, lass. Ye truly made my day."

The tower looked absolutely normal, just a crumbled circular wall of old stones and mortar. And it was supposed to contain a time traveling rock? What a weird story.

"And what about that rock..." She turned to Sìneag.

The woman had disappeared. Kate stood and looked around. Birds chirped, and wind rustled the leaves of the tree growing outside the perimeter of the castle.

"Sìneag?" she said.

The courtyard was empty except for her and Logan, who'd finished talking and was walking towards her, his eyes fixed on her. He looked like a blond wolf who'd seen a chicken and were about to devour it. Men normally weren't interested in her, and this attention made her throat clench. She rubbed her forearm, and took a step back. What was he going to do? Either devour her or kiss her?

Her life consisted of spending long hours at Deli Luck, then returning to the apartment above the restaurant and collapsing on her bed. Mandy and Jax would be long asleep by then. The next morning, Kate would wake up early and go down to make sure coffee was ready, pancake batter was prepared, and eggs and bacon were available for the early birds. Usually her first customers were Hank, their police officer, and George and Luke, who were both mechanics at the local tire factory and had the first shift.

There was no space in her life for romance. She'd only dated three guys in the last ten years, and she'd had sex just a handful of times. She had no idea how to flirt, or what to expect from a guy who was coming at her with wolf eyes like Logan was.

No. She was about to make a huge fool of herself or, even worse, of him. She needed to do something. To distract him. To reject him without rejecting him.

She backed away, hands shaking, until her back touched something hard. Metal rattled, and she turned around. The grating across the opening to the tower. The tower that had allegedly been built upon a time traveling rock. Yes, she could talk about that.

She went behind the grating and walked towards the gaping entrance to the tower.

"Do you want to take a tour of the dungeons, darlin'?" Logan pushed past the grating.

A crooked smiled played on his lips.

"Uhm, no." Kate smiled nervously. "I just had an interesting talk with someone who I assume can only be a local."

Logan came and stood by her.

Too close.

So close, it felt like he was looming over her, and she could smell his expensive body wash. Kate blinked rapidly and rubbed the back of her neck.

"Oh, aye?" he said. "What did they tell you, beautiful?"

He raised one hand and stroked her cheek. Kate suppressed an urge to jerk back. Instead, she laughed nervously and took a couple of steps to stand next to the tower entrance. Cold air wafted up at her. It smelled like wet earth, dust, and rocks. It was so dark, the only thing she could see was the round stairs that began a step or two below the entrance. The ruined steps led down—and she had no idea how anyone could even attempt to walk on them because they were crumbled. Some of the steps were almost worn away. Others looked like flat-lying rocks.

"She said somewhere there is a rock that allows people to cross time. Have you heard a local legend like that?"

Logan chuckled softly. His eyes half closed, he walked to stand by her side, with the same proximity as before.

"Nae," he said. "Havna heard anything like that. But sounds intriguing. Would you like to travel in time, darlin'?"

He reached out and cupped her jaw. Only with an effort did Kate manage to stand in place and not run from him.

"Dinna be afraid, darlin'," he said. "You're a bonnie woman despite your weight. You're just like your restaurant. Need a makeover to make you really shine."

A sharp pain pierced Kate's stomach. So he did think she was fat and ugly. Like most people. What did he want from her?

He leaned down, clearly for a kiss.

And the thought of him on her, thinking her a charity case, thinking she needed a makeover and he was the magician who'd turn an ugly toad like her into a princess, it was too much. Bile rose in her throat. She pushed him off, but he was much sturdier than he looked. She staggered and stepped back.

Her foot caught on something and she lost her balance.

The next thing she knew, she was flying backward into the cold, ancient darkness that smelled like a tomb.

She screamed, but the air was kicked out of her lungs as she tumbled down the stairs. She hit her head, her ribs, her arms and legs. When she finally lay still, her head felt as if it would burst from pain.

"Kate! Kate!" someone cried as though from another world.

As though from behind a grave.

She didn't know why, but she needed to get away from the voice.

Her head was killing her. It felt like a giant hammer pounded against an anvil, and the anvil were her head. The blackness surrounding her spun. She moaned and tried to stand. Nausea rose in her stomach, and she vomited violently.

"Kate!" someone called louder and closer.

No. She had no idea who called or who Kate was, but she knew she couldn't let him get closer. She wanted to get away from both the name and the caller.

She crawled away from the voice, away from the vomit, away from the pain. But her head was about to burst like a ripe watermelon.

"Kate!"

There might have been some light behind her, she wasn't sure because spots flashed before her eyes. She crawled ahead, having no idea where she went. She felt like a blind person in a malfunctioning helicopter, spinning out of control. She sank deeper into a reeling darkness and flashing spots and pain.

After a while, she saw something glowing blue and brown in the distance. A rock. She slowly advanced there—somewhere in the back of her psyche she knew that rock was hope. A direction. An answer.

She came to the rock and pushed herself up, wincing from the glow of a circle of blue waves with a straight brown line through it. Was there just one, or were there two or three of them? Her vision floated, doubling and tripling everything around her.

There was a handprint in the stone. As if someone reached out to her. As if someone wanted to help her. She needed help to get out of this dark, mindless world.

She put her hand in the handprint. It was icy cold and wet against her palm. Surprisingly, it calmed her, soothed her.

Help, she thought. *Hope. I need hope.* And she knew that it was on the other side of that handprint.

A vibration went through the rock, and a buzz went through her.

It was as though the rock lost all hardness and became something else. Like water, then thin air. She fell. Right through the stone. Tumbling down...

The impact of hitting something hard again slammed through her, and everything went black.

CHAPTER 2

Inverlochy Castle, July 1308

"WHO GOES THERE?" CRIED THE GUARD FROM THE WALL.

Ian patted the neck of his horse. A bridge across the moat separated him from his clan. They were all there, behind those walls, or at least, that's what his cousin Marjorie had told him when he'd gone to Glenkeld, their current clan seat.

Even his father was supposed to be in Inverlochy.

And no one knew that Ian was still alive.

"Ian Cambel," he cried.

He hadn't called himself that in years. The words sounded strange. They sent a tremor through his core, but his voice didn't give it out. It was as though he were an imposter about to take the place of a dead man.

Where was the feeling of coming home to freedom and peace? Where was the man he'd thought he would become once he returned to the Highlands?

Instead, he was ashamed of who he was. And dreaded his family's reaction to seeing what had become of him.

He was a monster who'd killed people for the pleasure of his masters. What would his father say if he learned that?

The guard turned to another man on the wall, and they talked briefly.

"Prove ye're a Cambel," one of them said.

Ian closed his eyes briefly and lowered his head. "I havna anything with me that can prove that. I've been on the road for months. If ye call my father or my uncles Dougal or Neil... Or any of my cousins—Craig, Owen, or Domhnall—they'll recognize me."

"Aye," the guard said and left the wall.

Ian patted his black horse, Thor, again—more to calm himself than the horse. Ian had named him after a warrior in Baghdad. The man had been from Norway, a giant with shoulders as broad as a ship. When the slave masters had tried to force Thor to kill a wounded Ian, the man had refused and was put to death for it. That was a lesson Ian had never forgotten.

So much had changed in the clan, he'd learned in Glenkeld. Craig had marrit. Lena, Craig's sister and Ian's cousin, was marrit as well, and Domhnall. Owen had grown up a strong warrior. Ian's father was weak and stayed in bed in Inverlochy, which was the reason Ian had come here rather than returning to his family home. Life had gone on without him. Everyone had evolved and grown.

He was the only one who'd taken a step back in development, lowered himself to a primitive state of survival. Life against death.

"Who calls himself Ian?" someone cried.

Ian looked up at the wall, but there was just that guard.

"Come closer!" the voice said.

Someone stood at the gates, which were open just enough to let a man through.

Ian's heart thumped in his ears. Was it Craig? He jumped

down from the horse and walked towards the gate, the ground shifting under his feet. Yes—dark hair, tall, broad frame...

He crossed the bridge without looking away from the man.

"Craig," Ian mumbled.

His cousin's eyes widened, his face blank. "'Tis truly ye?" Craig said.

Ian stood before him now, studying the face he'd known since he was born—older now, not a young lad anymore but a man, a proud warrior. A commander and a leader.

Would Craig understand?

Craig gathered Ian in a bone-crushing hug. Ian's eyes burned from tears. Craig slapped him on the back.

"Come in, come in." Craig ushered him through the gate. "How are ye alive? God, I canna believe my eyes. I ken ye're standing before me and 'tis ye, but I canna... All these years we believed ye were dead. We had a funeral. There wasna a day I didna think of ye, wishing ye were with us."

They went through the gates into the courtyard, where life was in full swing. Servants carried buckets with water from the well, baskets with food, hay, and wood. Chickens squawked and pecked at the grass. Warriors walked somewhere, played cards in the corner, talked. It smelled like stew, and oatcakes, and woodsmoke. Ian let a servant take the horse to the stables.

"What happened to ye?" Craig said while they walked through the yard towards what was probably the great hall.

"The MacDougalls sold me to a slave ship bound to the caliphate," Ian said. "I was a slave there."

Craig's features grew livid. "They what?" He stopped, his fists clenched till his knuckles whitened. "They told us ye were dead... Had I have kent, I'd have come for ye."

"I ken, Craig."

They entered the great hall, which was full of people eating the midday meal. Craig led Ian to the table in the corner by the fireplace.

Ian's gut squeezed as he saw his uncle, his cousins Owen and Domhnall, and other warriors of the clan he recognized.

Craig called for the clan's attention, and everyone turned their heads.

"Look who came back," Craig said. "Look who we thought was dead thanks to the damned MacDougalls. I swear, they'll pay for this, too."

Uncle Dougal was the first one to recognize him.

"Ian?" Dougal said.

Ian nodded, his chest tearing from a mixture of emotions he'd never thought he'd feel again—elation, relief, and even a hint of peace.

Dougal stood up from the bench, then the rest of them. Ian was hugged, hands clapped him on the shoulders, on the back. Noise rose around the table—questions. What happened? Where had he been? Was he healthy?

With his stomach clenching, he answered the same thing he had told Craig. Slavery ship. Baghdad. Slave.

How had he come back?

There was a battle and he managed to escape.

That it hadn't been a battle but a massacre, and that he hadn't seen any other survivors from the palace, he couldn't bring himself to tell them.

Because he didn't deserve to be alive, he thought, a cold emptiness spreading in him. He was a monster. A killer.

And that, he couldn't tell them, either.

"Where's Father?" he said finally, silencing everyone.

Their faces turned somber, and a bad feeling coiled in the pit of his stomach.

"Uncle Duncan is unwell," Craig said. "He's resting now. 'Tis good ye came."

"What's wrong with him?" Ian asked. He hadn't been able to get much information about his father's condition in Loch Awe.

"We dinna ken. But Ellair, the healer, doesna think he has much time left."

An iron knot formed in Ian's throat. "Take me to him," he said.

"Aye," Craig said.

They walked out of the great hall and went to the biggest tower on the northwestern corner. Up the circular stairs, they came to the second floor and stopped at the entrance to the lord's bedchamber. Craig explained it now belonged to Kenneth MacKenzie, who was appointed castle constable because Craig had resigned from the position. He wanted to be with his pregnant wife as much as possible. She was back in the safety of their home.

Kenneth MacKenzie had given his chamber to the dying man to make him comfortable.

"I will leave ye with him," Craig said on the stairs. "Have yer time with him. I'll be in the great hall."

"Aye."

Ian opened the door and stiffened, noting a small, thin figure lying in bed under the blankets. As long as he could remember, his father had always been a powerful man and a warrior. But his whole life, he'd grieved the loss of Ian's mother who had died in childbirth. Ian always wondered if Father had secretly blamed him for the death of the love of his life. They'd never been close. Ian had been raised in his uncle Dougal's house together with Craig, Marjorie, Domhnall, Lena, and Owen. They were more than cousins, more like real brothers and sisters to Ian.

With his father, there had always been this distance. And now, it seemed, they were almost out of time to change that.

On weak legs, Ian approached the bed, studying his father with wide eyes. His hair was now yellowish-white, not light red like before. Deep wrinkles covered his pale, weathered skin. Dark circles around his eyes were hollow. He looked more like a skeleton than the man Ian used to know.

Sharp pain shot through his gut, and his whole body went numb as he sank to his knees by the bed. He swallowed to relieve the aching tension in his throat.

"Father," he said.

The man opened his eyes. The whites were yellow, the brown irises dull gray. He glanced around, then focused on Ian. He frowned a little.

"Ye look like my son," he croaked. "Who are ye?"

Ian felt his throat work, his jaws tightening. "'Tis I, Ian. I came back."

"Ye came back for me? Will ye take me to my Mariot with ye?"

Ian shook his head. "I'm alive, Father. I wasna dead. I could finally come home."

Duncan exhaled softly and closed his eyes. "I thought ye were dead. I thought I'd lost everyone I loved."

Ian's heart weighed heavily. He'd never heard those words from his father. If Duncan knew what Ian had done to survive, he'd never repeat them again.

"What happened to ye, Ian?" Duncan asked.

Ian repeated the same story, and Father's eyes closed mournfully.

"A slave... They didna break yer spirit, though, eh, lad?"

Ian looked down, swallowing the pain and humiliation.

"Nae," he said. "I wouldna be yer son if they did."

Duncan lifted his hand from under the blanket. Ian squeezed it. It was the hand of an old man—bony and covered with age spots.

"I'm glad to see ye before I go, my boy," Duncan said. "Ye must take the estate now. Live there. My sword is yers now."

Ian bowed his head. "Aye, Father."

"Now go, Ian. I must rest."

"Aye."

Ian let his father's hand go and watched as he closed his eyes and breathed evenly but weakly. He was probably asleep. Ian couldn't move. He stood there taking every small part of his father into his memory.

Then he left the room, silently. He needed something strong

to dull the ache that was spreading in his body like a wound. Coming here, seeing everyone he loved and grew up with, and seeing his father dying was too much. He needed to get drunk and forget.

He asked someone in the courtyard where he could find some ale or *uisge*, and they pointed at the eastern tower.

"Cellar," the man said.

Ian went down the curved stairs to the underground storeroom. There, he looked through the casks and barrels and chests, and finally saw what he was looking for—a small barrel with an unmistakable scent.

And then he heard something. Like a moan or a quiet call. He looked around. There was a door. The moan repeated, and he could swear it came from the other side. Putting the barrel down, he took a torch from the wall and opened the door.

It was pitch-dark. The room was more like a cave going into the distance. The moan came from somewhere farther in, he thought. He continued into the room, shining the torchlight around the space.

Someone lay on the floor.

A woman.

She was blond, her shoulder-length hair spilled over the ground. She was dressed like a man, wearing tight blue trousers and a light-blue tunic that fell past her hips. She had a bag over her shoulder. She looked unconscious, although she moved her head a little and then moaned again, frowning but not opening her eyes. She wasn't a thin woman but curvy and long-legged. And pretty. So pretty he froze to marvel at her features for a moment.

Ian sank to his knees by her side. She had a small bleeding wound at her hairline, a large bruise at the top of her forehead, and scratches all over her face and hands. Her clothes were partially torn.

Ian cupped her face gently. "Lass!" he called. "Lass! Can ye hear me?"

"Mmmm." She turned her head.

"All right. I need to get ye out of here."

He put the torch on the ground so he wouldn't burn her and took her into his arms, then grabbed the torch, careful not to bring it too close.

He needed to find the steward and see if she was one of the maids, because there weren't many women in the castle, and all were maids. But first, he needed to get her help.

Now, with a purpose to aid someone, the ache in his chest diminished. He only hoped the lass was all right.

CHAPTER 3

She opened her eyes and immediately regretted it. Pain split her skull in two. She moaned and touched her head. Bandage.

She lay in a room with round stone walls. A simple slit window let daylight in. She turned and saw that there were more beds, some chests by the walls. Everything looked massive, heavy...

The word "medieval" came to mind.

Where was she? How had she gotten here?

She half rose on her elbows, wincing at the aches in every part of her body. Her head spun and she thought she was going to be sick, but thankfully it passed.

Did she remember anything at all?

Her head was empty. A gauzy curtain seemed to hang around her mind. She knew something was behind that curtain, but she couldn't seem to reach out and pull it away.

Someone entered—a man. A tall, gorgeous red-haired man in a knee-length tunic belted over narrow, woolen pants, a sword on his back. His hair was cropped short, and he had intense but kind brown eyes. His skin was tanned, as though he spent hours outdoors.

Something about him was familiar; although, she was sure she'd never seen him in her life.

"May I come in, lass?" he asked.

The sound of his voice was deep, melodic, and very pleasant. She nodded. He came in and sat on the bed next to hers.

"How are ye feeling?" he said.

"I—my head is killing me. Do you know what happened to me?"

"Nae. I found ye in the cellar, looks like ye've taken a fall."

"Oh." She touched her head again and winced. "Yeah, that sounds about right. I don't remember…"

"Ye dinna remember how ye fell?"

"No. Actually, I don't remember anything."

He frowned, studying her. "Even yer name?"

She shook her head, a cold wave of fear sweeping over her. She didn't even know who she was.

"Come, lass. What's yer name?"

"Kate," she said.

Her hand shot to her mouth.

"Oh! I remembered my name! Kate. Yes, I think it's Kate."

"Kate," he murmured. "A bonnie name. My name is Ian."

"And you don't know me at all?" she asked.

He rubbed the back of his neck. "Nae, lass, I'm sorry."

"Someone must know me."

"Do ye work here as a maid? None of the maids recognized ye, but mayhap ye were new and the steward just hired ye."

She shrugged. Something about it didn't sound right to her.

"I'll go and fetch him. He will ken ye."

Before she could think, she grabbed his big, warm, callused hand. He turned to her.

"Don't go," she said.

Something about him brought comfort and security to her. He was so tall and muscular, and he looked kind. He'd found her. He was trying to help her. He was the only person she knew.

He frowned. "Ye want me to stay?"

"Yes, please. I'm...I'm afraid to be left alone. I don't know who I am, and I'm not even sure if this is a dream..."

"I'll be right back, lass. I'll just find the steward. I promise I'm nae going anywhere."

He squeezed her hand reassuringly, and she felt better.

"Okay," she said.

He winced. "What?"

"Yes, okay."

"Strange word. Mayhap, people began speaking new words while I was away."

She smiled and leaned back in her pillows.

Soon, Ian was back with a man in his forties with a big beer belly. The man was bald and looked like he was in a hurry to be somewhere and Ian was wasting his precious time.

"Who are ye?" said the man, leaning over her as though she were a strange animal at the zoo.

Kate sat up, feeling vulnerable, and wanting to protect herself. "My name is Kate. I'm not sure how I got here. Do you know me?"

"Nae. Never seen ye in my life. Where did ye find her?" he asked Ian.

"In the eastern tower. In the underground chamber."

The man's face straightened. "Underground? Where the food and drink provisions are?"

"Well, not in that chamber, in the one beyond the door."

The man narrowed his eyes at Kate. "I have never seen ye. Why were ye there?"

"I don't know!" Kate said.

"Where are yer things?"

"She had a bag, a small bag."

Ian picked up a small, over-the-shoulder purse.

"Give it to me," the man, who must be the steward, said.

Ian didn't move, his eyes locked with Kate's. "Nae," he said. "I'll check it myself."

Ian opened the purse on the bed, then rummaged through it.

There wasn't much space in it, but he produced a plastic bag with a sandwich. A bottle of water. Napkins.

The men stared at them as though they were the devil's things.

"What is that material?" the steward asked.

Ian unwrapped the plastic bag and removed the sandwich. "Dinna ken. But this is bread, some salt pork, and some grass, I think. Or mayhap cabbage. And something else—something red... A berry?"

"Ye're a thief!" cried the steward. "Ye were stealing, weren't ye?"

Kate sat straight up despite the headache that was killing her.

"No! I never— I don't know what I was doing there, but it was definitely not stealing!"

"If she says she isna a thief, she isna a thief," Ian said.

He sniffed the sandwich. "This smells delicious, lass. Did ye make this?"

"I don't remember."

"Then what proof do ye have for not being a thief?" the steward insisted.

"I don't!" Kate cried. "I don't have any proof at all. I don't even know who I am."

"Ye canna just blame her for what she hasna done," Ian said. "Look at her. She canna even walk. Let her be, let her heal, and mayhap she'll remember something. Or mayhap, someone will recognize her."

The steward crossed his arms over his chest and gave a nod, although unwillingly. He turned and walked out of the room.

"Dinna fash yerself, lass," Ian said. "Ye will remember something. And in the meanwhile, I will try this. It smells too good."

He bit into the sandwich, chewed, and his expression changed to one of pure bliss.

"Heaven and hell, lass. Did ye make this?"

"I don't know!"

"This is delicious. Mmm. Do ye want some?"

"No, I couldn't even if I tried. I'm still nauseated."

"Mayhap ye're a cook?"

She shrugged, watching blankly as he continued devouring the sandwich.

"Aye, good. I will let ye rest. Ye need to recover. I will be back soon to check on ye. Aye?"

She nodded. "Thanks, Ian."

Her head pounded, and she felt like all the energy and life were sucked out of her. She turned onto her side, huddled deeper into the blanket, and watched Ian leave. She began sinking into the deep, dark waters of sleep, but the fear still lingered. Who was she? Why did the things in her purse seem strange to them?

And what if once she remembered all that, she wished she hadn't?

CHAPTER 4

Ian's head hung between his shoulders as he sat over the cup of uisge. He felt heavy, as though all his body parts were sacks filled with rocks. His mind was hazy from the alcohol. He felt numb in his chest and light in his head, and that was exactly what he needed.

Not to think about his dying father. Not to think about his terrible past. And not to think about what confusion his arrival must have caused in his family. And then that strange, bonnie lass who didn't know who she was... He felt for her.

And he didn't want to feel for anyone.

"I havna had a drop to drink since before that battle with the MacDougalls," he told Owen who sat by his side in the great hall and must have been as drunk as Ian was.

"Oh, aye?" Owen said.

Ian looked up and chuckled. "Aye. What do ye suppose, they throw feasts for slaves in the caliphate? The masters barely drink themselves."

Owen raised his cup. "To drinking! And to yer return."

They smashed the cups together. Ian threw back his drink, the liquid burning his throat and leaving a trace of fire as it slid down into his stomach.

Owen gave Ian a careful, probing glance. "What did ye do there exactly?"

It was as though he'd thrown a bucket of snow over Ian. He tensed, all light-headedness gone. He rolled his shoulders, his foot bouncing under the table. He stopped it, but the need to release the unease itched in him. He rubbed the back of his neck.

The dusty, square courtyard he'd seen countless times was in essence a large coffin. Swords flashing before him, his victims' screams as they were dying—their eyes always held surprise, then anger, and then finally acceptance. The memories pressed in on him from all sides, threatening to crush him like an ant.

He sucked in the air, released it, then took another deep breath and another. The cup was empty, and he poured some more uisge and threw it down his throat.

Only when his stomach burned, his mind clouded, and he could breathe easier, did he say, "What did I do? What slaves do."

Owen watched him with a concerned frown. Ian had to give it to Owen, he was smart enough not to press for more information. He simply nodded and poured himself another drink.

"I canna imagine how hard it was for ye."

Ian nodded. "That's one word for it."

"How did ye escape?"

The memories of crushed bodies under the rocks, of arrows piercing flesh burned his psyche. Then Abaeze. The friend who had saved his life...and taken his death.

"Someone attacked the palace. Destroyed it. Killed everyone. I was verra, verra lucky."

And he didn't deserve that luck.

"It wasna yer fault, brother," Owen said softly. "That ye were lucky. I can see 'tis torturing ye."

Ian stared into his cup, his back as hard as a tree. "Ye dinna ken, brother."

"I ken ye didna deserve to be sold to slavery. I ken ye were unlucky to be on that ship. I ken I'd have come for ye had I kent."

Ian nodded. "Aye. I'd have come for ye, too. For every single one of ye. No one deserves *that*."

They kept silent for a moment.

"How did ye come home? How did ye find the way?"

Ian chuckled. "'Twas easy to get out of the ruined palace with all the guards dead or on the run. Nae so easy to make it through the city in armor. I stole clothes, food, coins, horses. I fought my way through sometimes. Bought my fare on the ship from Constantinople. Then kept northwest. Stayed in Munich for a month or so, earning my wage by mending armor and weapons. Took care of horses in Cologne. Then took a final ship to Dover. Getting through England was more difficult than the whole rest of the journey. I kent they hated Scotsmen but this..."

"Aye. 'Tis war."

"Hm. I kept away from big roads and from towns and villages. 'Twas only when I inhaled the fresh air of the Highlands, I realized I'd made it."

"Ye mean, the freshness of sheep shite?"

They cackled. Owen hadn't lost his lightness through the years. But then his face got serious.

"On the morrow, Craig goes to Falnaird, his estate, to be with Amy. I go with him for a while, until Bruce needs me. He took the Highlands last year, little by little. The English aren't a threat nae more, it seems. The old King Edward died, and his son, Edward II isna as interested in Bruce as in the troubles in his own court."

But that couldn't be all. Ian was far too experienced of a warrior to think the war was over for Bruce. "What of the remaining enemies in Scotland?"

"We fought the rest of the Comyns in the west, so his major threat to the throne is gone. Now he chases after the last Comyns in the northeast to make sure no one opposes him again. The English may resume their attack at any time. The MacDougalls are still a threat, also."

Ian clenched his fists at the mention of the name. "I hope he crushes them."

"Aye." Owen's mouth curved in a grimace. "And I will be there when he does."

They exchanged a look, bound by bitter experience. The MacDougalls had done enough to hurt the Cambel clan. Kidnapping and raping Marjorie. Selling Ian into slavery. Killing their grandfather. Owen had plenty of his own reasons to want payback with them.

"For now, Bruce doesna need us as the battles are over for a moment," Owen continued, "but Uncle Neil, who's with the king, may send a message calling us to join the army. Will ye come with us if he does?"

Ian sighed. "Nae. I took enough lives. I canna take more. All I want is peace. And I pray that God forgives me for what I did. Although I dinna think he will."

"And what if the war knocks at yer door?"

"I hope that it doesna."

The evening ended quickly after, as Owen got distracted by a pretty servant girl, and Ian continued to drink until he forgot everything. He thought someone might have helped him off the bench and laid him in the corner, covering him in furs and blankets.

Then he passed out.

HE SAT BY HIS FATHER'S BED EVERY DAY. MOST OF THE TIME, Father slept. They talked a little, but it was clear Father was losing his mind. He kept asking Ian why he reminded him of his son, and Ian repeated the same story.

Three days later, Duncan was lucid enough to ask to be

propped up in the pillows. His eyes were brighter than before, and he seemed to be able to focus.

"My boy," Father said. "Give me my sword."

Ian stood to get his father's sword, which lay on the chest of clothes. He gave the claymore to his father, who held it with one hand. Father caught Ian's hand and squeezed it, fixing his eye on Ian's.

"I will die holding my sword and my son's hand."

Ian's eyes burned, and a chill ran through his body.

"Father—" he began, but Duncan interrupted him.

"Listen. I will tell yer mother what a great son she gave me. Ye take this sword after I'm dead and give it to yer son when yer time comes. Go back to Dundail and make it great again. Be well, Ian."

Father's hand weakened in Ian's grasp. His eyes lost focus, and he looked somewhere Ian couldn't see. His body went limp and still, his breast no longer rising and falling.

Ian sat for a while, barely breathing, watching for any twitch, any movement. Any sign.

Nothing.

"Goodbye, Father," Ian whispered.

His head dizzy, his heart skipping beats, his stomach turning in pain, he rose, kissed his father's still warm forehead, and closed his eyelids.

"I will take ye home and bury ye in Dundail, next to my mother. And then I will stay there and live in peace and wait until 'tis my turn."

But deep inside, he knew there would never be peace for him —not while nightmares haunted him and guilt the size of a boulder hung around his neck.

CHAPTER 5

K ate needed to find Ian. He hadn't visited her for the last three days, and something about that brought sadness. Sadness and fear. What if something had happened to him?

Her head still ached, as well as her arms, legs, and her left side. But after three days in bed, she couldn't lie in one place anymore.

The questions about who she was and where she was from were torturing her. Something about the castle, about the clothing everyone wore, about everything around her didn't ring true. She felt like she didn't belong here.

She'd asked the maids—whose room she shared—what year it was, where she was, and what was going on, but they seemed to be frightened by her questions and avoided her, claiming they had work to do or were too tired.

When she'd first arrived, the healer, Ellair—a stout man in his fifties—had dressed her head wound, stitched it, and given her a bitter drink that numbed the pain for a short while. Since then, the maids had brought her food and water and taken out her chamber pot. She felt bad that complete strangers took care of her. Though they didn't feel comfortable around her, one of them, Aisling, had been kind enough to give Kate one of her older dresses.

Kate had inspected her clothes and her purse for any clues. Inside her purse was a water bottle with a label—Highland Source. She also read that it was bottled in Inverness and was good till November 5, 2025. That didn't make any sense to her. Although the bottle was the one thing that looked out of place in this setting, it was the only item that felt right and familiar to her.

There was also a pack of tissues. A set of keys. A wallet. Inside, she found some paper money and a credit card in the name of Katherine Anderson, valid till 2024. Was she Katherine Anderson? Probably. She knew it was called a credit card, but she had no idea what to do with it. The money was in American dollars and UK pounds. The years printed on the bills didn't make any sense, either. No ID. No pictures of herself or her family.

Nothing.

All this had been more confusing than clarifying, and her head pounded again. Someone had begun screaming in her mind. She'd put the purse aside and tried to take calming, cleansing breaths. Finally, the screaming had stopped, exhaustion had taken over, and she'd slept.

The next day, she'd attempted to look through her clothes. The blue top had a label on it—H&M. The jeans were H&M, too. Made in Thailand, they said.

Made in Thailand? Wasn't she in Scotland?

Washing Instructions: Normal cycle. No bleaching.

Kate shook her head trying to recall anything, make sense of what any of that meant.

Nothing.

The pockets of the pants were empty. Her white shoes had even less information on them. While the clothes looked new, the sneakers looked well worn and had turned gray on the sides.

When all the maids had been out, she'd inspected the final thing she could derive any clues from.

Her body.

She'd stripped naked and sat on the bed, looking at everything. She wasn't a thin woman—there were rolls of fat on her belly, her breasts were full, her thighs were round, her ass was enormous. Was she beautiful? She had no idea.

Was she like this because she enjoyed eating? Because she didn't move a lot? Or simply because that was who she was?

The questions had made her headache return.

She was blond everywhere. There was a light mole on the right side of her belly, almost horseshoe shaped. Her fingernails and toenails were clipped short, and there was some dirt underneath her fingernails and scrapes on her hands. She looked clean otherwise, although she still would've loved a shower. Her hair fell to her shoulder blades. She wished she could see her face, but there were no mirrors.

Again, nothing.

Kate had beaten her hands against the bed in frustration. Then she'd put on her borrowed dress, fallen back into the bed, and cried. Was she really a thief? What was she doing in a place where no one recognized her? Had she been kidnapped, maybe? But why? And wouldn't the person who'd kidnapped her have showed themselves by now?

Enough! She forced herself to her feet, determined to find the one person who made her feel safe in this place.

Leaving the room, she gingerly made her way down the stairs to the courtyard. She inhaled the sunny air of the castle, the scent a mixture of freshly baked bread, woodsmoke, horses, and wet earth. There was something flowery there, too. Around the courtyard, people were busy carrying baskets with vegetables, heavy sacks, firewood. They stopped and talked to one another. Men with swords and bows strode between the towers and the gates, and she could see some of the archers up on the walls. In one corner of the courtyard, men trained at sword-fighting.

She stopped a man carrying firewood.

"Excuse me, do you know where I can find Ian?"

"Ian?" he said. "Is he a warrior? Warriors are usually on the walls or in the great hall, eating and drinking."

"Where's the great hall?"

He pointed at a separate timber building next to the biggest tower.

"Thanks," she said and went in the direction he'd pointed.

But she didn't need to go into the hall, because Ian sat on a bench in front. He was pale, forlorn. It broke her heart to see a physically powerful man like him look so lost, his eyes raw.

She came to him. "Ian," she said, and he blinked, focusing on her.

"Lass," he said. "What is it?"

"Are you all right?" she asked.

"I...I need to make arrangements...find Kenneth MacKenzie. My father just died..."

He said it as though he still couldn't quite believe it. Kate sighed. Something about it felt familiar, as though she, too, knew the experience.

"I'm so sorry, Ian," she said, covering his hand with hers and squeezing it reassuringly.

He blinked again and nodded, then got to his feet. Ian walked towards the southern tower, and Kate followed him.

"I need to arrange a cart for his body," Ian said. "I'm taking him home."

"Oh. You're leaving?"

"Aye."

She nodded, hiding her disappointment. She didn't know him at all, but it felt like she'd be losing the only person who'd cared about her in her life.

The life that she remembered, at least.

"Where are you going?" she asked.

"Home. Loch Awe. 'Tis south from here."

"What is it like?"

He sighed. "I...I havna been there in many years. I dinna ken how 'tis now, but I remember the vast loch, the mountains, the woods. Our house. Crazy Mary would cook haggis..."

She stopped abruptly as an image flashed in her mind—roasted leg of lamb in an ovenproof glass dish, glazed in honey—mustard sauce, with a filling of oatmeal mixed with minced vegetables and herbs. With the image came a feeling of home, of comfort, of security—and anxiety. Questions, doubts, the feeling of inadequacy...

"What is it?" Ian said, stopping as well. "Are ye well?"

"I remembered something," she said, turning the image in her mind again and again, holding on to it as though it were a lifeline. "Crazy Mary—it's the lamb roast, isn't it?"

"Nae. Crazy Mary is our cook."

"Oh...it's not the name of the roast?"

"Crazy Mary makes a great lamb roast. Aye."

"Yes! I know that lamb roast. When I think of it, it brings me a feeling of home. Maybe Crazy Mary knows where my home is. Or even someone in my family?"

Ian studied her. "I've kent Crazy Mary my whole life. I havna met ye before."

The steward walked out of the tower they had been heading towards. He threw an angry, suspicious glance at Kate, making her shrink inwardly, but she only raised her chin. Whatever the man thought, she knew for sure she wasn't a thief. He greeted Ian, then turned to her.

"What are ye still doing here?" the man asked Kate. "I dinna want thieves in the castle."

"I am not a thief, mister," she said.

"Ahearn, ye dinna ken she's done what ye're accusing her of. The woman needs help. Clearly, she's been unwell."

"I had thought ye left." He glared at her.

"It's the first day I can stand on my feet."

"Good," he said. "That means ye can go. Ye must leave the

castle immediately. Ye're nae welcome here. Go home, wherever ye came from."

Unwanted tears prickled Kate's eyes. She was now being chased away from the only place she knew. Where would she even go? She had no idea where "home" was.

"Ahearn, dinna ye think 'tis a little too harsh on the lass?" Ian said.

"These days, ye never ken who to trust, lord. I've been careful with people my whole life. And it's served me well. I must insist ye leave the castle today, lass. We have given ye enough kindness already. I canna risk thieves, spies, or whores."

"Ahearn!" Ian cried. "She's none of those things."

"My apologies, lord. Mayhap nae. Still. No one kens the lass. I canna take risks. Nae in the war."

Ian shook his head and looked at Kate.

His warm brown eyes under thick, ginger-tinged eyelashes seemed like the only familiar and dear thing she knew in this world.

"If she must leave, she's coming with me."

"What?" Ahearn and Kate said at the same time.

Ian swallowed hard, the hazy, pained gaze returning. "My father just passed, Ahearn. I was looking for Kenneth to make arrangements, borrow a cart for his body. I want to leave on the morrow and take him with me."

The man clasped his hands together. "I am so sorry to hear yer father passed, lord. But the lass?"

Ian didn't break eye contact with her, and that sad yet warm gaze gave her hope. Gave her strength. Told her she wasn't alone.

"Ye said Crazy Mary might be yer family. Come with me to find out. I'd verra much like to hire ye as a cook. Clearly, ye're good at it—the bread that ye made was delicious, and the lamb roast was the thing ye remembered. Crazy Mary may be yer family or ken something about ye. And I need someone else to help in the kitchen. Will ye come?"

Ahearn shook his head. "Lord, please, this isna wise—"

"Will ye?" Ian interrupted him, still looking at Kate.

A smile spread on her face, her vision blurry from tears of gratitude. "Yes," she breathed.

"Are ye strong enough to travel?" he asked.

"I think so," she said. "And thank you, Ian."

Being treated kindly was something she had never been used to. She had no idea how she knew that, but this felt strange. It felt unfamiliar. It felt like a rare, precious gift.

"Thank you," she whispered again.

Ian nodded and pursed his lips, perhaps his way of returning her smile. He turned to Ahearn. "Is Kenneth in the tower?"

"Aye. He was talking to the marshal."

"All right. I'll go find him and ask about the cart. Lass, dinna go anywhere without me. We're leaving today."

As he walked away, Kate couldn't help but admire his tall, muscular frame and confident stride. She wondered if he was married and hurried to his wife back home, or if he was in love with someone. Was *she* married? She had no idea.

But looking at Ian, something in her hoped she wasn't, and that he wasn't, either...

CHAPTER 6

Ian took a deep breath, filling his lungs with pure Highland air. Would it be able to finally clear his head of nightmares? The cart shook and wobbled on the road between the mountains of Glen Coe to his left and right. A waterfall streamed down the mountain slope nearby, its rushing cascade like sweet music. The sense of peace he'd been longing for during his years in Baghdad was almost within his grasp. Once he saw the calm waters of Loch Awe at Dundail again, he hoped that peace would finally come.

But would it really?

"It's so beautiful here," Kate said. "How long till Dundail?"

He looked at her bonnie profile. She sat by his side in the cart. The bruise at the top of her forehead had purpled. "Two or three days, I think," Ian said. "We might need to sleep in the woods but there's one village in between, I will try to get us lodging there."

"Okay," she said.

He chuckled. He'd started to get used to the strange way she spoke. In the caliphate, he'd heard countless accents and foreign speech from other slaves, so that wasn't new. But he'd never heard anyone who sounded like her.

"Did ye remember anything?" he asked.

She shook her head. "Nope. I've looked through my things, but they only confuse me and make my head hurt."

"Aye. Ye dinna have much with ye."

"I've banged my head for the last three days trying to figure out who I am and what I'm doing here. I hope Crazy Mary has the answer, or some clue."

"Aye."

"Thank you again, for helping me. I feel like you're the only friend I have."

Friend...

The sounds of the thundering rocks and screams, the images of torn flesh, of blood saturating dry dirt, of Abaeze's dying eyes... Abaeze was the last person who'd called him friend. Abaeze, who had saved Ian's life and then died in his arms.

"I'm nae yer friend, lass," he murmured, his voice a rasping whisper.

He looked straight ahead, at the black horse, at the reins in his hands, at the rocky, rubbly road. But out of the corner of his eye, he saw her tense and stiffen.

He didn't care. He *shouldn't* care if he hurt her feelings. He couldn't have another friend. Abaeze had known what it was like —he'd also killed to live.

Here, no one would understand. If Kate found out what he had done to survive... He couldn't stand the look of revulsion on her face, especially after she'd just called him friend.

And if others ever learned the truth, he'd be condemned as a monster—rightfully so. And he'd be fooling himself if he thought he'd have a normal life here. He'd see his clan for the yearly gatherings. He'd help them if they needed him. But other than that...

His way forward was the way of loneliness.

"Sorry," she said. "I didn't mean to overstep... I don't want to be a burden, though. I'll work very hard in your kitchen."

He nodded without turning his head to her. Her voice rang with hurt, but it was better to keep his distance from her and not give her any hopes. He felt for her, and he'd do everything he could to help her find out who she was and where she belonged. But that was it.

The rest of the day passed in silence. They slept in the woods and resumed their journey the next day.

As they set out, the road was a little rainy but otherwise easy.

Ian was glad they would arrive at the village of Rossely by the evening. The lass was still weak, and it would do her good to sleep in a warm bed at an inn, and not outside on the cold ground.

It was in the afternoon that he sensed something was wrong. Mayhap it was his warrior's instinct, or mayhap he'd caught the slightest movement—either way, he'd learned to heed the sensation during years of fighting.

He stopped the horse and listened. Wind rustled the leaves. Birds chirped.

And then there was a movement farther down the road and a man stood there, waiting. Ian eyed him warily. His sword was in the back of the cart with his father.

But he wouldn't kill another anyway, he reminded himself.

He needed this to go peacefully.

"Say nae word," he said to Kate.

He shook the reins and the horse resumed marching towards the man. He was tall and dressed like a knight, in heavy armor, a sword, and a shield.

"Identify yourself," the man said in Anglo-Saxon.

English.

"Ian Cambel, with my wife."

Kate looked at him sharply.

"Taking my father's body home."

The knight smirked. "Home? Everything from here to North Argyll belongs to King Edward of England."

Ian gritted his teeth.

Aye, war. People who wanted to kill were everywhere.

"I dinna want trouble, lord," Ian said, addressing the man

more politely than he deserved. Ian hated himself for cajolery. But if he wanted this to go peacefully, he needed the man to let them through.

"Home is Dundail, on Loch Awe. I return there to bury my father." He looked behind himself at the cart.

"Your home *for now*," the knight said.

He walked around the cart and looked into it. There lay Duncan's body, wrapped in cloth, the sword underneath his father's side. Ian's hands clenched into fists, his breath accelerated, and something began buzzing in his ears.

Just touch him with one finger...

But the man nodded and returned to stand by the horse. Thank God he had a decency to respect the dead and not look under the body.

He gave Ian a long look. "Come through, you bloody Scot. But know this. Your true king, Edward—not the spawn who calls himself King of Scots—will come and claim what's his. *Your home*. And if you dare to take up arms against him, your father won't be the only corpse your pretty wife has to bury."

The man leered at Kate. A low growl was born in Ian's gut, and he had to physically stop himself from letting it out. Something must have shown in his expression because fear flashed through the man's face, and his hand shot to the sword at his belt. Black and red filled Ian's vision, the urge to act gnawing at his bones.

A soft, warm hand covered his and squeezed it.

"Let's go, Ian," Kate said firmly.

Almost startled, he glanced at her. Her face looked calm, but in her eyes, he saw worry and even fear. That steadied him, made him take a deep breath that cleaned the fury away and brought him back.

"Aye," he said without taking his eyes off her.

Then, when he felt sober enough, he turned to the Englishman.

"Yer king will never be my king."

Then he lashed the reins, and the horse walked.

"What does it all mean?" Kate said when they were some distance away.

"It means, everything from here till pretty much home is infested with the enemy."

The enemy in a war he didn't want to fight.

"The English are the enemy?" Kate said.

"Aye."

"But why?"

"Because King Edward doesna want to acknowledge our rightful king, King Robert the Bruce. I didna ken all of that until I traveled through England. The English Crown pushed John Comyn as the next claimant to the Scottish throne. I was told Bruce opposed it and proclaimed himself king. Many clans supported him, although some, including the MacDougalls, still oppose him. The English king became furious. He sent an army to stop Bruce and succeeded. Bruce had to run with the few supporters that he had, including my uncle Neil. My clan has always been loyal to him and always will be. My uncle organized a galley to take Bruce to hide in the Western Isles. The Bruce came back last year, slowly winning his way through the Highlands and gaining more supporters. Now the course of the war has changed in his favor."

They were arriving at the village of Rossely now. Low stone houses with thatched roofs stood close to one another. The streets were wet with mud after the rain. Chickens and geese walked around, goats bleated, people carried buckets of water from the well or baskets with food and firewood. Somewhere, a blacksmith hammered at the anvil, *tong, tong, tong.* The air smelled of woodsmoke and freshly baked bread. Ian promised himself he'd never take the sights, sounds, and smells of home for granted again.

Among the villagers, there were knights in expensive armor bearing the red standard with yellow lions. The English.

Their speech hurt Ian's ears. He glanced around—everywhere were people who might come for his home.

"I dinna think we should stay here tonight," he said. "I'm sorry, lass, but we'll have to sleep outside again."

"That's okay," she said. "Don't worry about me."

"Are ye strong enough?"

"Yes, I'm fine." She pressed out a smile.

"All right."

As they drove through without stopping, Ian felt heavy gazes on him like hot coals. His hand twitched to reach out for his sword. He felt vulnerable and naked without a weapon.

He'd promised himself he wouldn't kill again.

But how could he keep that promise when the enemy was at his doorstep, he didn't know.

CHAPTER 7

T*wo days later...*

KATE'S HEART SQUEEZED ALMOST TO THE POINT OF PAIN WHEN she saw Dundail.

It lay on the coast of the loch in a green valley, secluded and backed by the mountains from the east. The almost still surface of the water reflected the square three-story tower of the mansion with an adjacent stone building. On the shore, a couple of small boats had been pulled up next to the path that led to the main entrance. Gentle grassy hills dotted with white sheep surrounded the grand manor. Smoke rose from the chimney.

It looked like a home. Not hers. But someone's.

Ian's.

She glanced at him, sitting by her side, driving the cart. His profile was stern, his eyes fixed on the house in front of them. There was something behind this mask. He looked as though he'd been tortured and was trying to hide the pain.

"'Tis nae where I grew up," he said. "I was raised in Innis

Chonnel before the MacDougalls seized it after they killed my grandfather, Sir Colin."

"So you haven't been here often?"

He shook his head, still looking at the house.

"Nae. Nae often. Mayhap once per year to see my father."

"Do you think of it as your home, then?" she asked.

He looked at her as though she'd said a foul word.

"Sorry, I just mean…I'm trying to understand, and maybe to learn what a home is for someone. Since I have no idea what mine is."

His gaze warmed. He looked like a handsome, tired, lost warrior. "I dinna ken if 'tis my home. I suppose I'll try to make it mine."

She smiled. "This looks like a wonderful place, Ian."

Once they arrived about half an hour later, Ian stopped Thor in front of the main building. Near it was a collection of smaller buildings: stables, a chicken coop, a cowshed, and probably a workshop and a storage house.

Ian jumped off the cart and helped Kate get down. He'd done it several times during their journey, and every time he touched her, every time his hands grasped her waist, she became a hot, melting ball of sweet tingling. He lifted her as though she weighed nothing, then put her gently on the ground. He smelled of sun and forest and something earthy and magical.

Then he'd walk away, and she'd whisper, "Thank you," standing there like a statue and watching him retreat. Somehow, the simple gestures of care and help along their journey had touched her so deeply she'd wanted to cry. But she had no idea why.

She wanted to crack her skull open and dig for those memories she couldn't find.

While Ian went inside, Kate looked around. On closer inspection, the house and the buildings looked distressed. Parts of the walls were crumbled, and the roof had holes—as did all the buildings on the property. The chickens wandered around looking almost wild. The shutters on the windows hung crooked. One of the planks of the small porch was missing.

Inside there was a great hall, similar to the one in Inverlochy but with fewer tables and benches. Everything looked as if it was decaying, and there was a faint smell of mold and mice.

How did she know what mice smelled like? A sudden flash of a kitchen with dirty yellow walls, a metal stove with gas burners, and chipped green cabinets invaded her mind. In that image, everything looked big to her. She put a chair by the stove, climbed it, switched on the gas burner and put a pan on it. She poured some oil.

She was about to make two grilled cheese sandwiches. Her mom wouldn't be home until very late, and Kate and her sister would already be asleep. She'd make another grilled cheese later for Mom and leave it for her on the table.

Kate climbed down and opened a kitchen cabinet to take out some bread. The scent of food gone bad hit her in the face. Mice feasted on the bread. She shooed them, and they scattered but left feces, urine, and dirt together with the bread crumbs.

The great hall smelled like that.

Kate held her head in her hands, although it didn't ache. The vision was so real and so normal, and yet so completely and totally foreign, she couldn't think for a moment. Her mind went blank trying to cope with it, trying to make sense of what she'd seen. Sadness and loneliness opened a hole in her chest.

And what of all the strange objects and materials in that vision? That big metal thing was a gas stove, she knew. A fridge kept food cool and worked with electricity, which also lit the light on the ceiling.

In the cabinet, there was also stuff to make the Crazy Mary, she remembered. The dish her mom had made once or twice, claiming it was a family heirloom recipe. The spices for it stood to the right, the oatmeal for the filling right next to the bread.

Kate sat down on a nearby bench, the wood cold even

through her dress. Her chest tensed, her heart convulsing. She couldn't breathe.

What was that? A vision? It felt like a memory, like it had really happened to her, but it made absolutely no sense. What she'd seen in it looked nothing like what was around her. Where had the electricity come from? The gas in the stove? The plastic and paper wrappings of the supplies? They looked similar to the things she'd found in her purse.

That was the only calming thing, the fact that she might not actually be insane. That there was some explanation for the madness in her head. But it would be best not to tell anyone about her visions, she realized, because the people around her would only think her more insane. She still needed to talk to Crazy Mary, and she had big hopes for that talk.

She should find the kitchen. The word sent a shiver through her. With her feet still weak, she stood. She had no idea where the kitchen was, but it must be somewhere on the first floor.

She found it relatively easily—it was right at the back of the tower. The room was the direct opposite of the kitchen in her vision: dark, with a big fireplace, and only a few small windows near the ceiling to let in the daylight. Torches on the rock walls illuminated the space as well. Around the lit fireplace, a starburst of black soot spread on the wall.

A massive wooden table took up the middle of the room. It was messy with peels and greens, the cutting boards dirty. Next to it, a large cauldron hung over the fire, radiating the smell of cooking vegetables and meat. A huge oven was built into the wall to the left. Pots, ladles, large spoons, and other utensils hung on the wall to the right. A large barrel of water stood next to the table.

Ian was talking to a bald man in his fifties with a bushy mustache and a dirty apron. His eyebrows snapped together, his eyes bulging, his mouth an angry curve, he held a kitchen knife in his hand like a weapon.

"Do ye think I want this?" Ian asked. "I would have kept him alive if I could. But now ye have me, yer new master. If ye dinna want me, I dinna wish to keep ye, Manning, where ye dinna want to be."

He glanced at Kate.

"Aye, in fact, I do already have a new cook." He gestured at her.

Manning turned to her with the same expression of wild fury, the knife pointed at her. He marched towards her, and Kate felt the urge to step back from him but resisted. He wouldn't stab her. And Ian wouldn't let him. She lifted her chin.

Manning came to stand right in front of her, reeking of sweat, onion, and meat on the verge of being spoiled.

"Who's the lass?" He studied her.

"My name is Kate," she said. "Ian hired me to cook."

"Did he now?" Manning said. "Did ye plan to get rid of me while ye were in Inverlochy?"

"Nae, Manning," Ian said. "I didna plan anything like that. The lass hit her head and lost her memory, but she remembered ye. Or rather, yer lamb roast."

Manning cocked his busy eyebrow and studied her from tip to toe.

"I didn't remember him, Ian. I remembered Crazy Mary."

"I am Crazy Mary," Manning said.

"Isn't Mary a woman?"

"Aye," Ian said. "Long story. Fact is, 'tis who ye came here for, lass. Crazy Mary."

"But..." She frowned, studying him, hoping for more flashes of visions or memories. But the bushy mustache and the bald head said nothing. She was seeing the man for the first time.

"I cooked your recipe, the roasted lamb. That's what it's called—Crazy Mary. I don't remember where I come from or who I am, but I remember that recipe. So I assume it's very important."

Manning narrowed his eyes. "Ye talk strangely, lass. Doesna she, lad?"

Ian raised one eyebrow. "Aye, she speaks differently. But she isna the first person I met who doesna speak like you or me. Doesna mean she should be abandoned or left without help when she needs some."

Warmth spread in Kate's stomach as he said that. *Oh, Ian...* That he had her back meant so much to her.

"Nae," Manning said slowly. "It doesna. But it means something. Something odd about her..."

He spun around and marched to the table.

"Ye want to work as a cook, lass?" he said and stabbed the cutting board with the knife. "Cook somethin'."

Kate's bravado disappeared into thin air. Cook something? What could she cook?

"The wee bread I ate from yer purse," Ian said, as though reading her thoughts.

She had no idea who had made the sandwich and what it was made of...

Wait.

Sandwich. It wasn't one of the words they seemed to use here. Maybe now that her memories—or some version of them —had come back, she would remember more.

"Okay," she said, and Manning looked confused. He probably didn't know the word "okay," either. She should stop using it. Why did she know so many words others didn't?

She came to stand next to the table. "I don't remember making that, but maybe I'll remember something else."

She ran her finger along the surface and shook her head. "But not until the kitchen is clean. I cannot cook in all these germs."

"Germs?" Ian said.

Hm. Another word they had no idea about. "Yes, you know. Bacteria. Viruses. Salmonella. Listeriosis. Food poisoning."

They watched her with blank faces, but as she said poisoning, both became alert and wary. "Mayhap she's a witch and nae a cook," Manning said. "Were ye casting a spell to poison the food?"

"Oh my God!" she cried. "I don't remember much, but I can definitely tell you I'm not a witch. All I'm talking about is cleaning the kitchen. You're not seriously working in this filth, are you, Manning?"

His face darkened and became dangerous. "'Tis a working kitchen, and I dinna have enough boys to clean it."

Kate sighed. "All right. Well, you have me. Let's clean first, and then I'll see if I can make something."

"'Tis nae to yer liking, lass, ye clean it. My food is fine whether 'tis clean or nae. Ye even heard of my lamb roast. I must be doin' somethin' right if strangers ken my cooking. Aye?"

She shook her head. "Sure. I'll clean. Can you at least point to clean water, a bucket, and something to clean with? A cloth maybe?"

He removed the apron and threw it on the floor.

"Find all that yerself. I wilna lift a finger to help someone insulting my kitchen."

CHAPTER 8

Ian helped Kate find the things she needed for cleaning and brought fresh water from the well into the water barrel.

He went out to take care of his father's body and start the arrangements for the funeral. Kate found some lye soap and vinegar, which she knew from somewhere was good for disinfecting things. After a couple of hours, the kitchen was as clean as she could make it. She'd used most of the water from the barrel.

The drain for the dirty kitchen water was a hole in the wall and she wondered where it went. She hoped not into the loch.

Her hands and lower back aching, her head spinning, she sat down on the stool to take a breath. What could she cook?

She'd looked in the cauldron before and seen that several things were boiling there wrapped in linen sachets: vegetables in one, eggs in another, and pork in the third. She'd removed them from the boiling water when she'd thought they were ready. Now turnips, eggs, and meat lay on the clean cutting board staring at her expectantly.

She looked around. Herbs hung in bunches suspended from the ceiling. Fish hung drying in the corners of the fireplace.

She went to look in the pantry. There were more eggs, and vegetables lay there already drying up and partly spoiled. Sacks of flour stood in the corners. There was also a bit of butter, cottage cheese, and milk in clay jars.

The milk was probably unpasteurized...

Pasteurized?

That was when the milk had been heated to kill the germs, she heard in the back of her mind. Again that word "germs," something that made the men think she was a witch.

She sighed.

Looking at what she had, she could make a meat pie. There was enough butter for puff pastry dough, and she'd use the boiled pork—she'd mince it and fry it with some onions and garlic and make mashed turnips with some potatoes... Oh there weren't any potatoes...or carrots for that matter. There were beans and peas, and she'd use them another time. But some mashed turnips with butter and salt would do nicely.

She had no idea how she knew that, but she knew. She got to work making the dough with some whole wheat flour, water, and butter. She minced the pork. There weren't any pans for frying and no stove, anyway, so she'd have to settle for using the meat and vegetables boiled. She found some dry parsley and cumin but no salt.

Somehow her hands knew what to do. And something inside her told her how much flour, butter, and water to use, and how to knead the dough, how much meat she'd need for the pie, and how to form it. How to chop the onion and the wild garlic.

More than that, she enjoyed the process. She loved every part of it, even peeling and the hard work of kneading. She knew instinctively how the food would taste and also how to make it better. And she loved it.

She made four pies to use all the meat available. She was sure there would be enough eaters for that many pies, and even if something was left, it would be better to have things cooked considering the lack of refrigeration.

Refrigeration...that big, clunky metal thing she'd seen in that kitchen in her mind.

She shook her head, willing the memories to fade away. She looked at the oven dubiously. How would she light it? Her hands itched to reach out for a round handle and turn it to 375 degrees Fahrenheit to preheat.

She needed someone to help her light the oven. While the pies baked, she'd make the mashed turnips. With the eggs, they'd be great tomorrow for breakfast.

Coffee...

She hadn't had coffee for what felt like ages. She missed the pungent, rich, roasted taste.

Could that be a hallucination, too? Could she have really imagined all those vivid details, the tastes, the smells? Something told her they were way too real to be just in her head. But wouldn't a crazy person think exactly that?

Was she really going insane?

No point of thinking of it now. The best thing she could do was to act. She released a long breath, stood up, and went outside. She found a teenage boy who was carrying firewood to the great hall and asked him to light the oven for her. Once he'd done so, she put the pies in there and closed the door. Then she set to peeling the boiled turnips and mashing them with butter. Then she added spices for flavor.

Soon, the pies were ready, and she took them out, inhaling the savory aroma.

THE MOUTHWATERING SMELL THAT CAME FROM THE KITCHEN made Ian stop, turn around, and enter. "Lass, if ye're going to cook something as good as this smell every day, I'm going to need to keep ye captive here."

She turned, her face lit up. She was so breathtakingly beautiful, her cheeks flushed from the heat and work, strands of blond hair framing her face, her eyes shining. It was the first time he'd seen her as happy as she was now.

"This kitchen has never smelled better," he said, and what he meant was, the cook had never looked better.

Fool. What was he doing, thinking of her like that? He'd just told himself he couldn't have feelings for the lass. He couldn't have feelings for anyone. He needed to concentrate on the estate. Clearly, his father, bless his soul, hadn't been managing it at all.

From talking to Crazy Mary and the few servants who still worked here, things were bad. And not just in the house, with the tenants, too. Of course, they didn't know the details, but those were the rumors. Both Dundail and its lord had been in decay for some time.

Uncared for.

And Ian didn't think he cared, either. He would do what he could, of course, but the last thing he wanted was to chase after the tenants and the tacksmen and collect rent.

He wanted peace. To be left alone.

His eyes fell on the four round, golden pastries which were probably the source of the divine smell.

"Are those meat pies?" he asked.

"Yes." She smiled. "You were right, I think I *am* a cook, Ian— although we'll need to judge that once we try the pies."

His stomach growled, and he realized how hungry he was.

"Let me be the judge then," he said, took the knife and then cut a piece.

It steamed, but Ian bit into it. He swore from the burning in his mouth and on his tongue but continued chewing. It melted in his mouth, the taste a divine combination of meat and soft-crunchy pastry. It was savory and a little sweet at the same time, rich in flavor and a little pungent from the garlic and onion.

"Oh, Jesu and Mary, this is delicious," he mumbled through a full mouth. "Ye are a cook, Katie. And what a cook..."

Her face changed.

"Katie?" she said.

Ian coughed, realizing he'd called her a nickname he had no right to call her. Something a husband would call a wife or a brother his sister—something intimate and loving, and not for a lord and his servant.

Something he wasn't looking for.

"Forgive me, lass," he said, shoving another piece of pie into his mouth. "I meant Kate."

But the nickname hung in the air between them, like a soft cloud.

"That's okay. I like it," she said.

She came closer and stood right next to him, leaning her hip against the table. The scent of cooking reached him, and the clean, sweet smell of her. The woman.

He hadn't had a woman since a couple of months ago. On the way here, in Germany, a willing widow living next to the black-smith he'd worked for, had taken a liking to him and took him to bed. She was the first woman he'd had since he'd been enslaved. And although his body had enjoyed it, demanding the release, it had been a soulless connection.

But Katie... Again that nickname. Kate—he corrected himself—even after knowing her for a short time, he felt in his bones there was more to her than just her beauty. She was like this pie. Pretty and ripe on the outside, and a mystery on the inside. But once one tasted, the whole world of flavor revealed itself, juicy, and fresh, and full of life.

"Thank you for giving me this opportunity, Ian," she said, looking into his eyes. Her hand lay on the table, one of her fingers almost touching his. His skin burned from wanting to take her hand and kiss it.

"I'd be a fool nae to hire the best cook in Scotland," he said. "And I'm nae fool."

And he also wasn't a saint. And he wanted this delicious, golden woman with eyes like blueberries and lips like sin.

He wrapped one arm around her waist and pulled her closer,

sealing his mouth with hers.

CHAPTER 9

His lips were surprisingly soft and warm. His whole body was as hot as the oven. He smelled like male musk and a midnight forest. When her tongue touched his, the most delicious cocktail of flavors spread in her mouth. He was delicious. Silky.

A low, sexy growl was born at the back of his throat. He gently sucked her tongue, and a velvet pleasure ran through her body. Her arms wound around his shoulders, and his hands glided up and down her back.

The whole experience was like a triple chocolate cake. Where she remembered the taste and the image from didn't matter now. She couldn't get enough of him.

As his tongue lashed against hers, teasing her and urging her to come closer, her bones liquefied, and her body sang.

He was so big, all-consuming, larger than life.

Dissolve with me, was all she could think. *Take me.*

He stopped.

Released her.

Stepped back.

She staggered and had to hold on to the table. He eyed her from under his brows, his brown eyes almost mahogany.

"I am sorry, lass," he said at the edge of his breath. "I canna. I shouldna have."

Kate blinked. The surprise from his withdrawal faded, replaced by a sense of being rejected. She'd enjoyed the kiss. She liked Ian. Clearly, he did not feel the same.

Her stomach hardened, her shoulders slumped, her chest hitched, and she stepped back.

"Thank ye for the pie," he said.

He opened his mouth as though to say something else but froze, then turned and left without another word.

Kate's gaze followed his broad back. He walked as though something heavy pressed on his shoulders.

She released a shaky breath and turned to face the table, supporting herself with both arms. Was she the heavy weight? Did he feel like he needed to take her in because she had nowhere to go?

That must be why he'd stopped the kiss. He had Manning, so he actually didn't need a second cook. He'd hired her out of pity.

She released a long breath to stop tears that threatened to fall.

Better make herself useful then. Manning clearly didn't do his job well. Maybe she was a burden now, but she could earn her keep by helping. She would finish cleaning the kitchen and then help tidy the rest of the house.

Just until she found out more about herself and could leave.

Then she'd free Ian of the burden she had become to him.

Kate set the pies aside, took a wet cloth and wiped a few crumbs off the table. Then she went outside to get another bucket of water. She noticed the cart was empty now and stood without the horse. Ian was nowhere to be seen.

Kate had just put the bucket on the hook above the well when a female voice called out, "And who would ye be, lass?"

Kate turned around. On a bench a few feet from the door sat a short, plump woman in a simple dress and apron, wiry gray hair sticking out from under her white cap. She had adorable rosy cheeks.

Kate wiped her hands. "My name is Kate. Ian hired me to cook."

The woman's eyebrows rose to the cap. "Lord hired *ye*? Oh, dearie, what about my brother?"

"Your brother?"

"Aye. Manning. The cook."

This woman was Manning's sister? Maybe *she* knew something about Kate.

"We both will be cooking. I hope Ian doesn't fire him because of me."

"Aye?" The woman looked her over suspiciously. "Mayhap so. Manning and I worked here our whole lives. My name is Cadha."

The woman stood up and walked towards Kate, wobbling on one leg a little. Stopping in front of Kate, she propped her hands on her hips.

"And where do ye come from, lass? Ye speak peculiar..."

Kate sighed. "I don't know. I lost my memory in a fall. I don't remember anything about myself, except that I'm a cook. But I did recall the lamb roast. No idea why."

"Ohhhh!" Cadha glanced her over with curiosity, then pity. "Ye poor lass. Losing all yer memory?"

"I was hoping Crazy Mary—well, Manning—would know something about me, since the name Crazy Mary was one of the first things I remembered. But he said he doesn't know me. Do you?"

Cadha cocked her brow. "Nae, lass, sorry. 'Tis the first time I see ye. But I can tell ye one thing. Ye're nae from the Highlands."

Kate looked down at her feet. It didn't surprise her—the memories that were coming back were way too different from anything she'd seen or experienced here so far. Still, the words sank in her psyche like rocks. She was no closer to understanding who she was. She was a complete stranger who couldn't even relate to people.

"Ah, dinna look so sad, lass," Cadha said. "Come on, let us get ye settled. If ye're goin' to work here, ye need somewhere to sleep. Aye?"

Kate pressed out a smile. "Aye. Well, yes. Thank you, Cadha."

"Follow me."

They went into the house again and climbed the circular stairs of the tower. Cadha told Kate that on the first floor was the lord's hall and a chamber, on the second were three bedrooms, and on the third was the biggest bedroom of all—the lord's bedchamber—and another small chamber. The stairs continued up from the third floor, and that was where Cadha led Kate.

"Maids sleep in the garret," Cadha explained through a strained breath. "We dinna have any currently. I do all the house-keeping, but as ye can see, I'm nae enough. Cooks used to sleep in the kitchen, but the old lord, God rest his soul, was kind enough to allow Manning and me to live in what used to be a larder. We're nae young chickens nae more."

She finally climbed into the attic and stood, panting, before a small door. Kate joined her, breathing heavily as well.

"I used to sleep here, too, with the maids, when we had any. Now 'tis for ye. A luxury, havin' a room all to yerself."

She opened the door into a room with a low ceiling, one side of which slanted down at a steep angle. There was only one small window on the opposite wall, and the shutters were closed. It smelled like dust and mice. Kate could see five beds in total.

"Sorry, dearie, 'tis nae tidy. No one has been living here since our Ian was gone. That was when the old lord started to decline." She sighed heavily, her face sad. "Everything changed that year. 'Twas as though the lord didna ken what to live for any longer. And didna want to. Stopped caring about the rent collection. About the household. What he ate. What he drank. Stayed indoors. He'd already been grieving his whole life after his wife died. But after Ian... All his lands became like him. Lost and uncared for."

Kate listened with an aching heart. She knew Ian had been away and had been assumed dead, but she hadn't given much thought to what it had meant for his family. Seeing this great house in such a condition of desolation said it all. Her hands itched to clean it and make it better.

"I'll help you with cleaning and tidying whenever I can. I like to be useful."

Cadha reached out and squeezed her elbow. "Well, aren't ye a dearie! Thank ye, lass. And dinna fash, 'tis only us four ye'll be cooking for—the lord, ye, Manning, and me. Mayhap the lord will have occasional guests. I take care of the chickens and the cows. There's a groom and a shepherd who come from the village. So 'tis just us."

She sighed again, then quickly narrowed her eyes.

"Do ye think ye're marrit? Have any bairns?"

The earlier kiss with Ian consumed Kate's mind, the heat of his body, the soft and delicious feel of his lips against hers. God, what if she were married? Kate blushed. She had no way of knowing, but something within her told her she was not.

"I don't think so."

"Aye. Good," Cadha said with a satisfied smile.

But why it was good, she didn't explain.

CHAPTER 10

Ian stared at Kate's meat pie in front of him. It was just him and the pie in the dusty great hall. Cadha had served him his dinner.

Not Kate.

He supposed it was Cadha's task, after all, as the house-keeper, not a cook's. But he wanted to see Kate.

He couldn't put the kiss from earlier today out of his mind. Her warmth, her softness, the luscious taste of her, the feel of her body—pliable and strong at the same time...

But there was more. She was a mystery. A beautiful, broken mystery.

And he knew what broken was.

Ian took the pie and bit into it, closing his eyes to shut out the devastating loneliness of the dirty, empty great hall. The stone walls pressed in on him.

He remembered last time he'd been here. His father had held a gathering of his clansmen, tenants, tacksmen, and friends. It was after they'd freed Marjorie and Ian had returned home with the clansmen who'd participated in the battle. There were the heraldic sigils of the Cambel clan on the walls, the chatter, the feast to celebrate their victory. His father had been less mournful than usual. The hall had been lit with candles. A lyre played and people sang. Then men had fought, which often happened after a few cups of uisge.

Did Ian want the great hall to ring with life like that again?

No. He couldn't face his father's people, look them in the eye and have them swear an oath of allegiance to him.

Not when he didn't have any intention of fighting anymore. Not when all he wanted was to be left alone.

But whether he wanted to or not, he'd need to face the people of his lands.

Because there was still one thing he owed his father's memory.

He shoved the last piece of the pie into his mouth and was about to stand up and find Kate when he heard footsteps from the hallway.

"Kate?" he called.

The steps halted, then she walked in, and he swore the dim room became brighter.

"Yes?" she said.

She wasn't smiling. In fact, her face was tense, her eyes distant. He hated that it was probably because of how he'd stopped and withdrawn from their kiss.

"Come, sit." He gestured at the chair next to him. "Please."

She hesitated for a moment, then sat by his side.

"Everything all right?" she asked.

"Aye, aye. The pie is..." He made an awkward gesture to describe how delicious it was, but the words stuck in his throat.

Instead, he gave a nod, already hating himself for such awkwardness.

"I will need to throw a wake and a burial for my father," he said. "To honor his memory, I'm going to invite all the tenants, clansmen, and friends from his lands. They would want to say goodbye."

Kate nodded. "All right."

"Can ye cook, please, Kate?"

She seemed to straighten her back a little as he said that. "Yes, of course."

"Thank ye."

"What should I cook?"

Ian scratched his head. He'd never had to entertain guests, and he didn't remember what was usually served at wakes. "Please ask Manning, and once ye've decided, tell me what I should buy in the village or hunt for."

"Okay. And how many people?"

"I dinna ken how many will come. I think about fifty."

Her eyes widened. "Fifty? But it's just the three of us: Manning, Cadha, and me..."

"Aye." Ian massaged his forehead. "Ye're right, I'm putting too much on ye."

"No," she said and straightened her back even more. "No. Don't worry. We'll manage. I'll think of something."

He felt her eyes on him, but he didn't look back at her.

"Don't worry," she repeated. "Just concentrate on your dad's funeral. I—we'll take care of the food. You won't even notice a hiccup, I promise. I won't let you down."

He glanced at her sharply. The soft golden light of the candles Cadha had set on the table for him played on her pretty face. The mixture of resolve and uneasiness in her features choked him, scraped at old wounds. She would clearly be making a big effort, mayhap bigger than she could manage after what she'd been through.

And he didn't deserve her.

"Nae," he said. "Dinna do more than ye can, Katie."

Her features smoothed in surprise. "I can. I can." She stood up. "Everything will be ready. Everything will be great. You have enough stuff going on, Ian."

She didn't let him contradict her but walked out of the hall, leaving him alone in the deafening, dark loneliness of the empty walls.

He'd been wrong. This wasn't home. This didn't feel like home. Not without Father.

Torn between the memories of the monstrous deeds he'd done and the emptiness of what he'd thought would bring him relief, he needed to forget. To numb the desperation that tore at the ragged wound that used to be his heart.

And he knew only one way to do that.

He went into the storage room and filled his waterskin with uisge from the barrel.

That night, the numbness took him even before he went into the bedchamber that used to belong to his father and was now his. It still smelled like his father—steel and leather, the tang of wool grease, and alcohol. Before Ian fell into oblivion, he dreamed of his father scolding him.

CHAPTER 11

T*wo days later...*

"WHAT ARE YE DOING?" MANNING YELLED.

Kate studied the dead chicken hanging upside down in her hand.

"What am I doing?" she said. "Trying to pluck it."

Manning scoffed and threw the dough he'd been kneading onto the table.

"Tryin'? Have ye never done this before?"

Kate raised her eyebrows. "I have no clue."

Although this was technically true, she had a feeling she hadn't. Her hands didn't know what to do with the chicken, unlike when she'd made the pie for Ian.

Manning's face grew red, his mustache moving. "How can ye nae ken? If ye're a cook, ye must have plucked chickens."

"I—" Kate opened and closed her mouth. The thought of removing the bird's feathers made nausea rise in her gut. And Manning's growling made her hands shake.

"Ye're useless!" he yelled. "I need twelve chickens plucked and then roasted. The wake is on the morrow. Do ye think ye could do anything useful? Or are ye going to stand around opening yer mouth like a fish?"

Kate glared at him. She hated that he was right. And his words hit too close to home, in a spot that radiated a familiar pain.

"There, there ye auld fool," Cadha said as she wobbled into the kitchen. "I could hear ye yelling from the cowshed. What is the matter?"

"The matter is, the lord has hired a worthless impostor. What kinda cook doesna ken how to pluck chickens?"

Cadha propped her hands on her hips and marched up to him. She flicked him on the forehead. "The lass doesna remember who she is, ye bullhead. How would she remember how to pluck a chicken?"

Manning's eyes bulged, and his face reddened even more. Kate suppressed a smile. Cadha had her back, and that made something melt in Kate like butter on a hot croissant.

"Here." Cadha took the chicken from Kate's hands and walked to the cauldron of boiling water. "This will loosen the feathers. But dinna hold it there for too long or ye damage the skin and the meat. Aye? About the time that takes ye to drink a mug of ale."

"No idea how long that is. Thirty seconds?"

Cadha threw a confused glance at her. "Whatever a *second* is, lass. Dinna fash yerself. Ye'll ken how long. 'Tis called scalding."

She put the bird in the boiling water and held it. After a short time, what felt like half a minute to Kate, Cadha removed the steaming bird and put it in a big bowl.

Manning was back to kneading the dough. "Ye're wasting yer time, Cadha."

"Ah, dinna growl, Manning," she said.

"Do ye even ken, how to roast a chicken, lass?" Manning

asked. "Or make a *normal* pie? Nae yer strange one with too much butter."

Kate's shoulders sank, her arms as weak as noodles. He was right. She didn't know if she could roast a chicken. And just because Ian liked her pie, it didn't mean that others would. What if her pie was completely strange for them?

"I—"

"I dinna have time to busy myself with teachin' ye. We have fifty guests comin'. Cadha shouldna take trouble, either. She has the whole house to clean and her back is painin' her."

He glared at Kate and stabbed a finger at her. "Ye're a liability. Ye're a burden."

Cadha gasped and burst into an angry tirade, but Kate didn't listen anymore.

The word "burden" echoed in her mind in another voice that said the same thing.

A female voice.

Her mother's voice.

An image flashed in Kate's mind, unraveling into a movie.

She was older now, and she didn't feel good. Her throat felt as though it were being cut with razor blades, her head aching. They were in that kitchen again—yellow walls, green cabinets. It smelled like cooked beans and sausages. Her mother hid her face in her palms and shook her head. In front of Kate was a plate with steaming green beans and sausages. Mandy, Kate's sister, sat to her right. She must be five or six years old, and Kate—ten.

"Can you not cut the ends off the beans, Kate?" Mom said without looking at her. "How hard can it be?"

"I didn't know..." Kate mumbled.

"Just buy the canned beans next time." Mom looked at her, her lips pale and dark circles under her eyes. "I don't have time to teach you these things. I have to get to my shift at Lou's in ten minutes."

"Sorry, Mom." Kate shivered, her skin aching. "I don't feel so good..."

Mom shook her head and chewed the beans. "Kate, I need you to be a big girl and take care of your sister tonight, okay? Do you think I never feel sick? Every day, honey. But I stand up and go to work to put a roof over your head and those damn beans on your plate."

"But I need to do my math homework today. If I fail, I'll have to repeat the year."

Mom sighed and threw her fork on her plate, where it clattered loudly. She hid her face in her hands again. "Kate, Mommy is so sorry, but she's so tired already. I have to go before I pass out."

Mom stood up, her arms bony where they showed below the sleeves of her blouse.

Kate felt so guilty. She didn't want to add more to her mom's troubles. Mom was doing so much for them. If it weren't for Kate and Mandy, Mom wouldn't need to work three jobs. Kate would just try to cut the beans correctly. How did one do that?

She took the green bean and the knife, but shivers ran through her in painful spasms. Her hands slipped and the knife sliced her palm between her index finger and her thumb. Kate cried out in pain. Blood flowed onto the beans. Mandy cried.

Kate ran after Mom, and opened the front door, holding the wound with her other hand. "Mom!" she called, her voice shaking. "Mom!"

Mom turned without a word and stood, looking at Kate as though she expected another task to be put on her shoulders.

That was the moment Kate realized she was nothing but a liability for her mom. A vampire feeding on her blood.

A burden.

No. She needed to put her needs aside and be strong.

"What?" Mom asked.

"Nothing," she answered, clenching her hand tight so that Mom wouldn't see the blood. "Have a good evening. I'll cut the beans properly next time, promise."

"Thank you." Mom turned and walked to the car.

Kate returned to the present moment, the medieval kitchen. Her head spun and buzzed from the memory. Manning and Cadha still yelled at each other. She looked at her right hand, and there it was, between her index finger and her thumb—a thin silver scar. She ran a thumb along it.

The line was harder than the rest of her skin.

Shock covered her from head to toe in an icy wave.

What was that? The vision seemed to be a memory—but there were so many things wrong with that. The car. The electric lights. The telephone. The sausages from a plastic wrapping. The beans in a can...

None of that existed today. Chickens needed to be slaughtered and plucked. Pies were handmade and baked in a fire oven.

And yet, the scar existed. Physical proof that said her vision was a memory.

Or she was going insane, and her mind had created that scene to explain the scar and drive her completely over the edge.

The differences in technology made no sense. But her mother did. Her sister did. The scars deep inside her that she couldn't see or touch did. The scars that tortured and crippled her soul from somewhere she couldn't reach.

"Ye are indeed a *Crazy* Mary, ye auld fool," Cadha cried, waving her hands.

"Ye keep talking like that, ye wilna taste a piece of that lamb come spring."

And before Kate could take a breath, another memory flew into her mind, unwrapping...

"My grandmother taught me this," Mom said. "And I got a bonus, so I thought I'd splurge on lamb. You won't believe this. It's called *Crazy Mary*."

Kate was older now, fifteen probably, and already chubby. She'd developed the habit of hoarding, food mostly, because she never knew when or what she'd eat next.

The kitchen was rich with the scent of braised onions, garlic, and spices. Ten-year-old Mandy, her dirty hair freshly brushed, a new secondhand dress on, sat at the kitchen table decorating gingerbread men.

A tiny artificial Christmas tree stood on the table. It was the only one they had in the house.

"Crazy Mary?" Kate giggled, giddy with excitement to have Mom all to herself for today. No work. No hurrying. Just a family day. "Hear that, Mandy? Crazy Mary!"

Mandy giggled in response, too. "It doesn't sound too yummy."

"Ah, it will be." Mom scratched her chin and looked dubiously at the meat. "If I manage to remember the recipe. Kate, write it down so that you don't have the same problem in the future. I think we prepare the oatmeal-and-spice stuffing first. Then the honey-mustard glaze. We need to tenderize the chops with this." She raised a mallet. "Do you want to do it, Kate?"

"Sure!" Kate took the mallet and it sank in her hand. She was eager to show she had been everything Mom wanted her to be— not a burden. Capable of feeding them, washing the dishes, cleaning the house, doing homework with Mandy, and not getting sick. The only thing she never managed to do was her own homework, but somehow, she was getting by. She was never going to be a rocket scientist anyway.

Mandy giggled again. "Is that why it's called Crazy Mary? Because you have to beat the meat?"

Kate laughed. "You're a Crazy Mandy."

Mom echoed the laughter. "No one's crazy, girls. I have no idea why it's called that. Grandma never said. But she did say the recipe was passed down from generation to generation. I'd love to know how it started."

Back in the medieval kitchen, with the creator of the lamb roast, Kate's chest squeezed in a sweet ache of loss. That must have been the only happy memory from her childhood.

Wait... Mom had said the recipe was passed down from generation to generation. Did that mean all her memories happened in the future? When Manning, Cadha, and Ian were long gone?

And if Manning had created the recipe, was Kate related to him after all?

Kate's head spun and the floor shifted. No, no, no. That head injury must have been worse than she'd thought. She needed a breath of fresh air. The smells of scalded chicken, pies, and meat suffocated her.

"Excuse me." She wiped her hands on her apron and left the kitchen.

"See what ye did..." Cadha's words trailed off as Kate walked out of the house and then out of the yard.

Kate didn't know where she was going. Tears filled her eyes and blurred her vision. Her chest hurt and her throat clenched in a painful spasm. Eventually, she found herself on the coast of the loch, the rocky soil mixed with reeds and grass.

Someone was there. She looked up. Ian.

Shirtless, his bare back glistening with sweat in the sun, he bent over the water. His biceps bulged as he washed a piece of clothing, the muscles on his side working.

Looking at him, Kate forgot how to cry. She even forgot how to breathe.

He wrung out the tunic, his muscles playing under the soft, ginger-colored hairs on his arm, and put it next to him in the small pile of wet laundry.

Then he looked at her and frowned.

Kate wiped her eyes.

He stood and walked to her, concern on his face.

"Are ye all right, lass?"

Oh, how could she be all right when he was about to stand right in front of her, with his glorious pecs and his six-pack covered in soft red hair? A sweet ache pierced her lower belly.

"I—"

"Why are ye crying?" He gently lifted her chin up and looked into her eyes.

The concern in his gaze warmed her. In fact, he was all warm, with cute freckles on his shoulders. The sweet ache pierced Kate's heart now.

"I just remembered something about my family."

"Oh, aye? That's good. What?"

"Actually, not that good. I'm not even sure it's a real memory. Maybe just a vision or something. It's from my childhood. If it is a memory, I didn't have a very happy one, for the most part."

He chuckled bitterly. "I didna have a happy one, either."

Kate nodded and looked at the loch because the more she looked at him, the more her legs turned into goo.

"Do ye ken where ye come from?" he asked.

She shook her head. "I'm sorry, I don't. I still need to bother you a bit longer."

He scoffed. "Bother me? Ye're nae bother, Katie. Stop sayin' that."

Burden... Ye're a burden. Ye're a burden.

Her eyes prickled again from tears, and this time even Ian's shirtless torso couldn't stop them.

"Okay, well, I better get back to the kitchen," she said and hurried away from him.

He called after her, but she walked faster. She wasn't just a burden. She was a crazy burden with strange visions and no idea where she came from...and the growing feeling that she was more of a stranger here than she could ever imagine.

THE DAY PASSED IN CONTINUING PREPARATIONS FOR THE WAKE: sending messengers to different villages and farms, buying more food, talking to the village priest.

In the afternoon, Ian went to the MacFilib farm to buy some of the uisge they were famous for.

The farm lay in a small valley surrounded by forest. Ian stopped the cart near the farmhouse. Several buildings were scattered around the property, among fields of oats that surged like a golden sea in the wind. Like all healthy farms, it smelled of warm earth, manure, and growing things. Ian couldn't imagine any better smell, except mayhap the scent of Katie's golden hair. In the distance, where the fields of oats ended, sheep grazed on the steep hills. Ian heard their weak *baa*s, along with the nearer sound of someone hammering at an anvil in one of the workshops.

Ian remembered that as a lad, he'd been out collecting rent with his father and had visited this farm among others. He recalled how much he'd admired his father then, how Duncan had dealt with the tenants—friendly but showing no doubt who was lord.

Ian didn't stand a chance of being the kind of lord his father had once been.

"Neacal!" he called, stepping to the ground. "Murdina?"

The door to the workshop opened and a man in his forties in a blacksmith's apron came out. Neacal. He'd aged, but looked strong and healthy. A tall, strong but lean lad of eighteen followed him. Ian narrowed his eyes. Could it be Frangean? Ian remembered him as a boy who could barely hold a pitchfork to help his father on the farm.

"Aye?" Neacal said.

The door to the farmhouse opened as well, and a woman came out—with her, the scent of fresh bread and stew.

"What is it, Neacal?" Murdina said.

Ian's chest tightened from both sadness and joy.

"Ye probably dinna recognize me," he said. "But 'tis Ian Cambel. Yer lord's son."

Neacal's face went blank in surprise. "Ian? Our lord's son is dead."

"Nae. I was sold into slavery in Baghdad. But I made my way back."

Murdina came closer to him. "Aye, I recognize ye, lad. 'Tis Ian! Look at his red hair and his mother's eyes."

Neacal and Frangean came closer, too.

"Lord." Neacal clapped him on the shoulder. "'Tis good to see ye alive and well. Welcome back."

"Thank ye." Ian nodded. "But I come with sad news. My father died a few days ago."

Murdina gasped and shook her head mournfully. Neacal and Frangean lowered their heads.

"I am sorry to hear that, lord," Neacal said.

"Thank ye. I was with him when he passed. I brought his body home to bury him. Ye're invited to the wake and the funeral on the morrow. Please, come to Dundail."

"Of course we'll come, lord," Murdina said and squeezed his arm. "Do ye need anything?"

"Yes, I was hoping to buy yer fine uisge for the wake."

"Oh, aye," Neacal said. "This year it turned out especially well. How much do ye need?"

"Two, three casks if ye have that many."

"Frangean, come with me," Murdina said. "We'll look, lord."

"Thank ye."

Murdina and Frangean went back into the house and Neacal patted the horse's neck.

"'Tis verra good we have ye, lord—a young, strong warrior. We need ye in these times of trouble. Have ye heard of the Sassenach troops lurking around?"

Ian's back chilled, and his shoulders tensed.

"Aye. I met some on my way here."

"Ye must bury yer father, of course. But forgive me for asking, will ye protect us from them? Do ye have a plan? Because whatever ye need from the MacFilibs, we can give ye."

Ian's mouth dried. How was he going to tell him he didn't have a plan of defense, nor did he intend to raise a sword again in his life?

Frangean appeared with a cask in his hands and carried it to the cart.

"Aye, here's good. I thank ye, lad," Ian said.

"Ma found two," he said.

"Aye, I'll take them."

Frangean nodded, a gleam of adoration in his eyes, then turned and walked back into the house.

"What do ye say, lord?" Neacal insisted.

Ian stepped back and threw a glance at the horse. "I canna think of it yet, Neacal."

The man raised his hands, palms to Ian. "Aye, I understand, lord. Forgive me. 'Tis just, we're all worried, hearing what the Sassenachs do around here. Kill and rape and plunder. Burn farms. Slaughter livestock."

Ian's stomach tightened. Had he been whole, he wouldn't have hesitated. If his people needed him, he'd be there.

But he couldn't. No man would die on his sword again. He'd promised himself.

Frangean appeared with the second cask and carried it to the cart.

"How much do I owe ye, Neacal."

The man waved his hand. "Nothing, lord. We regret yer father's demise."

"Nae. Please. I insist. He'd want that."

Neacal hesitated. "Aye. Thank ye. Four shillings will be enough."

Ian laid the coins in Neacal's hand and quickly climbed onto the cart, hurrying to avoid more questions he wasn't ready to answer.

"Thank ye," Ian said. "And I'll see ye on the morrow."

Neacal waved. "God bless, lord."

Ian visited other tenants after that to invite them to the wake. Back in Dundail, the large manor still didn't feel like home. He'd picked up some of the household chores, painfully aware of how much older Cadha and Manning had become. He didn't mind cleaning and washing his own clothes, repairing the tools, and doing some work in the smithy. Actually, simple labor brought him relief. Physical work made him feel like he was getting in touch with his land, and his house, and his people.

The day of the wake, the great hall was clean. Pastries, pies, bread, and cheese stood on the tables, roasted chickens already sliced, and cooked vegetables. The room didn't smell like desolation anymore.

His father's tenants and tacksmen, the rent collectors, began coming in. The men talked and drank somberly. The wives scolded running children and chatted with one another. Most people, he didn't remember.

There were claps on the shoulders and mournful faces and murmurs of condolence. People visited the body and said their goodbyes. Then they settled at the tables with their food and drinks. The hall was no longer silent and empty. It was filled with the quiet sound of voices.

A big, stout man with a bushy beard and long black hair came up to him. "I canna express how sorry I am, lord," he said. "I am Alan Ciar, yer tacksman in Benlochy."

Ian nodded. "I thank ye."

"Yer father was a good man. He'll be sorely missed. By everyone."

"Aye."

They stood in silence for a while. Ian had an uneasy sense that the man hadn't yet said what he'd come to say.

"'Tis a sad day to say goodbye to him," Alan said. "But a joyous day to see ye alive. We all thought ye were killed by the MacDougalls. I am certain ye will be as good a lord as he was."

Ian's jaws tightened.

"Gladly will I swear my oath to ye," Alan said.

Ian's shoulders stiffened as hard as rocks. No one should swear anything to him. If they knew…

"I canna think yet of that," he said. "But I thank ye for yer loyalty."

"Aye. Glad to. And I want ye to ken. I havna been stealing from yer father like the other tacksmen."

Ian frowned and looked around the room. "Stealing?"

"Aye. I suppose ye wouldna have kent. But why do ye think yer father didna do so well in the recent years? Why do ye think yer house is in this condition? 'Tis because after yer death... I mean, disappearance, yer father became a different man. He mourned ye so much he didna pay attention to what was goin' on around him nae more. So some of his tacksmen used him and kept part of the collected rent to themselves."

He straightened his back and corrected the belt on his big stomach. "Never I. I have always been loyal and honest and always gave all the rent and taxes collected."

"Hm," Ian said.

The man's dark eyes glistened. Ian studied him. Alan didn't look away or blink. He resembled a bull about to attack.

"Ye should ask around, lord," Alan pressed. "Ye should check. And they should face consequences."

Ian nodded. "I thank ye, Alan."

He gestured at the tables inviting the man to join the others.

"One more thing, lord," Alan said. "The English have been seen around. Knights and warriors. 'Tis good we have our lord back, a warrior who will protect us." He paused and frowned. "Ye will, aye?"

The weight of a mountain landed on Ian.

The enemy was knocking at their door, but Ian could not raise a sword again. He couldn't imagine what he would do once the English came.

Ian looked at his feet. "Alan, please honor my father's memory by eating some of the food."

As the burly tacksman nodded slowly and walked away to the table, Ian couldn't shake the feeling of betraying his people.

A movement in the corner of his eye made him turn. Kate came in with plates full of small, steaming pies. Her face flushed, no doubt from the heat in the kitchen, she smiled and greeted people. She put the plates down and asked groups of guests at every table something, and they nodded in approval.

How could they not like her cooking? Of course they approved.

She quickly glanced up and met Ian's eyes. She flashed him a quick smile, and he nodded, his gut filling with lightness just from seeing her. She nodded back, turned, and walked away.

What a bonnie, hardworking, skillful woman. She had just had some bad luck. If he could, he would help her find her way back home to make her happy. Or put the world at her feet.

Only, no matter how much he might do, she deserved better than a broken man like him.

And so did his people.

CHAPTER 12

T he next day...

KATE WIPED THE TABLE WITH A CLOTH TO REMOVE BREAD crumbs and the remnants of parsnip peels under the unhappy growling of Manning. She liked the kitchen clean and tidy, but even after several days she'd spent in Dundail, Manning still complained.

"She wants to wipe everything," he mumbled as he kneaded the dough for bread. "How many times must one go to fetch water? And how much vinegar did she waste?"

Kate tried to block out his complaints, but they started to affect her anyway. Her heart beat faster, and her jaws tightened in an attempt to stop her retort.

Don't say something you might regret. You can never take it back. And they will never forget it.

The words rang in her head, loud and hot, in her mother's voice. The voice from her visions.

Kate stopped wiping and leaned on the table, her heart

thumping in her chest. Well, she'd finally succeeded in having Manning shut his mouth. He stared at her with a frown.

"Are ye well, lass?" he asked. "Ye look like ye're in pain."

Kate straightened. "No, I'm all right."

He shook his head and resumed peeling. "Then dinna pretend to be. Get back to work."

"I thought you didn't want me to clean."

"I dinna want ye to make new rules in *my* kitchen. Ye come with all yer new recipes for pies, yer suggestions for food, yer... yer...telling me how to hold a knife. I have been a cook longer than ye've lived."

Kate sighed. "I only want to help."

"Ye want to help?" He stopped and looked at her, pure menace in his eyes. "Ye get out. Ye leave. I dinna need another cook. Ian kens me. He kens my cooking, and he likes it. Ye... Who kens who ye really are? Yer strange way of talking, how ye cook. Ye dinna ken how to light the oven! What cook doesna ken how to light the oven? And why do ye use so much salt, huh, when ye ken 'tis as valuable as gold?"

His scolding was getting to her again. She couldn't have felt more like an outsider, like an imposing fly, than she did at this moment.

"Look, if you want me gone, you'll have to talk to Ian," she said, fighting tears. "He's the one who hired me."

"Aye, dinna fash yerself, lass. I will talk to Ian. Ye will be gone from my kitchen. Ian has a big heart, and he felt sorry for ye. But everybody kens here, ye're not needed!"

He couldn't have pressed on a more painful spot. Right where she already hurt. And if he was saying the very thing she'd been afraid of, it must be true.

Ian felt sorry for her but, in truth, didn't need or want her here. And the last thing she wanted was to be a problem. Eating his food. Occupying his house. Taking his money—which, it didn't look like he had a lot of anyway.

She really should go. If only she knew where...

But for now, she couldn't stand being in a room with someone who didn't want her there. "You know what, Manning, I don't know why I remembered your recipe, but it certainly wasn't because you're a nice person. You want me out of your kitchen? Drown in filth for all I care."

She threw the cloth on the table, turned, and hit a hot, hard wall of man.

She recognized his scent immediately—that mysterious mixture of something exotic, and the midnight forest, and his own male musk.

Ian.

He took her shoulders in his hands and steadied her. The touch sent a current of excitement through her,. and melted her bones at the same time.

"Ye all right, lass?" Ian asked.

"Yes," she breathed out, all anger and disappointment gone, replaced by a sensation of playful bubbles in her stomach.

His brown eyes on her, Ian nodded and released her, then stepped back a little.

He glanced at Manning, then at her. "I wanted to thank ye both for what ye did for the wake yesterday. I couldna have wished a better feast to honor my father."

Manning glanced at Kate with a cold look, as if to say that she shouldn't even dare to take any of the gratitude on herself. "Aye, lad," he said. "Anything for yer father."

Kate wished she could have gone to the burial yesterday, too, to give Ian moral support. As she'd found out, women didn't go to the burials. He'd been pale and sad all day—understandably. But he was also withdrawing from the people and the world around him. He was respected by his tenants. She saw that in the way they talked to him. But he wasn't responding. It was as though he'd wanted it to be over as quickly as possible.

"Are *you* all right, Ian?" she asked.

He glanced sharply at her, his face tensing. "Aye, I'm all right."

"You look—"

"I said I'm all right, lass. 'Tisna yer concern. If everyone just stopped fussing about me..."

Kate stood still for a moment, unable to move. Something about that interaction rang a familiar tune. The slam of a door... the abrupt rejection of care...

"Looks like I'm nae the only one annoyed by ye, lass," Manning said slowly. Then he shook his head and returned to peeling parsnips.

"I'm nae annoyed, especially nae with Katie," Ian said. "But I must speak with ye, Manning."

"I can go..." Kate said.

"Nae, ye have much work to do," Ian said. "Manning. Please come with me."

They exited the kitchen, and Kate felt a small pang of regret that Ian had left.

She finished cleaning the table and picked up the bucket to fetch more clean water. But when she reached the door, Ian's and Manning's voices came from the hallway.

"Lord, ye must understand, she doesna belong here. 'Tis clear as day."

Ian sighed. "I ken that she doesna."

Kate's chest chilled.

"She will be gone when her memory comes back. She's already started remembering something."

So he wanted her to be gone. He didn't want her to stay, did he?

"Aye. Good. The lass has these strange ways of doin' things. I dinna like her meddling in my kitchen."

"It won't be for long. Be patient with her. She's been through a lot."

Yes, Ian only pitied her. All that care, all that kindness, it wasn't because he liked her. It was because he had a good heart.

"Aye, lord. 'Tis hard, though, with her around."

The bucket trembled in Kate's hands.

"Manning, ye'll manage. 'Tisna easy for her."

Steps approached the kitchen and Kate put the bucket on the floor and returned to the table. She found the cloth and wiped the table without really knowing what she was doing. Her heart was like a raging wound. The pressure in her stomach increased.

Manning came into the kitchen, and without another word, proceeded into his attached room.

Kate exhaled. She didn't think she could deal with him right now, knowing how much her presence was disturbing him. Ian came in, and something lightened in her heart.

"I—" he said.

"I need to fetch water." She picked up the bucket again and went to the door.

"Allow me."

Ian moved to take the bucket from her hands. Their fingers touched briefly, sending a jolt of electricity through Kate. She jerked her hand back.

"Don't worry, I'll manage," she said. "I'm perfectly capable."

Ian glanced at her, puzzled. "Aye," he said. "I am certain ye are."

She marched out of the house. Steps followed her, surprisingly.

She put the bucket on the stone wall of the well and turned to him.

"Listen, Ian, I really don't want to inconvenience anyone, least of all you. You've been kind to me, and I don't want to take any more of your patience. Just, please, tell me if you want me to go."

He frowned. "What?"

"I don't want to be a burden."

His jaw tightened.

"Ye are nae a burden," he said, his voice hard.

He definitely looked annoyed.

"Right," she said and put the bucket onto the hook. "Manning doesn't agree with you."

He sighed. "Dinna fash yerself about Manning."

"Easy for you to say."

Ian rubbed his temples and closed his eyes.

"Look, lass, stop thinking about this over and over. I ken ye're struggling, but I told ye I'm nae yer friend, and I canna always be making peace between ye and Manning."

Kate lowered the bucket. It flopped into the water and she waited until it filled. She pulled it up. Everything he was saying—or rather, how he was saying it—confirmed her fears. He didn't really want her here. He just pitied her. And now he was annoyed that she'd raised the subject over and over.

Lesson learned.

She wouldn't raise it again.

In fact, she should leave as soon as possible and relieve them all of her company.

"Won't happen again," she said. "I promise."

She pulled the bucket out and walked back to the kitchen. She didn't yet know when or how she would leave, but she'd rather poke herself in the eye with a sharp stick than have him look at or talk to her with that tone again.

She cared about him too much to burden him even more with her problems.

CHAPTER 13

I an went to the stables to tack up the horse and go out riding as far away as the day would allow. He needed to distract himself, to stop this nagging, sucking feeling of guilt and desperation. He hated being almost cruel to Kate. The headache after several days of drinking himself to sleep didn't help.

He opened Thor's stall and brushed the animal, then stroked his neck. Thor looked at him with his shiny black eyes.

"Ye lucky beast," Ian said. "Nae concerns, nae regrets. Just eat yer hay and gallop around."

Thor blinked and snorted gently, as though asking what was the matter.

The matter was a dark, heavy weight in the pit of Ian's stomach. He knew in the back of his mind that he'd snapped at Kate with no good reason. He knew he'd behaved like a cold, ungrateful shite. After what she and Manning had managed for the wake, he should have fallen on his knees and kissed her hands. It was she who'd done it, Ian was sure. The spotless great hall, the quick and delicious pastries, the clean cups and plates... Everything had been ready for the guests, neatly organized through and through.

Manning would have never put in that much effort. Cadha didn't have the physical strength anymore.

No, he knew it was all Kate.

And yet, Ian had hurt her—again. If he'd seen someone else talk to her as he had, the man would lie on the ground with his nose broken.

It was his cloudy mind, he knew, the hangover that made him act out. As well as his worry about the English invaders who threatened to knock on their doors sooner rather than later.

He put on the saddle and the reins, then walked Thor out. Summer was glorious in the Highlands, just like he remembered. It was never as hot as in the caliphate. Rather, the sun was warm and the wind brought the fresh scent of water from the bright-blue loch. The mountains and hills on both sides of the loch were lush with trees and grass.

Ian scratched Thor's warm neck, inhaling the air.

Since he'd arrived in Baghdad, he'd had the goal of coming home. Once he'd returned, he'd had to bury his father.

Now, for the first time since he'd been sold as a slave, he had no purpose. He could take Thor and ride anywhere he wanted.

Freedom.

He mounted the horse and let him walk out of the yard slowly. He savored every breath, every movement of the animal, the feel of his own body, still aching from the excess of uisge, but free nevertheless.

As soon as they were out in the fields of oats and barley, he spurred Thor, and they flew like a wind.

They passed the village of Benlochy, past the small church. In its backyard, Father had been buried yesterday with the customary wooden plate with earth and salt on it. Earth as the sign that the body would be returned to the earth where it had come from, and salt as the symbol of the eternal soul.

They galloped for a while—Ian didn't know how long. But with the effort of the exercise, the trees and ground and sky flashing before his eyes, he was able to forget, his mind going pleasantly empty, full of sunshine and wind and the rush of speed.

The only thing Ian wasn't able to forget, was Kate. But she didn't bother him. On the contrary, thinking of her brought something soothing and calming to his soul. Like a balm on a ragged wound.

By the time Thor needed a break, Ian had decided he'd apologize the moment he got back. He had been unfair, and she should know that.

He dismounted and led Thor to the loch to let him drink and graze on the grass nearby. The water looked so good, and suddenly Ian wanted nothing more than to plunge into it. Following the impulse, he undressed and walked in. Chill grasped his feet and ankles, the wind refreshing against his bare chest.

Ah, it would be freezing. Better not to wait. On with it.

He advanced even though the cold took his breath away and hurt his skin. He submerged himself completely and felt as if the loch embraced him like a babe against his mother's bosom. He let the waters of his motherland wash away the horrors of slavery and dissolve the painful memories of every life he'd taken.

He stayed underwater until his chest felt like it would burst, then swam up and gasped in the sweet air. Lightness he hadn't felt in a long while filled his body, and he wanted to laugh from the pleasure of it.

Voices from the shore made him still, then narrow his eyes. Englishmen, judging by their heavy metal armor. There were three of them. One dismounted, walked up to Thor and looked him over, checking his teeth. He lifted the animal's foot and looked at his hoof, then nodded with approval.

How dare he look at Ian's horse as though he was judging its quality? Something dark, ugly, and slippery turned deep in Ian's gut. Something he'd thought he'd left in the loch. He walked towards the shore, his hands itching for a weapon.

All three of them stopped talking and stared as he approached.

"Hey, you!" one of them cried. "Who are you?"

Ian didn't stop until he reached the rocky shore.

"I am the owner of that horse. And I will thank ye to get yer hands off him."

"A Scot," one man said quietly to another.

Ian raised his chin.

They looked him over and laughed. "It's a big demand coming from someone standing naked and dripping water."

"I dinna want trouble, man," Ian said. "Just let my horse go and be on yer way."

"What's your name?"

"Ian Cambel."

"Dundail?"

"Aye."

They exchanged amused glances. "Well, Ian Cambel of Dundail, since your estate is the next one King Edward's coming for, we'll spread the burden and relieve you of your horse now."

He could launch himself at them. He could take the dagger from the belt of the man standing by Thor. It would only take a moment to pierce the Englishman under his chin, then slice the second man's neck before he knew what hit him, hop onto Thor and gallop away.

He clenched his jaw so tightly, he thought he'd crush his teeth. Everything darkened and sharpened at the same time.

No.

He'd promised himself.

No life will be taken by my hands again.

The English chuckled. The man on the ground tied Thor's reins to his horse's saddle and climbed up.

"That's right, Scot, not a word. And be thankful I'm not taking your balls together with your horse. They aren't worth much anyway."

He spat and they continued on their way, slowly, as though they were already victors.

Ian shook. From cold, from helpless fury, and from the images of dozens of bodies lying in pools of blood on the Baghdad palace's dusty courtyard.

The peacefulness of being in the loch was gone, as though blown away by the wind. His chest tightened, and his stomach churned.

He refused to fight again. He refused to take another life.

But what would he do once the English showed up in Dundail? Could he stand by and let them harm the villagers who relied on him? And what of Kate? What would they do to the sweet lass who couldn't even remember where she came from but still managed to somehow warm his cold stone of a heart?

That thought chilled him more than the cold loch waters. He pulled on his clothes, then turned and ran towards home.

CHAPTER 14

Kate stared at the sloped ceiling of the garret. Although she hadn't remembered anything new the whole day, after Ian had left, something had lurked at the back of her mind. Like a shadow she'd seen a thousand times but couldn't recognize.

She held on to the vision of the kitchen, turning it in her mind over and over. She looked for more details of the furniture, her mom's face and voice, her clothes.

Nothing.

She turned to her sister and concentrated on remembering the color of her eyes—blue. The shape of her face—oval. Her nose—pointy. Her Mickey Mouse T-shirt was faded, and the seams had holes in them. Her hair was done in two messy ponytails, one on top of her head, the other hanging low by her neck.

The expression on her sister's face was mournful. She was afraid and—

New visions invaded her mind, so overwhelming all she could do was watch. Kate's breath was taken away, her heart pounding.

Kate was older now, probably eighteen. In black clothes, Kate opened the door to her and Mandy's shared bedroom.

"Mandy, do you want some cookies?" Kate said to a shape lying under the blankets on Mandy's bed.

Silence.

Kate came in and sat at the edge of her sister's bed and put her hand on the girl's back.

"Maybe a peanut butter and jelly sandwich?" she asked.

Nothing.

"Honey, are you sick?"

No response.

"The funeral was sweet. Mom's colleagues came. Her boss from the supermarket paid for the cremation."

"She would have wanted me there," Mandy's muffled voice came from under the blanket.

"Yes, but she'd understand you aren't feeling well. Are you still tired?"

"Leave me alone."

"It's been three days, Mandy. Something's wrong."

"You're not leaving me alone. That's what."

"I'm just worried."

Mandy turned and peeked out from beneath the blanket.

"I don't think we'll ever get better now that Mom's gone. We don't have anyone now."

"We have each other." Kate patted her hand. "I'll drop out of high school and start working. Don't worry. I got you."

Mandy hid her face in her palms and turned back to the wall.

"Now you're ruining your life for me. I just can't... I can't live like this."

A cold wave went through Kate. "Honey, you're not talking about—"

She couldn't say the words. Losing Mom to cancer was bad enough. Was her sister suicidal?

Mandy didn't answer.

"Talk to me, please," Kate whispered, desperation creeping through her in a dark cloud.

But Mandy didn't respond.

By the end of the week, Kate had found a job as a dishwasher and another as a waitress. Unlike Mom, she'd dragged Mandy to see the local doctor, who'd said this sounded like depression and recommended a psychiatrist. The shrink had confirmed the diagnosis. Kate had found a third job as a waitress in another town, where a few years later she'd be promoted to a line cook's position. All her earnings went to keeping the roof over their heads and paying Mandy's medical bills. Soon, Kate knew exactly how Mom had felt.

Back in Dundail's attic, Kate swallowed tears, staring at the dark wood of the ceiling. Her mom had died, after a life of hard work, which she'd done to support Kate and Mandy. Kate was a high school dropout. Neither she nor Mandy had been vaccinated when they were children because Mom hadn't had time to take them to the doctor. Kate had paid for herself and Mandy to be vaccinated when they were already grown-ups, she remembered.

And then, it was as though a dam had broken, and all the memories flooded through at once, choking her. They came from all ages in no order.

She and Mandy had moved out of their rental house and started a restaurant, Deli Luck.

At the age of sixteen, Mandy got knocked up and had Jax, becoming a single mother, just like their own mom.

Mandy had applied to be featured in Logan Robertson's *Sweet Burn* TV show, where he refurbished restaurants that didn't do well.

What bothered Kate the most about all these visions was the difference of the worlds. She knew she spoke a different language in these memories, English. She knew there were mobile phones, antidepressants that helped her sister stay afloat, and cars and airplanes. She knew that because she remembered driving, and then flying to Scotland.

But what had happened in Scotland, she had no idea.

Mice scratched in the walls of the garret. An owl hooted

outside. It was quiet at night in her Cape Haute apartment, despite them living on Main Street, where all the shops were located. Her window was at the back of the building, overlooking the alley.

Sometimes, she heard Mandy cry at night from the other side of the wall. She sobbed into her pillow so that she wouldn't wake up Jax. Every time, Kate knew what this meant. Mandy wouldn't get out of bed for a week, Kate would need to book an emergency session with Dr. Lambert, and hire a temp to take care of the restaurant. All that meant more costs. During those days, she also needed to be Mom to Jax.

Her heart weighed heavily for leaving them, for not being there to help. She knew from those memories that her life was dedicated to providing for them, to caring for Jax, to giving him a better future than Kate and Mandy could ever have.

But where was that world with cars and airplanes and stainless-steel kitchens?

The most disturbing thing of all was that the checks in the restaurant were dated with the year 2020. So was the plane ticket she'd held in her hand when she was in the airport.

The small window let in the pink light of sunrise. Kate managed to convince herself the visions weren't memories. They must be her imagination, no matter how real everything felt.

But the bottle, she thought. The bottle and the plastic wrapping in her purse. And the money in the wallet. And the credit card...

There must be another explanation for them.

If it was all her imagination, the verdict was clear. She was insane. She must be schizophrenic or something. Delusional.

And a burden.

Ian had just hired himself a crazy cook who thought she might be from the future.

And she was falling for him. Far too attached to him. She'd leave one day in any case, but the longer she stayed, the harder it would be to do so. The kindest thing would be to relieve him of her troubles. He was already tortured and clearly wanted to be free. She couldn't bear to make his life harder.

She had to leave.

She'd go back to Inverlochy and try to figure out why she had lain there, unconscious and wounded. There must be some way to convince the steward she wasn't an enemy. She should examine the underground area where she was found. Maybe there were more clues that would trigger her memory.

Or her imagination.

Her head spinning, Kate rose from the bed and dressed. She made her way down into the kitchen to take something to eat for the road. Ian hadn't paid her yet, and she didn't want to see him and explain why she was leaving. So she'd take some food as payment. That should be fair.

She took two loaves of bread, the remnants of the pies from the wake, and a couple of boiled eggs. She filled her water bottle from the well.

Kate looked around the kitchen for the last time. She'd hoped it might become her home, and despite Manning's growls, she'd been happy here. In a way, she was happier when she didn't remember those crazy things about the future, her sister and her restaurant.

Should she say goodbye to Cadha and Manning? Or Ian?

She hadn't seen him since he'd followed her out to the well yesterday morning. He hadn't asked for lunch or dinner. Had he even come home?

Didn't matter. Maybe he had a female friend he'd spent the night with. The thought stabbed her in her chest.

No, she shouldn't think about it. It was his business, not hers. She was no one to him.

But she had to leave some sign that she was all right and hadn't gotten lost somewhere or drowned in the loch. Not having a pen or paper, she took a handful of flour and sprinkled it over the clean table, then wrote with her finger:

"Thank you. I'm going home. Kate."

With a heavy heart, Kate walked out of the house. It was very early, and the loch stood still like a mirror in the crisp air of the summer morning. Birds chirped in the trees as she walked towards the woods from which Ian and she had arrived several days ago.

Several blissful days ago.

Kate turned back to look at Dundail for the last time. The sight was so beautiful it took her breath away. The proud house, the tall, square tower with the attached one-story building where the main hall was, looked magnificent against the long loch and the mountains, forest and hills on the other side.

"Goodbye, Ian," Kate whispered.

She turned around and continued up the hill and into the woods.

She always followed the loch, blue water glistening through the trees to her left. It felt good to walk, and her mind cleared as she breathed air scented with wood and leaves and flowers. She had walked till some time in the afternoon, with a couple of short breaks, when she heard voices.

Her pulse jumped a little, but she told herself there was no need to panic. It was probably just travelers like her. Still, she should mind her business and not attract any attention.

Her head high, her back straight, she walked. The voices grew louder, and she could distinguish the old English tongue that the knight she and Ian had met on the road had spoken. Through the trees, she saw men laughing and talking. The scent of woodsmoke, grilled meat, and stew hung in the air.

She could see them now. Most of them wore only tunics and pants, and armor lay on the ground next to them. Red coats of arms with three yellow lions were on banners and shields. Horses grazed here and there. The garrison was probably having a rest.

Kate's nape broke out in sweat. They weren't that far from Dundail. How many were there?

"Whose lands are these?" one of them asked.

"Lord of Dundail's—one of the Cambels, I reckon..." an older voice said.

"Doesn't matter whose lands," a third man broke in. "The instructions of the king and the MacDougalls were clear. We cut through the lands, taking anything we find on the way to Inverlochy. There, we wait hidden for reinforcements and attack."

"Bruce got too successful in the east," the man added. "Our king should have done something much sooner."

"What have you heard?" the first one asked.

"The Lord of Badenoch and all other Comyns were destroyed. With the MacDowells of Galloway gone, and the Earl of Ross having a truce with Bruce, the MacDougalls are the last opposition to Bruce in Scotland."

"So King Edward has finally come to his senses?" the older one said.

"Yes. Realized that Bruce is coming for the MacDougalls next. If they fall, there's no one else who'd oppose him. The whole of Scotland will be his. Edward will have a much harder time getting him under control."

"Right!" the first one said. "Hit him in the back while he thinks he's safe in the east."

"Exactly, lad," the third one said. "Take back Inverlochy, then Urquhart. That'll bring him back running. And with eight hundred MacDougalls, a hundred of us, and four hundred more coming soon from Carlisle, this time, we have a good chance."

Kate's thoughts raced. The MacDougalls had joined with the English. And now this hundred was marching through Ian's lands up to Inverlochy. Dundail was on their way.

Horror dripped through her veins. There was no question about it. She needed to run back and tell Ian.

Easy does it. Slowly, before they noticed her.

She'd turned back and taken just one step when someone cried, "Hey!"

She turned her head, her feet glued to the ground.

One knight was looking right at her. The same one who had

stopped Ian and her on their way to Dundail, she realized with a start.

She ran. Trees and bushes flashed, her heart drumming in her ears. Feet thumped behind her—several of them.

"Stop the Scotswoman!"

A strong arm grabbed her around her waist. She flailed with her arms and legs, but the man held her. She screamed. Then another one appeared before her. He held his sword to her throat.

"Shut up!" he commanded.

The sharp edge biting at her skin convinced her to do so.

"Let's take her to Sir de Bourgh," the knight said. "He'll be interested to know what Ian Cambel's wife has to say about Dundail's forces and the lord."

No! Kate couldn't possibly bring Ian even more trouble. She whimpered and wriggled, trying to free herself. Desperation dug its claws into her, but she firmly resolved to tell them nothing.

CHAPTER 15

A woman's scream pierced the air.

Ian stiffened and looked around. The woods near the path that led south to Dundail were calm, trees swaying peacefully, bushes barely moving. His hand swiped against his waist, where he'd normally have a sword, only to find empty air.

He listened again. Was he even right? Had it been the rustle of the wind? Mayhap, tree branches screeching against each other?

The wind brought male laughter. And the woman cried out again. The sounds came from farther down the path. The familiar beast of battle fury raised its ugly head, carrying a roar of anger through his blood.

He walked towards the sound without hiding, his body tense.

After a dozen or so steps he noticed red and yellow flashing between the trees. English colors.

Damnation.

Ian stopped and hid behind a trunk. His chest tight, he breathed heavily. Staying low and walking as quietly as he could, he made his way closer—from tree to tree, from bush to bush.

He reached grazing horses.

He saw a familiar black horse among them. "Thor," Ian whispered.

In some distance, he noticed men—way too many to fight. Mayhap, the woman was just a whore playing it a bit rough. As long as she was willing, that didn't concern him. He just wanted to get Thor back and go home.

The thought of home—of seeing Katie, of smelling her delicious pies or something else she'd cook for him—calmed him and made him breathe easier. He'd spent yesterday making his way home. Good sense had finally taken hold after he'd run until his lungs felt as if they would explode, and he'd walked from then on. He could never cover the distance the horse had easily crossed in less than a day. He slept in the woods, freezing without a blanket or a cape. Having no snare or a weapon to hunt with, he'd found nuts and berries but was mostly hungry. He couldn't get to Dundail fast enough.

The English were coming closer and closer. How could he avoid the fight and yet keep his people alive?

He still didn't know.

But by the looks of it, he'd need to decide sooner rather than later. His throat tightened at the thought. Black desperation scratching at the pit of his stomach.

First, he needed to free Thor. He approached the horse and undid the tie around the tree bark. He was just about to pull the reins and slowly lead Thor after him when the woman's voice stopped him.

"Let me go! I don't know anything."

Cold sweat trickled down his spine. He'd recognize that voice anywhere—the soft *r*, the way her vowels sang...

Kate.

Ian's fists clenched, memories of murder pressed all around him. Instinctively assuming a defensive position, he moved closer. Hiding behind one of the horses, he studied the camp.

An English warrior led Kate somewhere. A wave of painful tingling went through Ian. Her arms were tied behind her back, her face flushed. One cheek was red, her neck scratched, her bonnie golden hair in disarray. Her dress was torn at her side and at the neck.

Kelpie eat him alive, she'd been beaten. She struggled, mayhap for her life. Ian's breath rushed in and out, his throat going dry. Fire ran through his veins, just like so many times back in the caliphate, when he had been about to face a foe.

But unlike in the caliphate, he didn't have a weapon. And he had dozens of foes to fight, not just one. The concentration of yellow-and-red flags indicated the main camp was still some distance away. The man who was leading Kate was alone with her.

Why was she here at all? They were hours away from Dundail on foot. Had she come here? Had they kidnapped her?

In either case, she wasn't here of her own free will. That was verra much clear.

The Englishman with Kate started fiddling at his breeches. "If you know something or not remains to be seen."

Ian felt all the blood leave his face. Kate jerked at her hands.

"Just let me go! I can't tell you anything."

She stomped on his foot, whirled, and kicked him in the ankle. The man burst out in curses, turned, and hit her. Kate's head shot to her left, the slap loud in the air. She gasped.

Ian straightened. Kate's eyes were so wide she looked as though she'd seen a ghost, her face white, her mouth frozen in a large *O*. She shook her head slowly, staring at nothing.

Poor thing. She must be completely mad of pain.

Ian's vision turned from multicolored to black and red. Everything moved slowly, as though time itself had been wounded and all it could do was crawl. The sounds around him rang painfully loud.

He didn't have a chance to stop himself. All he could hear was the call of death. He wouldn't let anyone touch a hair on Kate's head.

He walked. Without a weapon. Without a shield. Without armor.

In a few broad steps, he reached the man. Ian's hand went to the handle of the sword that was still in the man's sheath and pulled it out. With a familiar effort, he made a broad swing, piercing the man's back and pulling the sword free in one move. The English bastart screamed, but Ian put his hand to the man's mouth and muffled the sound until he went limp and crashed on the ground.

Without the man between them, Kate came out of her strange state and stared at Ian.

But two more soldiers were coming at him.

"Turn," he commanded.

She did so, and he cut the rope that tied her hands, leaving the man's blood on her wrists.

"Step aside from the whore," one of the men yelled.

"You bloody Scot," the other said.

But Ian had no more capacity for words. He'd just killed a man after having sworn to never do so again. It was just like in the caliphate.

His ears filled with the bloodthirsty cheers of the crowd; his vision sharpened and intensified. He didn't feel his body anymore. Pure fire seethed his veins.

"Aaarghh!" He launched himself at the first one.

The sword light in his arms, he met the man's blade with a *clang*. Ian slashed again, and again, and again, every time meeting the steel.

The second man came at him now, from the other side, sword raised. Taking stock of his surroundings, he noted another man behind him pressed against a tree. A fourth man with a shield and a sword advanced.

Just like numerous times in the caliphate. Two, even three opponents against the unbreakable Red Death.

He went into another space. A space where he didn't exist,

where he was the spirit of the sword. Where everything around him moved slowly, and he was a deadly lightning strike.

He whirled and kicked and ducked. He cut. He slashed. He killed.

Two armed men lay dead on the ground. One man still leaned against the tree, but now his guts were spilling out, his eyes staring but not seeing. Ian's sword pressed against the fourth man's throat, about to pierce it.

"Stop!" Kate's voice broke through the red fog of death.

Ian stopped. The point of his sword still at the man's neck, one hand holding his collar.

His heart thumping in his ears, he panted. The man's wide eyes pleaded for his life. Ian's sword dripped with blood, sprays of red on his hands and his sleeves.

"Ian, you don't have to kill him," Kate said.

I dinna have to kill him. I dinna have to kill him. The words reverberated in his skull as he tried to make sense of them.

This wasn't the caliphate. Ian wasn't a slave anymore. He had a choice.

He glanced in the direction of the rest of the camp. The atmosphere there sounded cheerful. Men spoke in a hum of voices, occasionally bursting out in laughter. By some miracle, no one else had paid attention to them.

Ian looked again at the man. Now that he could think more clearly, he realized he knew the face.

It was the man who'd taken Thor.

"Ye whelp," Ian spat. "Ye whoreson. I'd gladly kill ye."

"Please..." the man whimpered. "I'll do anything."

"Aye. Ye will. Shut up." Ian looked up. "Kate, tie his hands behind his back."

She took the longer part of the rope she'd been tied with and did as he asked.

"Now tear some of yer dress and gag him," Ian said.

"Ian—"

"Do it. Or he'll alarm the whole camp the minute we're on the horse."

"But—"

"I'm nae killing him," he snapped. "Be happy."

She nodded. She tore a piece of her skirt and put it into the man's mouth.

Ian tied the man to a tree, then glanced around at what he'd done. The first man lay on his stomach, a dark flower of blood blooming on his white tunic. The second stared unseeingly into the sky, a long gash on his side, his insides peering out.

He waited for remorse to weigh heavily on his chest, but it didn't come. What was wrong with him? He'd just killed men in cold blood. Then he looked at the man leaning against another tree a few paces off. Not truly a man, but still a lad, he now realized. A waterskin and a loaf of bread lay on the ground nearby, no weapons. He didn't even remember killing the lad.

He truly was a monster, just as he'd suspected all this time. His throat tensed and stung. The skin of his palms itched, and his tunic scratched as though made of nettle.

He needed to move. He'd dwell on what he'd done later. Someone might come any moment.

Quietly, Ian undid the reins of other horses and gently slapped each on the hip to send them away. The English would be slowed down in their pursuit.

Mounting Thor, Ian helped Kate up. Then they went slowly through the trees towards the loch.

"Ian, what were you—"

"Shh," he said. "We're nae out of danger yet."

He was glad for some time in silence. He wouldn't have a lot of comforting things to say, anyway. The aftershocks of his rage rippled through his blood. Kate sitting in front of him, the scent of her, the feel of her soft, warm body against him, was a pleasant distraction from the memories tormenting his psyche.

They rode Thor slowly for a while in silence. Soon, the laughter, the music, and the voices from the camp vanished. Thor's hooves thudded softly, leaves rustled above their heads, and birds chirped. They descended to the shore of Loch Awe, gravel rustling under Thor's hooves. Ian looked carefully for shadows behind the trees or armor glistening, but everything remained calm. Once he knew they weren't being followed, he spurred Thor into a trot.

Dry blood covered his hands. He had tucked his enemy's sword into his belt.

Who was he now that he'd broken his own oath?

He was the beast he'd thought he was for eleven years. Just coming home wouldn't rid him of the death he'd brought to people.

Kate had seen him kill an innocent man and two warriors. She'd seen him at his worst. She knew who he truly was.

A cold-blooded killer.

The thought maimed him, gnawed at his soul, and lacerated his heart.

CHAPTER 16

Kate held on to the horse's mane, the trot sending shots of pain through her head. But for the first time since she'd arrived here, her mind was clear.

The slap had done something. Like with an old TV that didn't work, a hard hit had connected the wires. When that man had hit her, the detonation of blinding pain had come with a memory of another hit—of her falling into a blinding darkness while trying to get away from Logan Robertson, the celebrity chef.

That memory had finally brought the last two pieces of the puzzle together. Specifically, why she'd been with Logan Robertson in the first place.

"If nothing changes in the next two months," Mandy had said, pointing at the computer screen with many red numbers. "We're bankrupt, Kate. We're on the streets."

She'd said it in that lifeless voice she always got during her depression episodes.

"This Logan Robertson TV thing is our last chance. Please, don't screw it up."

Kate had taken her sister's hands in hers and squeezed them.

"I won't, Mandy, I promise. You know I won't let anything happen to you and Jax."

And then, in a flash, came Inverlochy Castle—or rather, its ruins. Logan talking on the phone by the gates. A red-haired woman in a green cloak enjoying Kate's sandwich.

Sìneag.

...the rock this castle has been built upon, that is saturated with the powerful magic of time travel.

Time travel... The ground had shifted under Kate's feet as she'd remembered tumbling into disorienting darkness, striking her head on the stairs, the shining symbols on a rock, and her placing her hand into the handprint.

And the feeling of falling through the stone. Another skull-splitting hit.

And then Ian.

After that memory came to her, the rest had followed.

She now knew who she was—Kate Anderson, a thirty-one-year-old woman from Cape Haute, New Jersey. The owner of Deli Luck, living with her sister, Mandy, and her nephew, Jax.

In 2020.

No matter how crazy it sounded, Kate knew she'd fallen through time. Just like Sìneag had said.

So Kate wasn't crazy. But she was living through a crazy thing. And she wasn't sure which one was worse.

She breathed easier now that the reality of who she was had become clear. Knowing that she wasn't crazy after all was soothing and released the tension in the pit of her stomach.

What she knew for sure was that no one in her life had ever taken care of her as Ian had. He'd freed her, for God's sake. He cared enough to kill for her.

No one in her life in the future would sacrifice so much for her. She didn't think anyone would ever care about her like that.

Oh yes, she'd seen Ian's livid face when he'd confronted those men. He'd become someone else. He'd been a death machine.

Every movement fast and calculated, efficient. Every hit meeting the aim.

He was terrifying. To others.

Not to her.

But was she safe with him? Should she be afraid of him? He'd killed an unarmed man in his battle rage. Could he have as easily killed her without even realizing it?

No. She didn't believe that. He would have stopped. Somehow he would have known.

She was safe with him. She knew it in her heart.

She'd never felt safer than she did with her back pressed against his torso, his arms around her as he held Thor's reins, his warm breath in her ear. A man like that wouldn't leave her in trouble.

Unlike Logan Robertson.

Or her previous boyfriends, who had sooner or later bailed on her. Who would want to go out with a woman who worked twelve hours a day?

She had so many questions for Ian. How had he found her in the woods? Where had he been last night? Had he seen her message? Where had he learned to fight like that?

But she had an even bigger question for herself: What now?

Now that she knew everything about herself.

Every day spent here brought bankruptcy closer to her family. Mandy and Jax might already be on the streets. What if Mandy got one of her episodes in the middle of it? How would Jax cope? Would social services take him?

The time traveling rock in Inverlochy was real. Knowing that, and how much Mandy and Jax were relying on her, there was only one thing to do.

She had to go back. Right now.

Even though Ian's arms felt so good, even though he made her melt like butter in a hot pan, even though he'd just been a hero—for her...

She needed to go back.

And she would, as soon as they were far enough away from the English.

It felt like a few hours had passed when Ian slowed Thor down.

"'Tisna verra long till Dundail," Ian said, "but he needs a wee bit of a rest."

He jumped off the horse and helped Kate down, filling her nostrils with his masculine scent. His hands on her waist, she lost the ability to breathe.

When she stood on the ground, he took Thor to the loch and the animal drank thirstily.

Ian sank into a crouch and washed his hands, rubbing them against each other and leaving the water dark from dry blood. Then he stood next to Thor, his shoulders tense, the large muscles of his back stiff and bulging. Something was bothering him. Kate came to stand by his side.

"Are you all right?" she asked.

He gazed at her, his brown eyes dark with anguish.

"Are *ye* all right?" he said.

Kate breathed out. Surprisingly, she really was. She knew what she needed to do. Knowing where she came from explained so much. She could finally feel like herself. Maybe not the "herself" she very much liked, but herself nonetheless.

He reached out and touched her cheek, his hand cold and wet, and pain pierced her skin. She winced and his arm fell.

"Sorry, lass," he said.

"You saved me. This is nothing."

"What happened? How did ye end up there?"

"You don't know?"

"Nae."

"I thought maybe you saw my note and came looking for me..."

"They stole Thor yesterday, and I had no means of coming home earlier. Why? What did the note say?"

She sighed and looked away. Was she silly to have just left without talking to him first?

"I decided to go back to Inverlochy and try to find my way home. Some memories have returned to me over the last few days. And now I know that people need me back urgently."

He looked at the loch. "Oh."

They kept silent. Kate wasn't sure what she could say without revealing too much. Or should she tell him everything?

No, surely he'd think she was insane.

"Did ye remember a husband?" Ian's voice cracked, and he cleared his throat. "Someone ye love?"

"No husband. No one in my...past life. Except for my sister and my nephew."

"So ye have a family."

"Yes."

"Where?"

"Far away from here. So far away, you won't believe me if I tell you."

He chuckled. "I've been far away. I lived in hell for eleven years. There's little ye can say that would sound unbelievable."

Kate sighed. "I need to go back, Ian. I cannot return to Dundail with you. You really should go and protect your people from the English, because they're making their way north from the MacDougall lands to Inverlochy and they're raiding and taking everything on their way."

Ian's jaws tightened, his nostrils flared. "Bastarts."

"Yeah. They are. But I must go to Inverlochy and reach my family. If I don't go back, my sick sister and my ten-year-old nephew will be on the streets."

Ian's face fell. "Ye want to go alone to Inverlochy? Through lands infested with the English?"

Kate's cheek stung at the word "English." She opened her mouth, but Ian interrupted.

"And ye think I will let ye go?"

"Ian, I have to try."

"To try and die?" he scoffed. "Nae. I'll tie ye to the horse if I must, but I wilna let ye go alone."

Kate gasped. "Tie me to the horse? Ian! It's my business. It's not your concern."

His chest rose and fell quickly as he glared at her, his fists clenching.

"Ye're wrong, lass. 'Tis my concern. Ye're my concern."

She was his concern? Did he care about her? Kate's heart fluttered in her chest.

"I wilna let another innocent person die because I failed to protect them," he said. "So 'tis what I suggest. Ye wait until I deal with the damned Sassenachs. Then I'll take ye myself. Make sure ye're safe."

Kate closed her eyes and rubbed her forehead. He was right. Of course he was right about safety. But could she wait even a few more days? She had no idea. She could only hope Mandy and Jax were still all right and that if she was delayed a little longer, nothing bad would happen to them.

But what about the well-armed English, who were a much bigger force? How would one man, however powerful, deal with them? Was it possible she was putting herself in more danger staying with Ian than leaving him?

But there was something about him that made her feel safe. Somehow, she knew that he would never let any harm come to her. He'd find a way.

"It's the wisest choice," she said. "You're right."

Besides, the thought of spending a few more days with Ian lit her up like a Christmas tree.

"Good," he said. "I wouldna want ye to go through that hell."

His eyes sad, as though he were carrying the weight of the world on his shoulders and there wouldn't be an end to it.

She wanted to share the burden.

"Tell me about hell," Kate said.

His eyes widened in surprise, then he frowned and looked at his hands. They were clean now, no more blood.

"Ye want to ken about hell? Picture what I did back there to those men and repeat it a hundred times."

Kate's mouth went dry—not from the knowledge that he'd killed a hundred men, but from the pain she'd heard in his voice. It was as though his very soul ached, torn by the memories of the deeds he'd done.

"Picture that," he rasped. "And tell me then that ye still want to ken."

She laid her hand on his forearm, and he jolted a little but didn't break the contact.

"I want to know, Ian," Kate pressed. "If you think the fact that you saved my life, by whatever means you could, terrifies me, it doesn't. If you think my opinion of you changed, it did. I respect you even more now. No one has ever done what you've done for me. All I have for you is gratitude. All I feel for you is—"

Love.

Was she crazy to think she was in love with him after knowing him for so little time? But her heart tap-danced inside her chest, and her whole body floated, as light as a feather.

She didn't say the word out loud, but Ian's eyes darkened, and a mixture of a hope and pain flashed through his face.

He turned to her, wrapped his arm around her shoulders and brought her to him. He paused, eyeing her, his gaze an intoxicating combination of admiration and doubt.

"Where have ye been my whole life, lass?" he said.

"So far away, you won't believe me," she whispered, then stood on her toes, reached out to him, and kissed him.

CHAPTER 17

H er lips were like petals—delicate, supple, and warm. Her body pressed against his was heaven, the feel of her stirring fire in his loins. He drank the kiss like a healing draft, sweet and fresh and magical.

He eased his tongue into the depths of her mouth, swiping it against hers with gentle strokes. She responded, the touch of her tongue sending a succulent wave of pleasure through him. She tasted of forbidden delights, of the secrets of the world, and he wanted to know all of them.

Her hands wrapped around his neck, and he tightened his arms around her, wanting to have as little space between them as humanly possible. And as few clothes...

He tugged her to the ground and they sank to their knees, then he gently laid her on the grass and stretched himself out next to her. He coveted her, wanted to cherish every part of her body.

He'd never imagined she would be so accepting of his confession just now, and not think him a monster after what she'd seen him do to the English. Her reaction humbled him. He didn't deserve a bonnie lass like her. She offered her acceptance so easily.

It was a streak of luck he'd encountered those Sassenach soldiers and could free her. If he'd returned home and found out she'd left without saying goodbye to him, he would have hurt more than he'd like. A painful heaviness formed in his chest. She was here in his arms now. The biggest blessing of all.

He brushed his hand against her unmarred cheek, marveling at the creamy, silky skin under his callused fingers. He trailed them down her neck to her tender collarbone, then stilled, pausing in awe at the curve of her breast under the material of her dress. Continuing his exploration, he cupped the deliciously ripe form. Kate gasped and arched her back a little to lean into his palm.

He massaged her breast, the abundant feel of her making him harden even more. Oh, the little golden-haired temptress. He leaned over her, nibbling at her nipple, then sucking the hardening bud into his mouth. Even through the damp fabric, he tasted her—a wee bit salty and sweet and a feast of feminine softness.

Kate tangled her fingers in his hair and brought him closer.

"Oh, Ian." The moan was born deep in her throat.

He'd never heard his name sound like a prayer before.

"Aye, lass," he rasped as he moved to her other breast. "Ye will see the moon and the stars."

She looked up at him. "I only want to see you."

His throat tightened to stop the heart-wrenching emotion from spilling out.

"I havna seen anyone so bonnie as ye," he said. "And I nae will."

He returned to worshiping her, grasping her waist, then kissing his way down her hips. He kissed every part of her— every inch of her sacred, every detail of her body a benediction.

He reached her ankles and ran his hands up her legs under the skirt of her dress, her skin there cool and smooth.

Crack.

Crack. Crack.

He looked up the shore, frantically trying to find the source of the sound. Thor looked in that direction as well, his ears moving to-and-fro.

"We better go, Katie," Ian said. "As much as I want to continue."

She bit her lower lip and sat up, flushed, her lips swollen and red. He would see her swollen and red like that in the most intimate part of her body.

Red and swollen from pleasure.

But not now.

First, he needed to bring her to the safety of Dundail.

He rose and gave her his hand. "Come, lass."

She took his hand and he helped her up, bringing her into his arms.

Crack. Crack.

He put her behind his back and picked up his sword.

A small deer appeared from the bushes and stared at them. Ian itched for a spear or a bow. He sighed out with relief.

"Ye would have made a great dinner of him, wouldna ye?" he asked.

"Well," she said. "I wouldn't feel..."

"Ah. I canna hunt with the sword. And anything ye cook is goin' to be heaven. Speaking of..." He climbed onto Thor's back and helped Kate up. "Let's go home. I'm ravenous—for yer food and for ye."

She giggled, and they trotted down the coast.

But the joy of seeing Kate's smile faded away as he started thinking about what would await him in Dundail. The troops were headed their way; although, he was sure they'd take several days before they reached Dundail—with all of their tents and supplies, armies moved slowly.

Still, he'd need to think quickly of how to defend his home and his lands. And it was painfully clear he wouldn't be able to do it without his tenants.

And his clan.

Sharp pain pierced his gut at the thought that he'd woken up the monster within himself and killed that innocent lad without even realizing it. How many more would he need to kill?

CHAPTER 18

"Ah, ye silly lass. What were ye thinking, leaving like that with nae word, alone?" Cadha lamented.

Kate was just getting off the horse in front of Dundail house, with the help of Ian's strong arms. Cadha wobbled towards Thor, waving her arms in the air, her cheeks flushed like two bright apples.

Was Cadha in such distress because of her? Kate's feet landed on the ground, and she raised her eyebrows in surprise.

"Sorry, Cadha," Kate said. "I didn't think you'd be so worried."

"Why of course I was worried, lass." Cadha clasped her hands. "Even Manning was, in his way." She turned to Ian. "And ye, where have ye been?"

The sun was setting behind the mountains on the other side of the loch, painting the sky in gold, orange, pink, and violet. The gray walls of the house were warm now, golden brown in this light, as though it had been freshly removed from the oven. The sight was homey and sweet, and something melted in Kate's chest at the image.

"Out," Ian said curtly and led Thor into the stables.

Kate followed him with her eyes. He glanced back briefly, his gaze lingering on her and launching a whirlwind of butterflies in her stomach. She hid a smile, then wheezed out a breath.

She returned her attention to Cadha, who studied her with eyebrows drawn together.

"What happened? Why did ye leave but now came together with the lord? Are ye playing at something, lass?"

Any trace of smile on Kate's face fell. "No, no. I wanted to go home but was caught by the English on my way. They thought I knew something about the local fortifications or something and tried to get it out of me. Ian saved me."

"Ye call him Ian?"

"Yes—what else should I call him?"

"What a servant should call their master. He's yer lord."

Kate nodded. "Yes. Well. Where I come from, people aren't always so official."

Cadha cocked her head and propped her hands against her hips. "So ye remember now? And where is that ye come from?"

Kate shrugged, uneasy now from the interrogation. "Far away. Listen, what do we do for dinner?"

"We?"

"Doesn't matter. I'll make something. Ian—I mean, *the lord*—hasn't eaten anything since yesterday."

Kate passed by Cadha into the house, feeling the woman's suspicious gaze on her like a heavy weight.

The kitchen was empty, but full of the smell of bread and cooking. Kate looked into the cauldron. In the now familiar medieval fashion, there were several linen pouches where vegetables, meat, and eggs were cooking. The water had already stopped boiling, steam rising.

The table was still covered with flour. And, like before, peels, crumbs, and dirt covered the surface.

Manning.

At least there was a bucket with fresh water. She poured it into the empty barrel where she did the dishes and took a clean cloth. Cleaning always brought her a strange sense of satisfaction, like she was blessing the house, and raising her worth by doing something useful. Wiping the table was something she'd done thousands of times in Cape Haute, working as a busser and a cleaner after her mom died. The familiarity brought nostalgia, her chest tensing and aching sweetly.

She wanted a burger, she realized.

It was one of the dishes she hated making on a daily basis because it was so simple, so uncreative—now she craved it!

Could she make one for Ian? He'd loved her sandwich, so maybe he'd love a burger...

But how would she make it without a stove? There was a cast-iron pan hanging on the wall, and she could put it into the bread oven and grill the patties over the coals. Not having a meat grinder, she'd have to mince the meat with a knife. She'd lack some spices, of course, like pepper... And she wouldn't have real buns, but bread would do. Without ketchup, mayonnaise, and pickles, she'd have to add moisture and a nice tang by melting thin slices of cheese over the patties.

Oh yes. Fresh parsley, garlic, and onion, and just a tad of rosemary would go a long way towards adding flavor.

Giddy with anticipation to have Ian try it, Kate went to work. She put on a simple linen headscarf that Cadha had given her to keep her hair out of the food. There wasn't any beef, so she made chicken patties.

Ian came into the kitchen as she was working. He picked up the edge of her scarf and fiddled with it.

"Ye look bonnie," he said. "I've sent Manning to the northernmost farms and a boy to Falnaird, my cousin Craig's home," he added. "He must be there now with his wife. Many of my clansmen being northeast with Bruce, I canna reach them in time. But I hope Craig and his men will come. Mayhap Owen if he's around. I need all the help I can get, and I ken my clan will do everything they can."

Kate nodded. "Sounds like a wise decision. Do you think you'll have enough time to prepare?"

"There's never enough time, but we probably still have a few days. The pigheaded Sassenachs dinna ken 'twas me. They wilna track us here, down the loch. The English dinna ken our lands. There are several farms on the way and Manning will warn them. Surely, the Sassenachs will want to replenish their provisions there. On the morrow I raise an army. But I canna do anything more today."

Kate sighed. "I'd say you've had enough adventures for today. You must be starving." Kate wiped sweat from her forehead. Heat from the coals blazed into her face as she stared into the oven to make sure she wouldn't burn the meat. "Wait another fifteen minutes. I'm almost ready."

He frowned. "Minutes?"

Oh darn. Did they not measure time with minutes yet? Right. She hadn't seen any clocks. They probably hadn't even been invented yet.

"I mean, soon."

He stood by her side. "It smells divine. What are ye cooking, Katie?"

Playfully, he laid his hand on her back and slowly ran it down to her bottom.

"Whatever ye're cooking, I verra much like *how* ye do it."

A pleasant shiver ran through Kate where he touched her. "A surprise. From home."

"As long as ye're eating with me…"

"Oh, I am. I'm suddenly so homesick, nothing will do but the food. Why don't you get us a bottle of wine?"

"Oh, aye. I'll put water to boil for bathing and set the table, dinna fash yerself."

He set to work bringing fresh water from the well and pouring it into the cauldron. A short time later, Kate held a plate loaded with medieval burgers. They were essentially sandwiches, but not bad considering the conditions. Who knew that after eight years of grilling dozens of burgers every day, Kate would be craving them?

She took the plate into the great hall.

Outside, night had already settled in, and the windows glowed indigo. Candles and flowers decorated the lord's table: bright-yellow marigolds, purple thrift, and white flowers she didn't know the name of. Plates and cups and a clay jug were already on the table. Ian stood up as she walked in.

Kate's heart thundered against her ribs as she set the plate of burgers on the table. This was like a date. A romantic, candlelit dinner date with a hot Highlander in a medieval castle.

Well, technically, Dundail wasn't a castle. But that didn't matter. Anything would be romantic, as long as Ian was by her side.

Oh God, if this was a date, she shouldn't be in an apron, wearing a torn-and-dirty dress, with hair that looked like a crow's nest. Kate wiped her hands against the apron and untied it. She put it on a bench, then took her seat by Ian's side.

"Sorry, I look like hell," she said. "You deserve a romantic dinner with a lady."

Ian was staring at her without blinking. In the light of the candles, his face was relaxed and full of wonder. His brown eyes were warm, his red hair ablaze from the light. Kate studied the thin scar crossing the edge of his left eyebrow, the slightly crooked bridge of his nose, the cut that started just above his bristle.

God, he was handsome. Handsome, and kind, and so wounded. Kate was torn between the urge to kiss every inch of his face while cuddling in his arms and the desire to listen to his heartbeat to make sure he was real.

"Ye're the only person in the world I want to share my evening meal with, Katie," he said. "And ye've never been more bonnie than ye are now."

Warmth rushed to Kate's cheeks, and she looked away, unable to meet the heat in his eyes. She exhaled sharply and smiled, picking up the plate with the burgers and offering it to him.

"Try this. It's from my homeland. I make these every day."

Ian chuckled softly and looked at the dish.

"I would have gladly skipped the meal, lass, as I am much more famished for something else." He picked up a burger, while Kate's face heated even more. "But I canna say nae to yer cooking. Especially since this came from yer home."

He put the burger on his plate and waited for her to take hers. Then he raised his cup.

"To home," he said. "'Tis nae the house that makes a home but people...a person."

Kate's smile fell as she thought about what he said. Was her apartment in Cape Haute really her home? Did her sister and her nephew make it so? Because it wasn't the building or the restaurant or the investors. She gazed at Ian.

Despite the short time she'd spent here, and despite the fact that she was a complete stranger in this land and this time, a feeling of home settled in her chest when she looked at him.

"To home," she echoed.

They clunked their cups and drank. The wine was sourer than what she was used to in her time, and it was probably diluted with water, but it would go nicely with the burgers.

Ian lifted his burger and bit into it, chewed, and nodded. "Aye, lass, ye've outdone yerself again. 'Tis delicious."

Blazing from the compliment, Kate bit into her own burger and chewed. Yes, not bad. The bread was a bit rough and tasted sour as any rye bread, but the meat had good flavor after being grilled over the coals, and the cheese was just the right combination of creamy, sour, and salty.

"These are even better with beef," she said through a mouthful.

"I will slaughter a cow for ye if ye make these every day," he said.

She chuckled. "Actually, I do make them every day back home."

He straightened. "Oh, aye? Nae wonder ye're so good at it. I swear, since I met ye, I've eaten the best meals of my life. Before the caliphate, everything is a blur, as though I didna truly live. In the caliphate, food didna matter. They fed us well, aye. Meat and fruit and bread every day. They needed to keep us strong and healthy for the fights."

Kate's chest tightened. "Fights?"

Ian stopped chewing, his face a bitter mask. He looked at the plate, then took his cup and emptied it down his throat, then poured more.

"Aye, Kate. Fights."

He met her eyes then, and Kate's heart broke at the pain and shame written on his face.

"Ye asked me to tell ye about hell. I think I can tell ye. But can ye accept me after ye've heard what I have to say?"

Of course she would. The real question was, if she told him the whole truth about time travel and everything, would he accept her? Or would he think her a mad woman?

CHAPTER 19

Ian held his breath as Kate took time to answer him. There was a gentleness in her face, and a kindness.

Would it still be there after he told her how much of a monster he'd been?

"Yes, of course," she said. "You can tell me anything. I want to know."

He nodded, then threw back the cup of wine. His hands shook as he poured another one. He was more terrified of reliving all that had happened than he wanted to admit.

"I was wounded eleven years ago, in a battle with the MacDougalls. Got a bad chest wound. My clan thought me dead, but the MacDougalls kent I wasna. They sold me to a slave ship. I dinna remember any of that. Afterward, the other slaves told me I was delirious with fever on the ship and they all thought I'd die right there. But I didna."

Unfortunately, he added silently.

"When we reached Baghdad, I was already recovering and could stand on my feet. In a slave market, the caliph bought me. My red hair and my size are verra rare and, therefore, valuable there. I'd thought I'd do construction or cut wood or stone. But the caliph had a different plan for me."

Ian's fist clenched around the cup uncontrollably, the metal felt like it would bend under his grip. Kate was just listening, her attention like a precious gift he couldn't repay. He hadn't realized how much he needed a friendly ear, how much he needed to share the heavy burden of his experience.

"What plan?" she said, her voice just above a whisper.

"The caliph had a secret kind of entertainment," Ian said. "Inspired by the ancient Romans, as I learned later. Only the richest and most important viziers and noblemen were allowed to participate. They bet their treasure on us. And nae just gold. Their women." His throat cramped, but he pressed out, "They won by having their best slaves fight each other until death."

Kate inhaled sharply.

"And you as well?"

"In the beginning, I was just a slave with exotic looks. The caliph had never owned a red-haired man before, not to mention a Highlander. But then, as I continued to bring him victory, killing my opponents one after another, I became his favorite. He even came to talk to me on occasion. I was invincible. Red Death, they called me."

Ian remembered the square courtyard brightly lit with a burning sun the first time he was sent to fight. The sticky sweat under his iron armor. His tightly clenched fist around the handle of the curved sword. The smell of hot dust and sweat. The other man, on the opposite side of the courtyard. It had been a taller man, brown-haired and heavy-built.

There were dozens of guests sitting along the long balconies on each side of the courtyard walls.

Ian's right hand shook. He still wasn't fully recovered from a piercing wound in his shoulder, just below the collarbone, that he'd received a moon ago. It ached constantly. The man was bigger and looked stronger than him, and the deadly threat on his face meant this wasn't his first fight.

But it wasn't Ian's first, either, he reminded himself amid the bloodthirsty cries and cheers of the spectators. All he needed now was to survive. He remembered, he prayed a Celtic prayer before battle.

WHEN THE MOUTH SHALL BE CLOSED,
  When the eye shall be shut,
  When the breath shall cease to rattle,
  When the heart shall cease to throb.

WHEN THE JUDGE SHALL TAKE THE THRONE,
  And when the cause is fully pleaded,
  O Jesu, Son of Mary, shield Thou my soul... [1]

THE FIGHT BEGAN. IAN'S OPPONENT LAUNCHED AT HIM IN A flash of golden hair and white flesh, with overwhelming power, like a battering ram. It took Ian all he had to not get killed. And even more, to wound his opponent. He didn't want to kill the man. They were not enemies, not by choice. They were both victims of bad luck, forced to fight against each other.

He slashed the man's thigh. The wound wouldn't bring death but was enough to immobilize him.

The man fell, clutching at his leg. Ian stood above him, panting. He'd expected the gates where he'd entered to open again and for him to be allowed to go back to the barracks.

But the crowd yelled. Their voices livid, men stood and waved their arms at him, urging him to act, to do something. Ian glanced at the caliph, the man in a white robe and a white turban, the only man sitting immobile. The caliph had a satisfied half smile on his face. He raised one hand, his ringed fingers glistening with gold and jewels, and archers appeared on the roofs of the buildings that were the perimeter of the courtyard, their arrows pointed at Ian.

The caliph said something in Arabic, which, as Ian later found out, meant that only one man would leave that courtyard alive that day. And it was up to Ian who that would be.

Then the caliph made a gesture of cutting his throat with his index finger.

That was enough to understand. Ian looked down at the giant, who was trying to rise but failing. His teeth bared in a terrible, desperate grin, he waved his sword helplessly at Ian, but Ian only stepped aside.

He had to kill the giant or be killed himself.

Understanding hit him like a cold shower.

It was one thing to fight for his clan, for his family, for the people he loved, for the cause he believed in.

It was another to kill people who hadn't done him wrong. To kill them because a man with gold and jewels on his hands told him to.

To kill them to buy his own life.

The caliph cried a word, and the archers pulled the strings of their bows back.

Ian couldn't hesitate. It was either his life or the blond man's.

"O Jesu, Son of Mary, shield my soul," Ian whispered and slashed the man's neck with his sword.

The spectators erupted in cheers. Some were happy, others angry. The archers disappeared. The caliph met Ian's glance and gave a barely noticeable nod, his face impartial and still.

Ian shook himself like a dog, shaking off the memory. He looked at Kate who eyed him with concern and compassion. The words poured out of him, painful and yet cleansing, like opening a rotting wound and cleaning it.

"The Red Death won every single fight," Ian said. "Eleven years. Dozens of lives. Husbands. Fathers. Brothers. Sons. From Africa. China. India. England. Egypt. Many, many Arabs. At times two or even three were up against me. I killed them all…"

He looked at his hands, surprised there was no blood.

"I'm a beast, Kate. A monster. I will never be whole, and there will never be redemption for me."

She took his hands in hers, and a soft, gentle current of tingling went through him. He met her eyes.

"You're not a monster, and you're not a beast," she said firmly. "The monster is the caliph. The whole system of slavery is the beast. You're a survivor, Ian."

A tremor went through him at her words, like the pus had been cleaned out of the wound and now the healing balm was applied, and it burned.

"Ye are too kind, Kate. I dinna deserve yer good heart."

"Don't punish yourself more than life has already punished you. I know you seek forgiveness, but it's not anyone else's to give. It's your own forgiveness that you need."

He shook his head. "How can I forgive myself when I vowed to God to never kill again and yet—"

He poured more wine.

"Ye've seen me."

"Ian," she whispered. "You stopped. I saw that it was the darkness that sucked you in, but you found it in yourself to see the light."

"Because of ye, Kate. Everything good in my life is happening because of ye."

She cupped his jaw, and he turned and kissed her palm.

"No one has ever done anything to save me," she said. "What you did for me... No one has ever protected me like that."

"I'll protect ye until my last breath."

And he'd love her even longer.

Their eyes locked, and he got lost in Kate's gaze. She stood up and came to sit on his lap, enveloping him in her delicious smell. Without another word, she kissed him. Her warm, soft mouth tasted delicious and felt like heaven. He wrapped his arms around her waist and pressed her against himself, her body pliable and responsive under his palms.

He wanted her whole, body and soul. He wanted to show her how much her acceptance meant to him. How much he wanted her. How much he needed her.

His heart expanded, his body light, his skin tingling as he picked her up and carried her to his bedchamber.

CHAPTER 20

In Ian's arms, Kate felt like a warrior's prize. Like she weighed nothing with her 170 pounds. Like he'd fight the whole world for her.

Surely this was just her wishful thinking. A dream or something.

If it was, she didn't want to wake up. Ian climbed one flight of stairs and pushed the door to his bedroom with his back. He laid Kate on a massive wooden bed. It smelled like him—leather and steel and woodsmoke.

The fire was already playing in the fireplace. Besides that, there were several chests and a table with a slanting top. A giant barrel stood by the fireplace. It looked like an oversize whiskey barrel with straight walls, and was big enough to fit two or three people.

Ian's arms pressed into the bed on each side of Kate's shoulders. He kissed her deeply, sending an electric current of pleasure right into her groin.

"I am going to wash ye," he purred when he stopped the kiss. "Then ye're going to wash me, and then I'm going to make love to ye."

The promise in his voice was heavy and intoxicating, and

filled Kate's whole body with bubbly anticipation.

"Aye?" he said.

Oh God, how did one construct words? "Yes, please."

He nodded, male satisfaction on his face. "I will bring hot water. Dinna go anywhere."

Her legs were like jelly, so she couldn't have moved even if he'd tried to chase her out with a stick.

Ian brought two steaming buckets of water and poured them into the barrel.

"Come," he said.

The prospect of undressing in front of him heated Kate's cheeks and neck, but she wasn't sure if it was because she was ashamed of being naked in front of him or because he stood by the barrel and looked at her with dark, hungry eyes.

In either case, she wouldn't back out now.

She stood up from the bed and walked to him on weak legs.

"Turn around," she said.

"Nae." He chuckled.

Oh Jesus. He'd see her naked and run away. "Turn around!"

"Nae."

Ian hooked the edge of his tunic and pulled it up and over his head. Kate's mouth dried at the sight of him. He was all lean muscle and male gorgeousness, with a broad chest and shoulders, firm pecs, and a triangle of muscle at the bottom of his hard stomach leading down under his breeches. Several silver scars caught her attention—a long one on his side, a ragged one above his heart and beneath his collarbone, and a few smaller ones across his shoulders, solid biceps, and chest.

Kate's throat convulsed at the thought of what those scars signified. The hardships he'd gone through, the pain, the constant fear and torture he'd been living for eleven years.

They also signified his strength, his unbreakable, unbendable spirit.

And they made her love him even more.

Kate reached out and gently stroked the big scar above his

heart with her thumb. "That's when all this started, isn't it? When the MacDougalls wounded you?"

Ian looked at her hand as though she'd touched him with red-hot iron tongs. Kate moved her hand, but he pinned it in place, pressing her fingers to the scar.

"Aye," he said, his voice rasping. "Touch me here. Touch me anywhere. Make the pain go away. Make me whole again."

Kate's fingers burned. She? Make him whole?

"How can I make you whole when I'm damaged myself, Ian?" she asked.

His eyes softened, and something connected between them on a level deeper and stronger than she'd ever imagined. Maybe their souls came together, maybe it was something else, but he became an extension of her, and she became an extension of him.

"I dinna ken. But ye're already doing it."

An unexpected tear crawled down her cheek. She? Healing anybody, making anyone's life better? She hadn't done anything.

"It's you," she said. "You're the one healing me. Not the other way around."

He stroked her cheek with his knuckles.

"And now, I'm going to wash ye, lass," he said.

He removed his pants and stood before her, completely naked, and completely breathtaking. Long legs with the muscles of a skier, narrow hips and...the biggest, most beautiful penis she'd ever seen.

How would he even fit inside her?

Kate breathed out softly. "You're...you look like a god."

Ian shook his head and laughed softly. The sound beautiful and dear and precious.

"'Tis a sweet way to try to distract me, Katie, but it wilna work. If one of us has a connection to the divine, 'tis ye, nae me. My soul is bound to hell. But I will show ye the stars before I go."

Kate licked her lips. She opened her mouth to protest. He

wasn't bound to hell. He was some sort of a Celtic god, the flame itself, hot and powerful and all-consuming.

But before she could say anything, he said, "Ye're thinking too much."

Then he drew her to himself and kissed her.

His hard body pressed against hers, but his lips were the softest things that had ever touched her. He eased his tongue between her lips and began a teasing game of stroking, licking, gently sucking, and nipping. Kate's bones turned to mush, and a deep moan built in the back of her throat.

"Aye, 'tis better," Ian mumbled approvingly.

He undid the girdle at her waist, then pulled the edge of Kate's sleeveless overtunic over her head. Then he did the same with the soft linen gown that had been under it. Kate tingled more and more as he got closer to her skin with each layer.

Was she ready for this? When was the last time she'd had sex? Must have been five years ago or so, with her last boyfriend, Jim. She wasn't even waxed or shaved—not that it would matter in medieval times, she thought.

Finally, she stood before him in nothing but her smock, and he bent one last time and pulled the fabric up and over her head.

Kate held her breath, fighting her instinct to cover herself. There she was before him, every curve, every pore exposed for him to see.

And he, a Greek god, a gladiator in the flesh, so gorgeous it hurt to look at his perfect form. If ever there was a model of a man's beauty, he stood before her.

Kate looked down, not daring to meet his gaze, and yet craving it more than anything. What would she see in his eyes? Disgust? A polite smile? Desire? Maybe he was into women with curves for all she knew. Then she'd be in luck.

Ian sank to his knees in front of her and wrapped his arms around her hips, taking her bottom in his hands, then pressed kisses to her stomach. He looked up at her.

"Never have I seen a woman more bonnie than ye, Kate," he said. "I want to worship every part of ye. Will ye let me?"

Worship her?

Her?

She was too disoriented from the hot desire in her veins and his male beauty to think of it, but distant parts of her psyche shook their heads in disbelief.

She shut them up and let her body and her heart take over.

"Yes," she whispered.

"Come," he said.

He rose and took her by the hand. He stepped on a small stool set by the washing barrel and climbed into the tub, then helped her in as well. The water was warm, just the right temperature, and Kate moaned at the wet touch of it on her sensitive flesh.

Ian sat on the bottom of the barrel and leaned against the wall. "Come here," he said.

Kate went to him and settled between his legs. His erection that felt hotter than the water, pressed against her lower back. He reached out to a small shelf built into the edge of the tub and took a piece of soap. It smelled flowery.

"'Tis a Castile soap," he said. "Made of olive oil, nae tallow as they do here. Father must have bought it a while ago. I canna imagine he'd have spent money on expensive soap in recent years."

He foamed the soap between his hands, put it back on the shelf, and massaged Kate's shoulders. She relaxed her head and sagged against him. His hands went down to her breasts and began massaging them, sliding over her skin, playing with her hardening nipples.

"Ohhhh..." she moaned. "This feels so good..."

"I wholeheartedly agree, lass," Ian said.

He washed her, rubbing and caressing her breasts, then ran his hands down to her stomach, her sides and her hips.

When he reached her hips, he slowed his movements down.

He gently kneaded her thighs and spread her legs. The gesture was so wanton, so sexy, Kate bit her lower lip. He slowly made his way towards her sex, every squeeze taking her higher into a cloud of delirious happiness.

Then his fingers were at her sex. He spread her folds and gently stroked her there. Kate arched her back at the intensity of the pleasure that shot through her. He began exploring her there, rubbing, slapping slightly, delicately tugging.

Kate hissed and moaned and shook while he found his way around her body.

"Ye like that lass," he murmured. "How about this?"

He applied more pressure against her clitoris, and a shudder went through Kate's legs. All she could manage, was a noise that resembled a meow.

"Oh, aye, I think ye like that."

He continued his game while Kate tightened more and more strongly in her core.

Then he suddenly withdrew, lifted her, and turned her to face him. She straddled him, his cock pressing against her stomach.

Ian undid Kate's hair, and the long tresses fell into the water and swam around her like sunrays.

"So beautiful, lass. How did I ever deserve ye?" he said.

He held her gaze, and there was a question in his eyes, as though, he was asking if she was really ready. She bit her lip and nodded. She wasn't just ready, she needed him.

Lifting her in one swift movement, he invaded her sleek core. He cursed under his breath, and Kate almost fainted from the wave of pleasure. He withdrew, then thrusted again, diving inside her, stretching her to the most delicious limits. He wrapped one arm around her waist to hold her in place and increased the rhythm, pounding into her with throaty, growly noises.

With the other hand, he reached between her legs and found her engorged clit. The moment he touched it, she was on the edge of an orgasm. He devoured her with his eyes, as though he were seeing the sky for the first time after years in prison.

In his strong arms, and under his sweet assaults, Kate was unraveling, being peeled open to the very core of her soul. Their eyes were locked. He looked at her as though he'd die if he didn't.

The orgasm took her like a hurricane, and as she tightened and convulsed around him, he stiffened, his hands digging into the flesh of her hips to pin her to him with every thrust he made.

She tightened and released, wave after wave in an eternity of world-shattering pleasure. The orgasm cascaded through her in a burning surge, and when it was over, she fell on top of him, into his arms. She hid her face in his neck, inhaling his delicious masculine scent.

As the aftershocks of their lovemaking were calming down, she stiffened.

She wanted to stay in his arms and have him at her side forever. She was falling deeper and deeper in love with him.

Loving him meant pain. Loving him meant her heart would be crushed. Because no matter how much she wanted to stay with him, there could be no forever for them.

Her sister and her nephew needed her. Without Kate, they'd end up on the streets.

The more she loved him, the more she'd be shattered into pieces when she had to leave. And she loved him more and more every minute.

CHAPTER 21

Thoroughly cleaned and satisfied, Ian held Kate in his arms. They lay in his bed after having made love two more times. He inhaled the scent of her skin and of her wet hair.

Thank ye, God, Jesu, and Mary for Kate.

Ian had never been so happy in his entire life. His body expanded and light, his blood flowing easily through his veins. The intensity with which she'd given herself to him, the responsiveness of her beautiful body, made him love her even more.

He stroked her arm. "Ye're a blessing to me, lass," he said.

She looked up at him. "Me? A blessing?" She snorted.

"Aye. And it pains me that ye doubt it."

She hid her face against his chest, her hair tickling him slightly. "You just like my cooking."

"Aye, I do. But 'tisna just that." He put a finger under her chin and raised her head so that she looked at him. His throat spasmed as he met her eyes, big and blue and so bonnie. "Ye came into my life with nae warning and brightened everything. Like a light in the darkness. I didna have hope before ye. Just desperation. But ye... Just yer presence, just seeing ye walking around my house, doing simple things. Homey things. It cracks my heart open."

Tears filled her eyes. "No one has ever said that to me before."

"They're all pigheads."

She breathed easily against his skin, her breasts caressing him slightly as her rib cage moved. She traced her finger down his chest.

"Tell me about yer home," he said. "Tell me about the far away."

His lungs stopped working as he waited for her answer. This all felt too good to be true. He'd need to take her back to Inverlochy. Destiny wouldn't let her be his forever. If God was willing, Ian would protect his lands against the Sassenachs. But then she'd be gone, too.

And that would be his punishment for the countless deaths he had caused so that he could live. For keeping the lass here, despite knowing that the enemy was coming. For these selfish acts.

KATE BRIEFLY CLOSED HER EYES, GATHERING HER INNER strength. She needed to go to save Deli Luck, she needed to go to take care of her sister and her nephew. She needed to take part in that TV show if it wasn't too late.

Sooner or later, this magical dream where she had fallen in love with a Highlander would be over. And Ian had told her the truth about himself. He'd told her the most difficult thing he'd ever done.

She wanted to tell him the truth, too, no matter how crazy it would sound, no matter if he believed her or not. It was important that she was honest with him.

Because that was what they were. Honest with each other.

Would he believe her? Her purse with the only objects she

had from her time was now with the English; otherwise, she could have shown him the date on the bottle, and the money, and the credit cards. He wouldn't have doubts then.

But he'd asked her, and she'd tell him.

Kate pushed up from his chest and propped herself with her hand on the bed. She gathered the blanket to her chest to cover her nakedness and also as a gesture of protection, to shield herself from the pain she was about to inflict on both of them.

"I must tell you where I really come from, Ian," she said. "But you may not believe me. In fact, you most probably won't."

He frowned and sat straight up, all easiness gone.

"Do you remember I told you I was from so far away you wouldn't believe me?"

His gaze grew so intense, his eyes were like black coals in the semidarkness of the room. "Aye."

She swallowed. "It's not the distance that's far. It's time."

He shook his head. "Time?"

"When you found me in Inverlochy, I had just traveled in time. I was born in 1989 in another country, the United States of America."

He narrowed his eyes, studying her as though he was struggling to understand her.

"What are ye saying, lass?"

"In Inverlochy, there's a rock... It was carved by the Picts, and there's some sort of magic that allows people to travel through time."

He shook his head again in disbelief.

"Lass—"

"I know, it sounds crazy. But however crazy it is, it's true. Back in 2020, I met this woman—Sìneag. She told me about the legend of a rock that opens a tunnel under the river of time. In 2020, Inverlochy stands ruined, and I—"

She remembered the rude advances of Logan Robertson.

"I slipped and fell and hit my head. I think I had a concussion and probably that's why I lost my memory. But I remember crawling through the darkness, disoriented, panicked, looking for a way out. And there, in the darkness, glowed that carving of a river and a tunnel, and there was this handprint in the stone. And I laid my hand there. I touched it. And I felt like I literally fell through the stone."

She sighed. "The next thing I remember, is you."

She let out another long breath.

There. All the cards were on the table, and it was up to him whether he'd pick them up or not.

Ian blinked. "I want to believe ye, I do. Aye, that does sound like madness. Or like ye hit yer head verra hard. But I..." He shoved his fingers through his hair. "Ye havna judged me or rejected me after I told ye the worst part of my life. And I wilna judge or reject ye, either. I see ye believe ye are from the future. I will assume—at least for now—that ye are."

Kate squeezed his hand.

"I believe the Highlands are full of magic, and we are a super-stitious people. We still believe in faeries and kelpies and loch monsters. Mayhap, there's the time traveling rock somewhere in Inverlochy."

Kate smiled, lightness filling her chest. Did he really believe her? "Thank you."

"Aye. Well. Yer strange manner of speaking. Yer unique cook-ing. The strange materials in yer purse."

She nodded. "Yes. It's all modern. I can't help it. That's what I know from back home."

His face went blank. "Home..."

Kate's smile fell. "Home."

"Tell me about it."

Kate looked at her hands.

"Home is with my sister, Mandy, and my nephew, Jax..."

She then told him everything. Even about her workaholic mom. Her childhood full of neglect and struggle. About Mandy's depression. About Deli Luck.

Kate remembered the day Mandy and she had bought the restaurant.

They'd walked into the building, and Kate's head had spun from happiness. There was nothing in there, just empty walls, big windows, and hardwood floors. It smelled like dust.

"I like the blinds," Mandy said, looking at the windows. Jax, who was three, sat in his stroller and played with a police car that went *wee-oww wee-oww*.

The sun shone through the windows and the blinds left striped shadows on the walls and the floor.

"They look very retro," Kate said. "Very diner. We want something more unusual."

"But this town wants retro and diner."

"No, there are enough of those places. You know I want to cook something more creative than burgers and spareribs."

"I know, hon." Mandy shook her head and shrugged. "But I don't see any of our customers enjoying a vegan quinoa bowl with avocado, either."

Kate's stomach tightened. A part of her agreed with Mandy, but she didn't want to give in to negativity. Mandy seemed to have felt well over the past couple of weeks. She took her medications regularly and didn't miss therapy. But there wasn't any way to know if she was thinking clearly.

"Only because they've never tried one," Kate said.

"And they've never tried one because they don't want one."

Kate didn't want to stress out Mandy with unnecessary arguments. She'd better change the subject. She walked towards the back of the space. "Here's a good place for a kitchen door."

"Yeah. That looks good. Nice central place for the waiters to move quickly. That's what you want."

Kate smiled. "Yeah. Agreed. And there are also stairs leading to the first floor where we all can live. Do you want to see it?"

A smile blossomed on Mandy's face. "Of course!"

She let Jax out of the stroller, and the three of them went up the stairs and into the apartment. Like downstairs, it was big and empty. The old windows, hardwood floors, and flower-patterned wallpaper made Kate think of old times.

Kate finished the tour and they stood in the living room. "We don't need much. Two bedrooms is enough, right?"

"Absolutely. I'll share a room with Jax. And it's so convenient that it's in the same building as the restaurant."

Kate hugged her sister, her small frame feeling fragile in Kate's arms. "I'm so relieved you like it." She sank to the floor and stroked Jax's full cheek with her knuckles. He giggled. "And don't worry, I'll take care of you two. With money coming in, Jax can go to preschool. You can go to college like you wanted."

She picked up Jax, set him on her hip, and kissed his sweet, plump cheek.

"Actually," Mandy said, and her eyes sparkled for the first time in a long time. "What would you think if I were to help you in the restaurant?"

"Help me?"

"Yeah. With anything. Waitressing. Cleaning. Running the business."

Kate frowned. "Are you sure you're well enough? And what about college?"

"I want to go to college to be able to run my own business one day. But here we'll *have* a business, already. And I could always get an online degree, part-time."

Kate bit her lip. "I'd love nothing more than to do this together, but I don't want to overburden you. I'll take care of you, don't worry."

Mandy's smile fell. "I'm not worried. I just want to do something. Feel useful."

"Does Dr. Lambert think it's a good idea?"

"I don't know yet."

"Tell you what, let's talk to her and if she clears you for work. We'll figure something out, okay?"

The doctor had cleared Mandy for work, but Kate still had trouble delegating and giving her sister tasks, afraid that anything might trigger another episode of depression. Mandy's episodes became less frequent with time, and she became more help than Kate had admitted to herself.

Kate told Ian how Mandy had gotten a celebrity interested in their restaurant—it took a bit of explaining about what TV was and that a TV cooking show was widely popular. Ian blinked, disbelief written all over his face, but he didn't interrupt.

She told him how she'd wound up in Scotland. How this was their last chance to save the restaurant and keep their home. Ian didn't ask questions but listened intensely. His face solemn, he nodded from time to time.

Telling someone about her life was strange. She didn't usually like to talk about herself or her past, but sharing with Ian was freeing, and surprisingly easy.

When she finished, the last word drying out like a drop of water in the fire, Ian was looking at her, his jaw muscles working.

"Say something," Kate said finally, unable to wait any longer to hear what he thought.

"So ye want to go back to... 2020? Is that so?"

She clenched her fingers together till her knuckles whitened and hurt. She didn't want to go back. What she wanted, was to stay with him forever. But she had to leave.

"Yes, Ian," she said, her throat painful.

He nodded.

"Aye. It makes sense now."

"What does?"

"God wouldna have sent me a woman like ye to make me happy. He sent ye to me to punish me. To give me the biggest happiness of my life only to take ye away."

Pain pierced Kate's gut. "No, no. No one is punishing you. You were already hurt enough. You should stop beating yourself up for something that was done to you. For something beyond your control."

"'Tis all right, lass. At least I'll ken ye'll be alive and safe, even though in the future. I never expected to be happily marrit. My life is destined to be lonely, lass."

Kate's chest tightened painfully. To hear a man like him saying that was so sad.

And yet it reflected her own thoughts about her future. She'd never thought she'd be one of those women who found their soul mate. Somehow, in the back of her mind, she'd always known she wasn't worthy of true love. She wasn't lovable.

Maybe that's why her mom never took care of her. Something about her made her simply unworthy.

"So is mine," she said.

"Yers?" He chuckled. "Ye should be praised and worshipped and loved every single day, by a man who's worthy of ye. 'Tis nae me..."

But it was him. Kate knew it like she knew her own name, if anyone could make her happy, it was Ian.

"I promised ye, I will take ye to Inverlochy," he said. "And I will make sure ye get back to yer time."

Kate's heart shook and trembled, threatened to break into a million pieces. She loved him for promising to take her back, but the idea of leaving him tore her chest apart.

"Well, I'm not leaving yet." She crawled to him and straddled him.

The blanket fell off, and Ian looked her up and down with the eyes of a ravenous predator.

"Nae, ye're certainly not. Not if I have any say in the matter."

He drew her onto his chest and kissed her hungrily, and Kate forgot everything but his body and her shivering need for it.

But she knew it would never be enough. Leaving Ian would be like leaving a part of her soul behind.

CHAPTER 22

T he next day...

BANG. BANG. BANG.

Ian hammered at his father's sword in the workshop that stood by the house. The edge glowed orange red, the heat emanating from it bringing droplets of sweat to Ian's forehead, bare back, and chest. The scent of hot iron hung in the air.

He'd need the sword verra soon, and the blade had some indents and scratches, so Ian set about repairing it.

Earlier this morning, he'd taken his father's claymore from where it hung proudly on the wall of the great hall, and carefully brushed his hand along the length of its blade. It was a simple sword. Leather bound the handle, the pommel was a circle, and the ends of the cross guard had rings welded together forming two four-leaf clovers on each side.

And it was blessed by his father. Ian would honor his father and the whole clan by using it for good.

He hadn't had any uisge since the day before he'd gone

riding on Thor. He didn't need any. The night with Kate had made him drunk from happiness, despite the threat coming ever closer.

"Lord! Lord!" cried a male voice outside the smithy.

Ian raised his head. "In here."

Steps pounded against dry dirt-packed ground. A thin figure appeared in the doorway. It was Frangean MacFilib who Ian had seen a few days ago. The lad's clothes were torn, and dried blood sprayed his face.

Ian straightened, the hammer hanging heavy in his hand. "What is it?"

The lad dropped his hands to his knees and panted. "The Sassenachs. They raided the farm." He lowered his head. "Killed Da."

Ian's fists clenched. He'd been so wrong to underestimate how fast the army could move. "Manning didna reach ye?"

"This morning. We tried to defend ourselves, but there were too many of them. Went like a knife through butter."

Ian's pulse pounded against his temples, darkness welling up inside his gut. "How many?"

"A hundred, I think."

"A hundred..."

That must have been the garrison he'd encountered with Kate. They made it so fast. Too fast. A hundred wasn't a large number for a war, but for a small landowner like Ian, with only about seventy tenants, this was an overwhelming force.

And now they'd started killing his people...

A mixture of guilt and dread weighed on his chest. He'd already broken his vow to never kill another man again. And God would punish him for it. But whatever was in the future, Ian couldn't live with himself if he let any more of his people suffer.

Mayhap, all that he'd been through was for this moment. Mayhap, he'd become a ruthless killer because his people would need him to lead them. Mayhap, he needed to take responsibility for his clan so that they wouldn't lose their freedom even if it meant giving up his own.

Ian laid the hammer down and wiped his forehead with the back of his arm. "What is happening at yer farm now, lad?"

"I got away without anyone seeing me. I heard talk that they'd occupy the farm first before moving south."

Ian came to stand by the lad's side. "I am sorry about yer father, Frangean."

"I am sorry about yers, lord."

"Thank ye. Do ye have a sword?"

"Nae."

Ian nodded. "I have one for ye. 'Tis time to raise the fiery cross. Will ye come with me?"

The lad's Adam's apple bobbed under his sparse scruff as he swallowed. His eyes watered and reddened, but he lifted his chin. "Aye, lord."

Ian clapped him on the shoulder. "Good. I wilna let another Sassenach pig touch more of my people as long as I still breathe. Come. Let's show them whose land 'tis here."

Frangean followed Ian into the house, and Ian gave him the sword he'd taken from the English warrior.

"I'm coming with you," Kate said from behind him.

Ian turned, and his heart leaped like it did every time he saw her. She'd braided her hair today, exposing her bonnie face and big eyes, highlighting the most kissable lips he'd ever seen.

"You're going somewhere, right?" she said, looking at the sword.

"Aye, lass. The English raided and occupied the MacFilib farm."

She nodded. "I know you can't stand by and watch people lose their lives and homes. It's not who you are."

"I'm going to raise the fiery cross and ride to all the farms and villages and call my people for battle. We can only defeat the English if we are together."

"I'm coming," she repeated.

"Nae."

"Yes. I'll cook. I'll clean. I'll do stuff to help. But I can't stay here and wait. I don't want to be without you."

Her words warmed his heart.

"I'm coming," she said firmly.

Who was he to contradict her? He'd be on the road for a couple of days to reach all the farms and villages. Besides, she'd be safer with him than alone, here, without anyone to protect her.

But the main reason was, he couldn't stand the thought of separating from her, either.

"Aye," Ian said. "Ye're coming with me."

With the help of Frangean, Ian made the fiery cross. He took two straight sticks and bound them together, then lit them up to have them scorched and burned.

As he saw the cross burning, he remembered the last time he'd seen one. It was when his grandfather Colin was still alive and chief of the clan. They'd stood before Dunollie Castle, ready to fight for Marjorie, Ian's cousin, who'd been kidnapped and held by Alasdair MacDougall.

The cross had brought them victory then, and they'd retrieved Marjorie, who'd been raped and beaten. The cross was the call for war, for bloodshed, the call to stand and protect their land and their families.

Seventy farmers and one warrior against a hundred trained knights and soldiers. Their odds were bad. Only if Craig with his men came would they stand a chance.

If not, Ian would have even more deaths of innocent people on his hands.

CHAPTER 23

K ate stirred the soup in the cauldron hanging over the campfire. The night brought a chill to her body. In the darkness, campfires around the farm were burning. The air was loud with clanging swords and men grunting and cursing as they trained at sword-fighting.

Kate glanced up to find the tallest figure of all. There he was, the man she loved, fighting like a lion, his hair gold-red in the light of so many fires. He was the dance. The dance of battle, the dance of war.

The dance of death.

The flashes of his arms, the lines and angles of his legs as he stepped, whirled, and cut with the sword were beautiful. Mesmerizing.

He was the Highlands itself. A gorgeous warrior of might and power. And heart.

Of course she'd fallen in love with him. And he believed her, for God's sake. Who would believe the crazy story of time travel? Had they switched places, she certainly wouldn't have.

And he was damaged, like she.

He'd never be whole, he'd told her. That's how she felt, too.

And now the pain was even worse because Ian was doing his

duty, taking care of his people. And she? She'd selfishly abandoned hers in order to stay with the man she loved in a place where she could be killed.

What would happen to Mandy and Jax then?

She should have never come back with Ian to Dundail. She should have insisted she'd leave.

But the day had been busy. After they'd left Dundail, they'd visited three farms today. Ian had been magnificent, sitting on his black horse, the charcoal cross in his hand, his hair like a flame itself. He'd called for his people. He'd called for them to rise together with him and to die protecting their lives and families or be victorious.

He'd said a Gaelic prayer, and they had all answered. Fire kindled in their eyes, their chests puffed, their chins rose, their shoulders straightened.

"*Cruachan!*" Ian cried. "To our land! To Scotland!"

Cruachan was the Cambel clan war cry, as Kate learned.

"*Cruachan!*" they echoed.

And so now there were twenty people here. Ian had been training them in sword-fighting and archery ever since they arrived. Ian said they all lacked battle training. Half of them didn't even have swords, so they were assigned to bows and arrows.

Finally, Kate saw, they were all getting tired. One by one, they came to her and she served them the soup.

She liked to feel useful and there was gratitude in their eyes.

Ian came and sat next to her by the fire. He accepted the bowl of soup and kissed her hand.

"Thank ye," he said.

His forehead glistened with sweat and his tunic was wet under his armpits and on his chest. He still breathed heavily, but satisfaction played in his eyes.

"No problem," Kate said. "Eat up."

"Mmm." Ian closed his eyes and shook his head appreciatively. "Verra good soup, lass. Better than anything I've eaten in a camp kitchen."

Kate smiled, joy blooming in her chest from the compliment. "How is it going?"

Ian's face darkened. "They're nae warriors. Just honest farmers. They'd need months of training to stand a chance against a trained enemy like the English. We only have days at best."

The reality of the war became apparent to Kate for the first time. They did face death, faced the real horrors of violence. Things she'd only heard of and seen on TV and in movies back in her life in the twenty-first century. Kate's skin chilled and prickled.

But she wouldn't be a coward. She wouldn't make Ian's life more difficult than it already was.

"Listen," she said. "I was thinking, wouldn't it be better that I leave, now that you need all your strength for your people? You have enough people to think about. I don't want to add to your troubles. And I really need to get back to help my family."

His face fell. "Leave now? My reluctance to let ye go aside, lass, 'tis verra dangerous."

Kate looked into the fire. "But I don't want to—"

He set the bowl of soup aside and took both of her hands in his, making her look into his eyes. They were dark brown in the dim light, framed by his long, light eyelashes, and both concern and heat shone through them.

"Ye dinna add to my troubles," he said slowly and firmly. "Never."

Her eyes prickled.

"But I...I can't function in this century. I don't know how things work. I didn't even know how to light that bread oven, for God's sake. If you hadn't started a fire, I couldn't have cooked... And now I'm worried you will always need to look over your shoulder to see if I'm protected instead of having your full attention on saving your own life."

Ian chuckled. "Women born in my century canna start a fire,

either. Noble ladies canna cook. And they certainly wouldna have accompanied their man to a war, too afraid of the field inconveniences. And if ye're worried about protection."

He stood up and held his hand out to her. "I'll teach ye how to protect yerself."

Kate put her hand in his and stood up. Ian reached behind his back and removed a long, sharp knife.

"There are six vulnerable areas in a man's body," Ian said. "Eyes, throat, nose, solar plexus, groin, and knee. Now, most likely, those men will be in armor, so it wilna be as easy to reach those areas."

He held out the dagger, handle towards Kate.

"So this will be yer best shot to protect yerself. Take the dirk."

"Ian, I can't. It's your weapon."

"Aye, lass, ye can. Take it. I have my sword. I'll be calmer knowing ye have this."

Kate swallowed and took the dirk. It had an antler handle and felt warm against her skin from Ian's body.

"So ye must aim for the slits of the armor. Like I said, for the eyes, throat, nose, groin, and knee. The solar plexus will be unreachable if they are in armor. Aye?"

The blood drained from Kate's face. Was she seriously going to stab a human? On the other hand, some of those humans had no problem slapping her and almost raping her.

"The trick I'm goin' to show ye will be useful if yer enemy doesna have the armor, aye?"

Kate nodded, her hands shaking.

"If they grab yer wrist, remember the 'rule of thumb.' Rotate yer arm in the direction of the enemy's thumb. Then pull yer arm back and ye'll be free. Let's try."

Ian grasped Kate's wrist, but panicked, she forgot what direction to turn it.

"Here." Ian gestured to Kate's left.

"Oh." She rotated her arm, feeling awkward and useless.

"Good. Now pull it."

She pulled and freed her hand.

"Good," Ian said. "Dinna fash yerself. Ye wilna become a warrior in one evening. But ye will learn some movements to help ye."

"Okay."

They continued training, and Ian showed her how she could hit the attacker with her elbow if they were on her side and how to hit them with her forehead and then into their solar plexus if they were in front of her.

"Ye need to bend yer knees like that, then put yer free arm vertically, like that, in front of yer body to protect the vital organs. Also, ye'll be able to move more." He jumped back and to the side to demonstrate.

"Ye remember the weak points: throat, eyes, groin?"

He bent his knees and stabbed upwards from a crouched position. He made her try it. Her whole being protested against hurting another person.

They would come after you. Or worse, after Ian. Be strong.

Kate repeated the moves diligently, praying that she wouldn't need to use them. Ian showed her what to do if someone kicked her, if someone launched at her, if someone stabbed at her from above.

By the time they finished Kate was exhausted, not just from the physical exercise but from the mental images of what those stabs, kicks, and cuts would mean.

Potentially, taking someone's life.

But no matter how gruesome the prospect of that was, Kate would breathe easier knowing there was something she could do to defend herself, so that Ian wouldn't put himself at risk worrying about her. And maybe to defend Ian if she had to.

CHAPTER 24

An icy splash of water hit Ian in the face, together with the pungent scent of the sea. The cold drops cut across his burning skin, and he opened his eyes to the gray sky. He lay wrapped in furs and blankets. The floor beneath him sank and rose, over and over. Around him, men sat among barrels watching the coast.

His chest hurt, torn apart.

He was going to be sold into slavery, Ian realized.

He was going to kill many, many men to survive. They were going to make a monster out of him.

No.

He had to stop them before they got to the shore.

He stretched his arms with an effort, pain piercing him, but the tangle of blankets and furs kept him in place like a cocoon. He wriggled, suppressing groans of agony. The dressing on his chest slipped away, and the rough wool of the blanket rubbed against the wound. It felt as if swarms of furious hornets stung him in the chest.

But it was the pain that gave him strength and set him free.

He roared and tore the cocoon off. The men looked at him, surprised.

But he didn't need to concern himself with them.

Just the captain.

Ian stood in the bottom of the ship. The angry sea pushed and played with the vessel. Ian held on to the main mast and saw the captain.

He was at the bow, staring, waiting. On weak legs, Ian made his way through the sacks, the caskets, and the barrels. Through other slaves who lay helpless.

If he could only kill that captain, just that one person, he'd never go to Baghdad, he'd never be a cold-blooded killer. And once he met Kate, he could just be happy with her.

If he only killed this one person, his life would be completely different. The ship careened left, then right, splashes of seawater shocking him.

"Ye bastart," Ian spat, balancing on the escaping floor. "Ye wilna take me to slavery."

The captain removed his dagger, the same dagger Ian had given Kate. "I will kill ye, even though I'm unarmed."

He roared and launched himself. The dagger swooshed past his side. Ian blocked the captain's hand and kicked the man to the floor. The dagger fell and slid across the ship towards the center. Ian straddled the captain and wrapped his fingers around the man's throat.

The captain's neck was surprisingly thin, the skin soft. His fingers tightened around it and he pressed. The captain's eyes bulged.

"Ian," he choked. "Ian..."

The beard disappeared. The gray hair replaced by long, silky golden tresses. Red, weathered skin turned fair and smooth.

"Ian," Kate's voice croaked. "Stop. Wake up."

He blinked.

And he was no longer in the sea. No longer on the ship. The cloth of a small tent was on both sides of him. The light of the fire outside played against it.

His hands weren't wrapped around the captain's throat. He was strangling Kate.

WITH AN APPALLED EXPRESSION, IAN LOOMED OVER HER. HE withdrew his hands and rolled off her.

"Katie." He knelt before her. "Jesu, Mary, and Joseph, are ye all right?"

Her throat tight, the horror of suffocation chilling her body, she crawled back into the other corner of the tent, as far away as possible. Her neck and throat hurt, feeling raw and bruised. She rubbed her neck.

"I'm okay," she croaked. "What was that? Did you have a nightmare?"

He looked so lost and forlorn. But it didn't diminish the very real death she'd seen before her when he'd suddenly rolled on top of her with a wild stare and clasped his strong hands around her throat.

"I...I think so, aye. 'Tis happened to me ever since I got away."

Kate inhaled deeply, enjoying the freedom of being able to fill her lungs with air. He watched her with such remorse that her heart broke.

"If anything had happened to ye, if I had...with my own hands... Ye, the woman I love... I wouldna be able to live with myself..."

The woman he loved... All the tension in her body released, and she sighed. "I know, Ian. I know you didn't mean it. I think it's PTSD."

"What?"

"A post-traumatic stress disorder. You can't help it. It's like a mental illness in a way, although treatable. It's not your fault, Ian. Many soldiers get it after a war. It's no surprise you have it."

Her neck and throat already felt much better, although still sore. She crawled towards him and he backed up.

"Nae, Katie, better stay away."

She chuckled. "You aren't going to hurt me now that you're awake."

She sat on the blanket with her legs crossed and opened her arms to him. "Come here."

He hesitated a moment. "Are ye certain, lass?"

"Yes, I'm certain. Come."

He exhaled and came to her. He lay on the blanket and put his head on her lap. The weight of his head pleasant on her legs, she gently brushed his hair and the side of his face with her palm. He closed his eyes.

"Tell me about the dream," she said.

"'Twas on the ship. I had to kill the captain so that he wouldna take me to Baghdad. I thought if I never landed there, I'd never become a slave. I'd have a chance with ye. The chance to spend a lifetime with ye."

Kate's chest throbbed. He wanted a lifetime with her. And she wanted a lifetime with him, too.

"I thought, if I killed just one person, him, I wouldna need to kill so many more innocent ones. I wouldna need to become a monster."

Kate shook her head. "You're not a monster."

"I almost killed ye. I killed that unarmed lad while getting ye away from the damn Sassenachs, and don't even recall attacking him. How can I nae be a monster?"

"You're just wounded in your soul, and healing. You're a good man. The best man I've ever known."

He rubbed her thigh gently. "Ye're too kind for saying that, lass. I dinna deserve ye."

She shook her head. "No, that's definitely not true. You deserve every good thing in your life and more. You've suffered enough."

Unlike her.

At least, that was what she'd grown up believing.

Kate stroked his scruff. "Would you feel better if I told you about my nightmares?"

"I dinna want ye to relive something that frightens ye."

"It's nothing like yours." She chuckled. "Compared to your struggles, mine were minor."

He looked up at her. "I want to ken everything about ye."

"Okay. Well. In my time, people have developed vaccines. It's medicine that helps prevent certain dangerous diseases. Parents need to take their children to a doctor to have them vaccinated. Some choose not to—it's a big debate... Anyway, my mom was not someone who opposed vaccination. She just...didn't have time to take my sister and me."

"Aye. Ye said her work was heavy."

"Yes. And so, one day—I was already seven or eight—I got whooping cough. It's a sickness that can be prevented with vaccination. And not just me, my two-year-old sister, too. I still remember lying at night, in a fever, coughing my guts out. Wanting my mom. Realizing, she didn't want me. She didn't care about me. She didn't love me."

Like Kate knew no one would. She was unlovable, unworthy of care. Even though Ian said he loved her now, he'd come to the same conclusion. So it was good that their relationship would soon end, no matter how wonderful it was now.

"She shouldna have been yer mother. Not caring for her bairns... There's no one more loving or caring that I ken, Katie, than ye."

She flushed a little. "I don't think so. I often think there's something about me that people find cumbersome. Eventually, she realized she had to take us to a hospital. We spent a couple days there, but she took us home because she couldn't afford to pay more medical bills. The doctors said the illness was already advanced enough that there was nothing they could do to heal it that she couldn't do at home—steam, soup, air humidifier. She lost one job because she stayed at the hospital and at home caring for us, then had to find two more to pay the bills that she got because of us. Anyway, I know now she was doing the best she could. I took care of my sister my whole life. I know what it means to have someone depend on you for everything. Especially as a single parent with no one else to help. But still... I sometimes dream about that hospital, lying there alone. Mom isn't there, and doctors and nurses pass me by. I cough and cough and cough, and no one can hear me or wants to see me."

He rose from her lap and took her in his arms. "Lass..."

His arms were heavy and warm around her, like a protective shield.

Kate leaned against his chest. "See, I also have nightmares. Everyone does."

"Aye. But nae everyone tries to kill another human being."

She looked up at him and cupped his jaw. "It'll pass, Ian. If only you can forgive yourself. And let yourself live. At least for now. For tonight."

"Aye." He kissed her briefly. "For tonight. And every night with ye."

His face grew somber and gathered that darkness with the edge of desperation she'd seen in his most violent moments.

"But if I try to hurt ye again, I want ye to use the knife and do what I showed ye. Aye?"

Kate's skin chilled at the thought. She'd never be able to do that.

"Promise me," he said. "That'll give me peace of mind."

Kate swallowed. He looked intensely at her, waiting. If it would give him some peace of mind, she'd promise him, but she'd never go through with it.

"Okay, Ian," she said. "I'll do it."

He kissed her again, deeply, hungrily, stirring desire in her blood. Oh yes, that was what they were good at—forgetting the pain of their souls through their bodies.

For tonight, they'd forget and be happy.

What tomorrow would bring, Kate didn't want to know.

CHAPTER 25

T*hree days later...*

THE GREAT HALL OF DUNDAIL SWARMED WITH PEOPLE. IT WAS dark again, the indigo of the late night outside fighting against the warm light of the candles.

But it wasn't an easy atmosphere. The men frowned, speaking in low voices, hunched over their cups of ale and wine. The food on the tables was modest but delicious. Kate and Manning had prepared an excellent stew of vegetables and wild-fowl that Ian had hunted earlier.

This wasn't a celebratory feast.

It was a war gathering.

Tomorrow, they'd fight.

After three days of his campaigning with the fiery cross, every single one of Ian's tenants had answered the call. Alan Ciar was among those who supported the cause the most, and he alone brought twenty-five people. The man had battle experience and sat by Ian's side at the lord's table.

Alan's eyes shone brightly. "We will make the bastarts leave," he said. "'Tis a good plan, lord."

Ian nodded, looking around the hall. There were more people than he had hoped. Eighty men—including young'uns and older men who could still hold a sword. Ian realized this was what they must have missed. Uniting for a common cause. Doing something to protect their families and livelihood.

Ian rose from the table, noting out of the corner of his eye that one more man had joined the hall—Crazy Mary. He'd been distant and observing everything skeptically, but now he stood leaning against the wall near the entrance to the great hall. He scowled at Ian, his arms were crossed over his chest.

But he was there.

"My father would have been proud of ye all," Ian said, and every single pair of eyes turned to him. "He would have sat where I sit, in his lawful place. He would have drunk with ye and ate with ye. And he would have considered it an honor to go with ye to battle."

The men nodded, straightening their backs and raising their chins.

"And I know in his spirit, he's with us. What is a better way to die than protecting yer loved—" A movement caught Ian's eye, and he saw Kate join Manning. She was in the headscarf she always put on when she cooked. It framed her bonnie face making her look so sweet. His throat clenched.

Ian locked eyes with her, happiness blossoming in his chest just from seeing her. "Protecting yer loved ones from the enemy that wants to take everything from ye?" he finished.

He looked around the room again.

"I hear our rightful king, Robert the Bruce, was in a position not much better than we are right now. Verra few people. Nae resources. Nae hope against a powerful enemy, the Sassenach king. But look at him now. He's winning. And so will we."

He took his claymore and put it on the table, leaning with his arms against the surface.

"He uses clever Highland tactics—swift movements, apt concealments, artful stalking, and silent execution. And so will we. He takes advantage of the Highland terrain, knowing the land like the English never will."

He looked in every single pair of eyes that he could meet. "And so will we."

He straightened his back, his heart thumping.

"The English are still garrisoned on the MacFilib farm, and Frangean, who's our spy there, tells me they await reinforcements in a few days. They dinna ken we have united as a force. We must act now, before more men arrive. 'Tis our only chance."

The men stuck their fists in the air and roared.

"But lord," said an older man, once the din had abated. "Many of us dinna have swords or bows. We canna fight steel with pitchforks."

He was right. That was one thing Ian still hadn't found a solution for.

"We dinna have just pitchforks," Crazy Mary said.

Everyone turned to him. Ian frowned. Manning met Ian's eyes and slowly separated himself from the wall and stood closer to the men.

"Yer father, he had weaponry. He was safeguarding many swords, in case a moment like this would come. Ian didna ken of it. But I kent."

The hall filled with the murmurs of many voices, people staring at one another in astonishment. The old fox, his father. Although he had let his home and his lands fall into disrepair, he hadn't failed to prepare for trouble.

"How many? Where are they?" Ian asked.

"Hidden. I'll show ye. I advise that no one else follows."

Ian went with Manning to the kitchen, where he pushed a large barrel aside. There was a round iron handle right in the floor. Manning pulled it, and it lifted up, opening to what looked like a small root cellar. Except, it wasn't filled with parsnips and cabbages.

There was a heap of claymores.

"'Tis enough for an army," Ian murmured.

Manning nodded, bent down, and picked up a sword.

"Aye. And 'tis time yer army grows by one more."

CHAPTER 26

Later that night, when dinner was over and men lay down to sleep in the great hall, Ian and Kate met in his bedchamber. They lay in bed after making love, her body warm and soft and pliable in his arms. If they won tomorrow, the way for her to go home would be open. If he died, he hoped it would be after he'd taken most of their enemies.

In either case, this was likely the last night they'd ever spend together.

And it would never be enough.

"I want to ken everything about ye, lass," he said. "What is yer world like in the future?"

Kate chuckled. "Well, the world, at least where I live, is generally safer than your world, I think. It's more comfortable. There's electricity that helps us save tons of work. It provides light and warmth and helps us cook without fire. A lot of what one has to do by hand in your day and age is done by machines."

"Machines?" Ian said. "'Tis like listening to a fairy tale. Sounds like magic."

"I know. It does. I've already forgotten how it feels to have a washing machine do your laundry. Medicine is much more advanced. Many diseases have been cured. Most developed countries don't have plague or pox or cholera outbreaks anymore, though we do have new diseases. Surgery is very advanced. They can now do eye surgery and improve vision."

Ian shook his head. "Sounds like a much better place to live than here."

The world she described sounded like a magical place. He was glad that in about seven hundred years, there would be such a different life. Fighting diseases, fighting death, making hard work easier.

"Slavery exists, unfortunately," Kate added carefully. "But it's against the law."

Something tightened in Ian's stomach. "Good. Verra good. A world without slavery is a better world."

"But things are not perfect. There are still wars. For the same reasons: power, money, territories. Resources. Honestly, I think in many ways your life here is simpler and easier. It's hard, physically, but there's something so satisfying about cooking from scratch, working the land, taking care of your tenants…"

"Fighting the English," Ian added. "Fighting for freedom. 'Tisna simple or easy."

"No," she said. "But it's worth fighting for."

Ian didn't think he could love her more in that moment. Some things were worth fighting for. His people.

Her.

"Women and men have equal rights where I live. It's not like that everywhere in the world, though. In the Western world, women earn money, go to work, and can even choose a life with no children."

Ian frowned. "A woman's place is with her husband," he said. "I do appreciate a woman's freedom, but 'tis her husband or her father that must—"

"Not in the future. This is a very conservative point of view. Women are their own bosses."

"I dinna ken if I agree with that. If ye were mine—" He

suddenly swallowed his words. Speaking of a future with Kate, one he could never have, was hard. Painful.

But she looked at him with her big, bonnie, kind eyes full of hope.

"If I were yours, then what?" she said.

"If ye were mine, I'd want to protect ye. I'd want to boss ye around so that ye wouldna work too hard. I'd have a hard time sharing ye with anyone. I'd want ye all to myself."

She blushed. "There are so many things that are wrong with those statements for a modern woman. You can't boss me around, and you can't keep me to yourself." Then she hid her face against his chest. "At the same time, it's so unbelievably hot..."

He kissed her, devouring her mouth, suddenly hungry for her on a new level. She leaned into him with her whole body, turning his veins into flowing fire in an instant. He became hard for her right away, his cock hot and firm and needy.

This might be the last time that he'd have her. *The last time...* Pain pierced his gut, opening a dark, bottomless pit.

Nae yet. She isna gone yet.

She put her leg over his hip, her sleek sex touching his erection. His skin flushed and burning, he crushed her to himself.

"What are ye doing to me, lass," he whispered hotly.

"What are you doing to *me?*" she echoed.

He covered her neck with kisses, her skin like the finest silk against his lips. He went lower, to her lush breasts, and cupped them with both his hands. He took one nipple into his mouth and sucked it gently, and was rewarded by a low moan as she arched her back. He repeated it with the second breast, and the nipple hardened right away in his mouth. He played with her breasts longer because he knew that would give her the most pleasure.

"These breasts should be cherished and loved every day," he said. "Should be caressed and licked and stroked."

"Oh...I agree."

Ian went lower, to his favorite place on her body—although he loved every inch of her. The scent of her there drove him mad with desire. So feminine, so wanton. He spread her gentle folds and put his mouth on her. A shudder went through her. She put her hands on his head, brushing her fingers through his hair, the touch sending soft waves of pleasure through him.

He kissed her there, in her most sensitive spot. She felt hot and silky and soft against him. She was the sweetest dessert he could ever get. He licked against her folds, and her legs tremored around him. He continued teasing her, right where he knew she loved it, and she awarded him with a satisfied, guttural moan.

She was his fae, the goddess of summer, Bride. And he was frozen and broken and in need of warmth.

He inserted a finger inside her, and her tight entrance took him in gently, bringing a surge of desire into his veins. She sucked in air, and he inserted another finger and found the most sensitive spot inside and began massaging her. She wriggled and writhed, rubbing herself against him with the rhythm of his movements. He licked, and sucked gently, and pinched the swelling bud of her sex.

She grew tighter and tighter around him and breathed faster and faster. Her voice grew louder and more and more needy.

She was close. And he wanted her to have more. He wanted to show her all the stars in the sky.

She'd said she found the commanding man desirable...

Ian withdrew, and in a fast move, flipped Kate over on her belly, dragging her delicious arse in the air, and bit her playfully.

"This arse is better than yer food," he murmured, taking two handfuls, kneading the firm, abundant flesh.

She sucked in a breath. Ian bit her again on the other cheek, and couldn't stop a growl from the sweet slide of her silky skin against him.

He continued to bite her softly, here and there, feeling himself harden even more. He didn't think he had ever been this aroused. His balls would burst if he didn't have her right now.

But this wasn't about his pleasure.

This was about her.

His bonnie, kind, golden goddess from the future. Broken, like him.

He slid his hand between her thighs and found her sex again. She shuddered as he spread her folds gently and rubbed her while biting her at the same time.

"Ye like that, lass?"

"Oh God, yes," she breathed.

"Ye will like this even more," he promised.

He stood on his knees and placed his throbbing erection at the entrance to her sleek, wet sex. She gasped softly and made a circular movement with her arse, rubbing against him, and sent a lightning bolt of bliss through him.

He made a sound that was similar to a bear's roar, then guided himself into her.

Oh dear lord. She was tight and sleek and took him in as if made for him. With one hand, he grabbed a handful of her hair, careful not to hurt her. With the other he held a handful of her hip. She was gorgeous, all his, and he all hers.

Oh, how he wished this was not the last time. But he would make it one to remember for a lifetime. A memory he could hold on to in the nights spent without her.

He moved out of her, then came back with a thrash, bursts of sunlight spreading through him. Then another thrust, and another. He bent and began fondling her engorged little bud. Kate whimpered, letting out small noises that made him drive into her even more wildly.

He sped up, the need to have her, the need to own her and be owned by her burned through him like a wildfire. She squeezed him, and he knew she was right there, on the thin blade of the orgasm.

He tightened, her excitement always spurring his own. With a violent wave of ecstasy that pulled him under like a storm surge, he spilled into her. He grabbed her hips to steady himself, thrusting over and over, wanting to give himself to her whole.

Till his last drop.

Her body shuddered, rocked by waves of delight as she cried his name again and again.

Then they both stilled, panting.

Kate flopped forward, then turned over and lay on her back, pulling him on top of her. She wrapped her arms and legs around him, meeting his lips in the most gentle kiss. They lay like that and breathed together, being one.

Even if just for a few moments.

She looked at him after a while. "I don't want to go," she said. "I also don't want you to go to war. I want this to last forever."

Ian brushed her head with his palm. "I wish this, too, lass. I wish this, too."

And as he squeezed her tighter to himself, willing the borders between their bodies to dissolve, he knew that his whole life was worth it, just because of today. Just because of this night.

But as time passed, as the first sunrays illuminated the room, he knew that the fairy tale was over and that when Kate left he'd be back to his old destiny.

The destiny of a broken man.

CHAPTER 27

In the darkness of the night, the MacFilib farm was quiet. Tents stood around the house and in the oat fields that spread like giant silver blankets on the ground. Two camp-fires burned, and Ian guessed they were where the watchmen would be. The rest must be sleeping.

Arrogant bastarts. Must be so sure they wouldn't meet any opposition.

Craig and Owen hadn't shown up. Mayhap, Craig didn't get the message or he wasn't able to come because he was dealing with his own issues. But Ian just couldn't afford to wait any longer or he'd have to deal with the English reinforcements as well.

"Is Frangean ready?" Alan asked, crouching next to Ian behind a boulder.

"As soon as I give him the signal," Ian said.

"Aye."

The troops stood hidden in the woods around the farm, swords and bows at the ready.

Ian looked back into the forest. Somewhere there, Kate hid. She'd refused to stay behind in Dundail, sure that she could be useful, too, somehow. She'd take care of the wounded, at least give them water and bandage them, as well as steer the horse-drawn carriage with the wounded if need be. Ian had taught her how to do that.

Ian's heart thumped in his chest. This wouldn't be a straightforward battle. Nor a fair one. The English were a stronger force, battle-honed and armored, whereas most of the Highlanders lacked armor and experience. Attacking in the darkness and using their cunning was their way to even the chances.

Was Ian truly going to kill again? So cold-bloodedly, cutting the throats of distracted men?

Yes, he was. Because they'd come for his land and the land of his people. They'd come to kill.

Because they were about to take Ian's freedom and the freedom of many more Highlanders. And Ian wouldn't let that happen.

If he was going to be a monster, freedom was one thing he was ready to go to the depths of darkness for.

His stomach as hard as rock, his blood pulsing in his temples, he murmured the prayer for victory:

*A*LL-SEEING *G*OD,
   Satisfy and strengthen me;
   Blind, deaf, and dumb, ever, ever be
   My contemners and my mockers...

*A*LAN'S VOICE JOINED HIM, THEN MORE AND MORE MEN echoed, until everyone whispered together:

*T*HE TONGUE OF *C*OLUMBA IN MY HEAD,
   The eloquence of Columba in my speech;
   The composure of the Victorious Son of grace
   Be mine before the enemy.[1]

· · ·

THEY FINISHED AS ONE. ONE CLAN. ONE PRAYER. UNITED LIKE one sword. Silence hung over the woods. Only the wind rustled the leaves and the branches, which seemed to carry the last words and pass them to one another.

It felt like the verra land was on their side. The trees, the rocks, the sky watched over the farm, waiting, ready.

And so was Ian.

He curved his hands around his mouth and hooted like an owl. "Hoo-hoo. Hoo-hoo. Hoo-hoo."

He counted the six hoots in his head, then repeated the call.

The Highlanders around Ian rose from their crouched positions. Ian narrowed his eyes, trying to see through the darkness if there was any sudden activity or movement, which would mean Frangean had been discovered.

But everything remained silent.

And then, thick smoke, gray against the black sky, rose from the building. Then orange-gold flames glowed behind the thatched roof. Sparks flew like flies with fiery wings into the darkness above and disappeared.

The English ran around the camp. Worried outcries filled the air. They went to the well and passed the bucket of water towards the house.

Alan leaned towards Ian. "Now?"

"Nae yet," Ian said. "Wait."

Tension crackled around the Highlanders like a lightning charge. They leaned forward, their postures stiff like wolves about to launch, faces tense, eyes dark in the growing glow of fire before them.

Ian could barely hold his own body back, his legs taut as bowstrings.

And then the moment came. There was not a single man down in the farm who wasn't trying to put the fire out.

Ian raised his arm high for everyone to see, then swung it down.

"*Cruachan!*" Ian said, not quite a cry and not quite a whisper.

It had enough strength and power for his men to echo it, but they all did so quietly enough that the enemies would not hear.

Like wolves, they moved stealthily through the night, claymores glistening in the light of fire.

Ian slashed his first sleeping man with no more sound than the gurgling of a cut throat, ignoring the twitch of guilt in his chest. He slayed the second one, who was lying next to the first. His men around him were doing the same, and soon, the air filled with the sounds of quick death.

A third man raised his head and opened his eyes, but Ian cut his throat. Pain and the realization of death in the man's eyes bruised Ian.

More and more were waking up. More swords gleamed orange in the light of fires. More and more screamed as steel cut their throats and sank into their flesh. The metallic clash of swords combined with the roar of flames as dark figures fought and the red-orange storm consumed the farmhouse.

Ian's lungs filled with the acrid, smoke-filled air. Chaos spread around him. There were so many more English than Highlanders, and Ian could only hope that the courage and spirit of his people would help them win when everything was against them.

Out of the darkness and smoke, a man came at him—a knight, wearing chain mail but no other armor. Flames shone against the bright metal as the Englishman raised his sword. Ian's claymore met it with a loud *bang* above his head, the impact going through his muscles like ripples on the water. The man pulled his weapon back for the next strike, and Ian spun out of the way and hit him against the chain mail. The man grunted, and Ian used the moment to thrust his sword into the man's face. But his claymore was blocked at the last moment, and the man hit Ian in the cheekbone with his elbow.

Ian's bone cracked from the iron-heavy hit, white spots flashing against his vision. His head spun, and another hit sent him back.

No. Not like this.

He called for all the might he had, for all fury. He roared, louder than the screams around him. Louder than the howling fire. He came at the man with downward strikes, his muscles light and singing with purpose. With one final strike, he crushed the chain mail and planted his sword in the man's chest. The knight fell, and Ian didn't watch the moment of death in the man's eyes.

He didn't need to.

Looking around, he saw many more fallen Highlanders than fallen English, and fear mixed in with his fury, like a splash of poison.

No. He couldn't let fear sway him, or allow himself guilt or compassion towards the enemy. They had none towards him or his people. They would have none towards Kate.

He screamed again. "*Cruachan!*" He called for the last bits of courage and strength left in him and his people.

His blade flashed red before his eyes as he ran into the skirmishes.

"Here!" he cried. "Here, ye English bastarts. Ye pig cocks. Here, take me!"

And as heads turned to him and three men ran at him, he went somewhere else. To the place where his head became empty. Where body and his instincts reigned, where his claymore sang its uneven, deadly song. Where he was free of thought and doubt.

He set the killer within him free.

Bodies fell. His blade sprayed blood. He sweated and ached. And his sword wanted more.

He didn't know how long he fought before a familiar face staring up into the sky made him stop. Alan. Dead. A gaping wound in his stomach.

Ian turned around and saw more Highlanders wounded or dead. Alpin Mac a' Bhàird, Caden Rosach, Donal Umphraidh... Many, many more. He became aware of the smell of burning flesh and woodsmoke in the air, so thick he could taste it on his tongue. Nausea rose in his throat.

They were losing.

They'd already lost. He could see only half of his men still standing, and many more English.

His stomach sank. What had he done—he'd sentenced his people to slaughter. Two men fought with Frangean, and Ian went towards him to help.

Ian didn't see the man coming until he was upon him, a big Englishman with a wolfish grin. A huge, black-haired monster of a man. His sword gleamed as it came towards Ian's throat. He wouldn't even have a moment to block him.

Goodbye, Kate.

He closed his eyes.

A low, pained grunt came... But Ian didn't feel anything. He opened his eyes. A spear pierced the man's stomach, his hand grasping the end that protruded.

"*Cruachan! Cruachan!*" called dozens of voices over the rumble of horses' hooves.

From the darkness of the woods, the fierce riders descended, swinging their swords, cutting down the shocked English.

Who?

Craig's drawn face among the first row of the riders said it all. Owen rode right next to him, taking down the English one after another.

They came.

With renewed strength, Ian called, "*Cruachan!* Our brothers have come!"

But whether that would be enough or he'd be sentencing even more people to death, he didn't know.

All he knew was that he was not ready to say goodbye to Kate. And all he could do was fight.

~

KATE PACED THE WOODS. WHEN SHE'D SEEN IAN AND HIS MEN go into battle, she'd brought the horse closer to the action in case they needed immediate help.

Her hand on Ian's dagger, she paced between two trees, her eyes glued to the orange-red glow in the small valley below.

Shadows and figures flickered there. Men fighting with swords, with fists, men throwing each other in the fire. The scent of burning hair and flesh was like a sickening barbecue. Cries of pain, fury, and surprise reached her, as well.

She didn't know how long she waited. Time lost its meaning while the images of Ian wounded and hurt invaded her mind. They knocked the air out of her lungs and made her gasp like an asthmatic.

"Oh, Ian," she whispered over and over again, "please be all right."

Then, surprising herself she prayed, "God, please keep him safe."

A tall, muscular figure walked towards her from the direction of the farm, holding a sword in one hand. She couldn't see the man's face, but his broad-shouldered stance, like he was ready to take on the world, could only belong to Ian. Relief flooded her, filling her lungs with freshness and life.

"Oh, thank God!" she cried and flew into his arms.

He wrapped his arms around her in a bear hug. He smelled like smoke and iron and sweat.

And he was alive.

She leaned back to look at his dirty, blood-sprayed face. From behind him, two more men approached, and Kate tensed.

"We won, lass." He grinned. "My cousins arrived with help. Owen was in Falnaird with Craig and Amy. We won."

"Oh, thank God," she whispered again, mindlessly stroking his dirty, bloody coat which served as armor.

He kissed her, quickly, almost roughly. The rush of the battle must still be thundering in his veins. Kate's head spun, her body weakened, but one of the men cleared his throat, and Ian stilled. Then let her go unwillingly. He turned and shook his head with a friendly chuckle.

Kate studied the men. There was an undoubtable resemblance between the three of them, although the other two looked more similar. All three were tall—giants compared to her. Ian was the most muscular. One of the cousins was a little older and had dark hair reaching his jaw, whereas the second one had hair the color of pale gold. Although it was hard to see their color in the darkness, both had catlike eyes. The three shared gorgeous, high cheekbones, square jaws, and straight noses any Roman statue would die for. Both of his cousins were handsome, strikingly so, but she only had eyes for Ian.

"Craig, Owen, meet Kate Anderson," he said, gesturing at first the dark-haired and then the blond cousin. "Kate is the best cook I've met in my life."

The cousins studied her, assessing, and Kate felt an urge to make them like her. In another life, if she were from this time and she didn't need to go, maybe she'd hope for his family to accept her, to welcome her. She felt Ian straighten next to her, his shoulders tensed and rose. Did he want them to like her, too? The thought warmed her cheeks.

"Good evening, mistress," Craig said with a small, polite smile. He watched her intently, and Kate had a strange sensation of being under an x-ray machine.

"Good evening," Owen said and flashed a smile. "I canna wait to taste some of yer cooking that has impressed our Ian so much."

Kate's face flushed a little and she smiled, fidgeting with the edge of her dress.

"It's so nice to meet you," she said. "I've heard so much about you from Ian."

Craig's smile fell and he frowned. So did Owen. Both glanced at each other, then back at Kate.

"Where do ye come from, mistress?" Owen asked.

Oh no. What should she say? Again, her accent must have betrayed her. She glanced at Ian but then raised her chin. She'd just be evasive.

"From far away," she said.

"How far?" Craig took a step towards her.

Ian moved closer to her. "Why, Craig? What does it matter?"

Craig continued drilling Kate with his eyes. "It matters because the lass speaks with a peculiar accent and manner. So peculiar, I've only heard it from one other person."

One other person? Could it possibly be he'd met another American? A time traveler like her?

"Who?" Kate said, her throat dry.

"My wife, Amy."

Kate cleared her throat. "Your wife?"

"The one and only."

"H-how did you meet?" Kate said.

"'Tis a good story. Involving an underground storage room in Inverlochy Castle. And a tunnel."

"Through time?" Kate exhaled.

A smile spread across Craig's face. He clapped Ian on the shoulder. "Ye bastart. Did ye find yerself a woman from the future, too?"

Owen eyed Kate with an open mouth.

Ian raised his eyebrows. "Ye marrit one?"

Craig nodded.

"So she's staying with you—forever?" Kate said.

"Aye."

Ian looked at Kate, and she returned his gaze, which was full of sadness. "I'm envious," she said. "I can't."

Ian's jaws played, pain thundering in his eyes.

"Let us go, lass." He turned to Craig and Owen. "I must deliver her to Inverlochy. She needs to return home."

Both men nodded in understanding.

Kate's throat clenched. "To Inverlochy?" She swallowed to relieve the feeling of sandpaper in her mouth. "Already?"

"Aye. Fortifications will arrive soon, and I'll be needed here again to throw this attack back. We'll have to call the MacKenzies and other allies for help."

He took her by the elbow and led her towards the horse.

"Goodbye, lass," Owen cried after her.

"Take care of her!" Craig added.

Kate's heart sank. This was it. She needed to go back to her duty, too. And sacrifice her happiness.

They came to the horse. "You're right," she said. "It's just that I thought we'd have more time..."

He shook his head and looked down, hunching. "I had hoped for more time with ye, too, Katie. But we both kent this wouldna be forever. I promised ye. 'Tis time."

He was right, damn it. Of course he was right. She was so caught in the ocean of happiness and joy with him, in a little honeymoon. But Deli Luck was about to go bankrupt and Mandy and Jax still needed her.

And now he'd need to leave his people during a difficult time for her. She couldn't give him more concerns than he already had.

Kate took a step back.

"Look, I can go myself then," she said. "Your people still need you."

"The battle is almost over, lass. Owen and Craig are handling it. We won. The Sassenachs are fleeing."

Kate fiddled with her hands.

"If there's no more danger, I can go alone."

"There's nae way I'm letting ye go alone."

"I don't want to burden you with my troubles. Clearly, you have more things to think about here."

"Ye are nae burden, Katie," he said, his tone almost angry. "Now stop yer ninnying and let us go."

And let us get this over with, said his tone. He most definitely wanted to get rid of her, the sooner the better. Even if he did have some feelings for her, they both knew their relationship would never last forever. He could go on with his life then. He'd come back from the dead, and now he had a second chance at life. And she wasn't part of it.

Anyway, she had her own life to go on with. Her own people to take care of and save. He had done his duty. It was time for her to do hers, no matter how heartbreaking.

Kate nodded. "All right, Ian. Let's go. You're right—the sooner I leave the better."

CHAPTER 28

Thor's powerful body moved steadily under Ian, and Kate sat in front of him, distracting him in all kinds of delicious ways. Her lush arse between Ian's thighs, she was warm and precious pressed against his torso. Every rub of their bodies, every touch, every slide was an exquisite torture.

They'd traveled the whole day after the battle at the farm, slept in the woods, then rode another day and another night, and had been on the horse half the day today. The wind was strong, and it murmured in the branches of the trees. Stern rocks watched them go. The birds were silent, and there were no animal tracks that Ian could see. Every living creature had probably been scared off by the English forces as they had moved through.

Ian leaned forward and, without touching Kate's head, closed his eyes and inhaled the smell of her hair. He tried to memorize the scent. These would be the last days he'd spend with her, and there couldn't be enough lifetimes.

She'd mostly been silent, and he didn't want to push her to talk to him. They'd slept under his cloak last night to keep warm, but he'd dared not kiss her or caress her. He'd barely slept since the night he'd attacked her in his sleep, not wanting to start dreaming, terrified he wouldn't be able to stop himself from hurting Kate again. Lying awake next to her, being enveloped in her sweet scent and doing nothing, was a hot agony.

It was better this way, anyway, keeping his distance. What was he thinking? He should have never fallen for her, should have never let them grow close. He was about to deliver her to Inverlochy, where she'd go back to her own time. There could never be a future for them. Even if she didn't need to leave, a killer like him would never deserve a lifetime with her. She wouldn't want to tie herself to him forever, and he'd never let her ruin her life by doing so.

They hadn't stopped yet for their midday meal. "Lass, are ye hungry?" Ian asked.

Kate nodded. "Sure. I could eat."

"Aye." He spotted a small clearing between two trees ahead of them to his right.

When they were on the ground, Ian set about making a fire. They still had the last pieces of oatcakes from home and the roasted fish Ian had caught yesterday.

"I'll warm this up," Ian said.

"I can do it," Kate said.

"Dinna fash yerself, Katie."

She looked down. "Thanks, Ian."

They ate in silence, and its heavy weight hung between them. He hated it. After what he'd confided in her, and after he'd gotten to know her better, this felt unnatural. He wanted to ask more about her, what she liked to do when she wasn't working, what she hoped to do with her inn. The thought of a woman managing an inn by herself was strange, but he respected her strength and determination. Knowing how well she cooked, he did not understand how it could be failing.

Ian shamelessly devoured Kate's every movement with his eyes. Her bonnie face as she ate, the way she held the fish as she took her bites. Her posture, the curves of her breasts under her dress as she leaned forward to avoid fish juice dripping on her. So graceful in every movement.

"How long till Inverlochy, do you think?" Kate said when she had finished and wiped her fingers on the cloth.

Inverlochy... The word pulled him out of the sweet trance of watching her. "We'll be there tonight," he said.

"Tonight?" Her face twitched, as if in shock.

"Aye, lass, 'tis our destination. Ye seem surprised."

"I thought it would take longer, that's all," she said coldly. "Excuse me if I cannot read the horse's mileage per hour." She stood up. "Let's go then. Why wait?"

Ian's gut twisted painfully. Why, indeed? While he wanted every moment with her to stretch into eternity, all she wanted was to be gone.

He stood up as well. "Thor needs rest. So do ye. Ye must be hurting all over from two days on the horse's back. Are ye so eager to leave?"

She crossed her arms. "I am, of course I am. I'm not going to restrict you any more than necessary. In fact, why don't I continue the rest of the way on my own?"

"What?" He frowned.

She clearly couldn't stand a moment longer with him. His cold-blooded killings had finally gotten to her.

"Look, I release you from your obligation of honor or whatever still keeps you with me. I can make it on my own now, if it's only a few hours of walking."

"Ye think I'm taking ye because I feel obliged?"

"Obviously."

"Lass, I do feel obliged to protect ye, but 'tisna why I'm taking ye to Inverlochy. If I could, I would have kept ye with me forever."

Her eyes widened. "Don't feel like you owe it to me to be courteous, Ian. You probably think you need to protect my feelings after what I've told you about my childhood, but really, I'm fine. It's not the first time I've been unwanted. I know the signs. I'm fine."

"Unwanted? I couldna have possibly wanted anyone or anything more than I want ye."

Kate hugged herself, tears glistened in her eyes. Ian covered the space between them in three steps and grasped her upper arms.

"Stop this at once," he said. "I want ye. I love ye. Ye're a treasure. Ye're like the source of life to me."

She blinked, staring at him with a mixture of hope and disbelief.

"Then why are you chasing me away?" she whispered.

"Because ye dinna belong here, lass. Ye belong to the world with great healers, the world where women own inns, the world where majestic iron creatures fly in the air and light comes to life with the movement of a finger."

His lungs squeezed. He didn't say the main reason, and it weighed deep inside of him like a sack of rocks.

"I need to go back for my sister and my nephew. Not for the conveniences. I couldn't care less about conveniences. If I was happy with someone, I'd give up all that..."

Her voice trailed off. She cupped his jaw, and he leaned into her soft, warm hand.

"You know that, Ian, don't you?" she asked.

He swallowed a painful knot in his throat. "Aye, I ken ye would. But I wouldna have allowed ye to stay anyway. Nae for me."

"Of course for you. Who else would I stay for then?"

He shook his head. "Nae for me, lass. 'Tis right that ye're leaving. There is nae future for us—nae in this century, nae in the future. Ye're too good for a man like me, after what I've done."

Her face went blank. "*I'm* too good? Ian, we've talked about it, it's not..."

"Aye, 'tis. A man like me, a cold-blooded killer, I must be

punished, Katie. God must punish me. He canna allow me to take so many lives, then find the biggest treasure in this life and just be happy. 'Tisna how life works. 'Tisna how I am going to accept it. And I wouldna wish ye to spend the rest of yer life with someone like me."

Kate shook her head. "Ian, stop blaming yourself for this. You can't keep punishing yourself your whole life."

"I will never be whole, lass. Ye're better off without me. I canna make ye happy. I dinna deserve ye, and I dinna want to make ye miserable."

"You don't need to be whole to be happy with someone, Ian," she whispered. "You just need to find someone who helps to fill your broken parts."

Ian's head spun from the healing promise in her words. He leaned down to kiss her, but a sharp pain in his shoulder threw him back.

He looked up.

It took him less than a moment to evaluate the situation. An arrow pointed at him from behind a tree. There must have been another one that grazed him. Swords glistened here and there among the trees—five or six.

His muscles stiffened momentarily, fire rushing through his veins. Then his instincts took over, kicking fear away. He grabbed Kate and launched for a tree, shielding her with his body.

An arrow hit the place where they'd just stood. Ian cursed and looked carefully from behind the trunk.

"Ian, you're hurt," Kate said.

The English. Five swordsmen and an archer. Their hair was singed, the edges of their tunics black and sooty. They must have come from the farm. Had they tracked Ian and Kate?

"'Tis a scratch."

"It's not nothing—" Kate said, but Ian interrupted her, turning to her and looking deeply into her eyes.

"Lass, listen. Ye follow every word I say if ye want us both to survive this. There are six of them. All warriors. Where's yer dagger?"

She paled even more and reached for the dagger, which was in the sheath on her belt.

"Good. Take it out and remember what I taught ye. They have no armor, they're survivors from the farm."

He glanced to the left, where Thor grazed, away from the camp. If he dealt with the enemy quickly, they'd have a chance to run for Thor and—

But they didn't have a chance. Not with six against one.

The only chance was for Kate to go alone.

"Ye have to promise me, lass," Ian said. "If ye see me fall or if I tell ye, run to Thor and get away. Go alone to Inverlochy."

"No, Ian! Never."

"Aye. Promise. If ye care at all about me, run."

"I can help you—"

"Nae, ye canna. We're losing time. Promise. Now."

Her chin shook, and her neck became red and blotchy.

"Ian, no—"

He already hated himself for the pain his words would bring her.

"Ye *are* a burden to me," he said. "I canna protect us both now. If ye want to help me, ye must go."

She gasped without a sound. Pain distorted her face, and her eyes filled with tears. She shrank visibly, her shoulders curling inward. Her hand clutched her stomach.

Ian's fists clenched helplessly. He wanted to hit himself for hurting her like that. But it was for the best. It was to keep her alive. He would likely die now. He couldn't bear the thought of her being left alone to them.

"Promise," Ian hissed. When she said nothing, he pressed. "Relieve me of yer burden. Now."

She looked down and hunched.

"Yes," Kate said. "I'll go."

Ian breathed out. "Thank ye."

He looked from behind the tree again. The English were advancing towards them. He had to protect her.

He looked over his shoulder at her. "When I tell ye to go, ye go. Ye promised me. Aye?"

Kate nodded solemnly, hurt and fear in her eyes. He nodded back. Then he turned to his attackers, unsheathed his claymore and went.

He didn't even have time for a prayer. Just the war cry must do. "*Cruachan!*"

They looked surprised as he launched at them, probably because he attacked them alone instead of running. Ian used that surprise to his advantage. He slid to the left, slicing the outermost man's side, then ran farther behind them, making them turn around away from Kate.

Five.

The bowman shot, his arrow missing Ian by an inch. One of the swordsmen came at him. They clashed together in a scrape of iron against iron. The man attacked swiftly, but he wasn't experienced. Ian slashed him in the chest, and he fell. Two more came.

They were different. Heavy bangs met Ian's sword from both sides, and he barely jumped back in time to avoid the soldiers' following thrusts.

It was when the third man joined, and arrows continued to fly at him, barely missing him, that he knew that he was finished.

"Goooooo!" he yelled as he danced with death.

A flash of gold and gray in his side vision told him Kate ran. Iron-hot pain burst in his side—he'd missed the thrust of a sword as he'd allowed himself one look at her.

She was on Thor, staring at him.

"Go, my love," he mouthed, and resumed the fight with double the strength. He couldn't let them see her.

"Ye bastarts!" he cried, calling on the reserves of his strength.

And with the sound of hooves fading away, he sank into the bloody sea of battle rage.

CHAPTER 29

Kate let Thor lead the way down the path. Her eyes burning, she swallowed the tears as the woods around her blurred in flashes of dark green and brown.

Ye are a burden to me, rang in her head. *Relieve me of yer burden.* And then, *Gooooooo!*

Her chest was on fire. Her stomach a bottomless pit. Her worst fear had come true—he'd said she was a burden. Before, he'd said he loved her. He'd said she was a treasure, making her whole world light up like fireworks.

No one had ever said they loved her before.

Not her parents. Not her sister. Not a man.

No one.

Hearing those words, it had felt as though he'd been saying them to someone else. Like he looked at her, but he actually meant another person.

As it turned out, she had been right about that all along. He didn't love her. He only needed a clear conscience, only wanted to be kind to her. Because he was a kind man. A strong, wonderful, kind man. Bigger than life. Stronger than death. Greater than slavery.

Unbreakable.

Until now.

She'd left him to fight four people. Four! He was already wounded. What chance did he have?

In her mind's eye, Kate saw Ian lying on the ground, blood on his face and a gaping wound in his chest. Dead.

Pain tore her apart at the image, like a bomb exploding, shredding her to pieces. A world without Ian wasn't a world worth living in. She loved him. Even if he didn't—even if he'd never—love her.

She loved him.

Love unraveled in her heart, a mixture of unearthly lightness and wrenching pain. There was nothing more important than keeping him alive. Not that he'd hate her if she came back. Not that she had any idea what she'd actually be able to do against warriors. Not that she might get hurt herself.

All that mattered was that Ian survive.

"Thor, stop!" she commanded.

But he continued his stride. Remembering what Ian had taught her to do when driving the cart, Kate pulled on the reins—lightly at first, then stronger. Thor slowed down, then stopped.

"Good boy," she said and patted him on the neck. "Now, let's go back."

She pulled the reins all the way to the left. Thor turned his head left but didn't walk.

"Left, Thor!" Kate cried desperately.

She had no idea how long they had ridden, but she knew they were losing precious time.

"Your master needs you, Thor," she whispered. She kept holding the left rein, and Thor kept looking left. Then he took one tentative step.

"Yes, good boy. Keep going!"

She pressed her left leg to his side.

He walked left!

"Oh, yes!" Kate exclaimed.

She released her pull and her leg when Thor turned and faced the way they had come from. She squeezed his sides with her legs, and made a "tsk, tsk" sound, something she'd seen and heard Ian do. Thor was a good horse—he obeyed her signal and sped up a little.

"Oh, Thor, well done!" Kate kept saying under her breath, amazed she had any control over him.

They strode for a while, Kate shivering from the images of Ian being hurt that flashed through her mind from time to time, blinding her. She tried to concentrate on the road, on not falling from Thor's back. Thankfully, he didn't need much direction and followed the path.

What felt like an eternity later, she heard them. Screams, groans of pain, and iron clashing against iron. Her pulse accelerated. He was still fighting. He was still alive!

She stopped Thor, who obeyed her at once, luckily, and jumped down rather awkwardly, twisting her ankle a little. Pain stabbed her, but she could still walk, and she limped as silently as she could towards the sounds of a fight.

She removed the dagger from her belt and held it like Ian had taught her—easily but securely. She breathed. There was no doubt in her mind that she'd use the dagger if she had to protect Ian or herself.

There he was, Ian. He waved his sword before just one opponent. Five men lay on the ground, not moving.

Ian had his sword in his hands and danced a slow circle with his opponent. It was the archer, Kate thought, who also had an ax. Ian had a big gash on his shoulder and a slice on his side, with his tunic torn and hanging. He dragged one leg—his thigh was cut, too. One eye was swollen completely shut. Cuts darkened on his face, and blood covered one of his ears. He moved slowly, clearly tired. He swung the sword with an effort.

His opponent was in much better shape. His quiver was empty, and the bow lay on the ground, useless. But his ax gleamed in the daylight.

Kate's hands shook. How was Ian still alive?

How was she going to help him?

The dagger... But she had to approach so that the man didn't notice. He had his back to her now. He lunged at Ian, who jumped back, luckily.

She needed to hurry. Still holding the dagger, she walked towards the warrior, slowly advancing, making sure she stepped quietly and didn't alert the man.

She was about five feet away when Ian's eyes locked with hers for just a split second before returning to the man in front of him. But in that split second, his eyes widened for a barely noticeable moment and a fear like she'd never seen in him before flashed through them. His gaze on his opponent again, his shoulders tensed, his eyes filling with determination.

"Come here, ye Sassenach bastart," he growled.

Step forward, one more.

"Burn in hell, dirty Scotsman," the man answered.

Three more steps.

The man swung his ax high in the air above his head for the last, deadly blow. Kate launched forward. *Whack.* Just like Ian taught her, she pierced him in the side of his neck. The dagger went in, meeting the resistance of flesh. Kate let go, nausea rising in her stomach.

The man froze, the ax fell from his hands and hit him on the head, then landed on the ground. The man followed, collapsing like a sack of wheat.

Kate and Ian stared at each other for a moment. Relief and pain on his face, he sank to his knees on the ground. Kate rushed to him and hugged him, supporting him so he didn't fall.

"Ye shouldna have come back," he croaked.

"I should have never left. We must hurry. You're injured. And don't you dare say it's just a scratch."

She helped him up, her heart leaping, triumphant. He was alive. At least for now, he was alive.

CHAPTER 30

"Open the gates!" Kate cried.

Up on the massive walls, warriors moved. Kate tightened her arms around Ian and prayed they'd be let in quickly.

After the last warrior had died, they'd gone down to the loch and cleaned and bandaged Ian's wounds as best they could with cloth torn from Kate's dress. Kate had been astonished at how strong Ian had seemed despite the number of wounds on his body and of how much blood he must have lost. Afterward, Ian had managed to climb onto the horse, but a short time later, he'd almost slipped off. Kate had found a rope in his travel pack and tied it around him and then herself, so that he was strapped to her and sat between her arms. She'd managed to keep him on Thor's back in this way, though it had been extremely difficult.

"Who goes there?" one of the guards responded.

"Ian Cambel," Kate said. "He was wounded in a battle with the English. Please, let us in. He needs help urgently."

"Let them in!"

The gates opened slowly.

Kate pressed her fingers to Ian's neck. His pulse was still beating, thank God. He'd come to consciousness from time to time along the path, raised his head, mumbled something, then fallen unconscious again. She'd asked herself a thousand times if she should stop and let him rest.

But she was terrified he'd die without immediate medical help. She could bandage cuts and cook him a nourishing soup, but she had no idea how to deal with deep wounds.

With a sinking heart and a dark, heavy feeling in her gut, she'd spurred Thor on, desperately looking for any sign of Inverlochy Castle. She was grateful they'd arrived before dusk had settled.

Kate let Thor walk in the courtyard. The familiar gray walls pressed in on her from four sides. This was where they'd thought she was a thief and where she'd thought she was going insane for the first time.

In many ways, that situation had been better than the current one. When she'd had amnesia, she'd had nowhere to go, and could stay with the man she loved...

Now, she had a purpose, somewhere to go back to. Mandy and Jax needed her to provide for them. They must be worrying like crazy by now. Thor stopped, and Kate glanced at the eastern tower, where in 2020 she'd fallen down the stairs and stumbled upon the rock that would bring her to Ian. A shiver ran through her at the thought of going back to that dark, dank cavern again.

Men hurried towards Thor with a litter, and Kate helped them take Ian carefully down. Ahearn, the steward, hurried towards them.

"'Tis ye again!" he cried. "The thief."

Kate climbed down and walked after the men carrying Ian. "I'm not a thief. I'm a cook. I never took anything from you. Ian needs your help, and I brought him here, that's all. Now, will you help me take care of him or will you continue your baseless accusations?"

"Someone call Ellair!" he yelled.

"Already done," one of the men said.

"Take him to my bedchamber," Kenneth MacKenzie said.

The castle constable had appeared from somewhere and watched Ian with a concern.

"Thank you, sir," Kate said.

He glanced at her with a frown but only nodded.

The men walked to Comyn Tower, as they'd called it, and Kate followed them. They put him on a giant bed in the lord's bedchamber, which was bigger than Ian's bedroom in Dundail. He lay so pale, almost gray against the pillows. Kate's heart squeezed.

Ellair came in.

"Please, help him," Kate whispered.

He barely glanced at her and continued into the room. He proceeded to clean the wounds, then sewed the ones on Ian's side, thigh, and head. He put some herbal poultices on them and covered them with clean cloths. Kate stood in the corner, clenching her hands. Tremors of worry went through her, and she almost threw up when she saw the crooked needle piercing Ian's wounded flesh.

But she couldn't look away. She was afraid if she did, he'd die, or he'd disappear, and she'd wake up and learn all this was a dream.

Ellair finished and put his things away. When he left the room, Kate followed him. "Is he going to be all right?"

"That is now in the hands of God. He lost much blood, but his wounds didna touch the organs. Still, he may die of blood loss or rot-wound."

Kate nodded solemnly and returned to the room, praying silently to God or whomever would listen, to save Ian. A few minutes after the healer left, Kenneth MacKenzie came in.

"How is he, lass?" he asked. ·

Kate stood paralyzed by the door. Seeing Ian ashen and immobile in the bed brought darkness all around her. "He lost a lot of blood, but Ellair says the wounds have missed major organs. Now all we do is wait."

"What happened?"

"The English," she said in an expressionless tone. "They're making another attempt to capture Inverlochy and other castles north. A garrison came through Ian's lands, and he defended his people. On the way here, six of them attacked us."

Kenneth's jaws tightened. "Thank ye for telling me, lass. The vultures are probably thinking 'tis a good time to attack while Bruce is busy in the northeast."

"Yes. That's what I heard them say."

"Aye. Well. 'Tis smart. But I wilna let them take the castle."

"Ian, Craig, and Owen managed to fight off this one garrison, but more are coming, I heard. And they might even attack together with the MacDougalls."

Kenneth shook his head. "Pigheaded MacDougalls. Fighting on the wrong side of this battle. They should be on our side. They're Highlanders. But I suppose I understand them a wee bit. If someone had killed my nephew, I wouldna have been happy about it, either."

"Who do you mean?"

"Bruce killed John Comyn, his main contestant to the throne. He was the MacDougall chief's nephew. 'Tis personal for them. I suppose they're true Highlanders in that way."

"They were the ones who sent Ian to slavery in Baghdad," Kate said, suddenly furious with the MacDougalls, people she'd never seen in her life. "It would be personal for me, too, if I ever saw them."

She looked into Kenneth's eyes. "If they ever come here, you make them pay."

Kenneth held her gaze solemnly, then nodded briefly and left.

Kate finally found the strength to move. She went to Ian's bed and sat on the edge on the other side, then climbed onto the bed and lay next to Ian. She stared at his profile, which appeared to be lifeless. No flutter of eyelashes or flicker of eyelids. His chest rose and fell, but barely. Kate carefully reached out and put her hand on his forehead. His skin was cool and dry. She moved a bit closer and inhaled his scent.

"I love you," she whispered. "I'll do anything so that you live. I'll stay with you forever if that's what it takes. Mandy and Jax will somehow do without me. I want you to live. Please, live. I love you."

She whispered it all like a prayer, like a charm that would keep death away. Then, the exhaustion of all that had happened claimed her, and she slept.

When she woke up, the sun had already risen and colored the sky in the pale gold and blue of an early summer morning. Ian was looking at her, his eyes cloudy but awake. She smiled and cupped his jaw.

"How are you feeling?"

"Like I've died and came alive to an angel," he rasped.

She snorted. "Only if I'm one of those fat angels from Renaissance paintings."

"I dinna ken what ye mean, Katie."

"Forget it. Are you in pain?"

"Aye, but it doesna matter."

She touched his forehead. "You're a little warm. I'll call Ellair."

She moved to stand up, but he reached out and caught her by the hand. "Wait. Stay with me just a wee bit longer."

"Of course."

She lay back down.

"Ye shouldna have come back for me," Ian said.

"I should have never left you. I was a coward, but I came to my senses, thankfully, not too late."

He shook his head.

"Ye should have been in yer time by now."

She smiled. "I have good news for you, buddy. I'm staying until you get better."

He made a movement to sit up but didn't have the strength. Anger and fear mixed on his face. "What?"

That didn't look good. Kate hadn't known what to expect

when she would say this, but she'd hoped it would be more than an unpleasant surprise.

"I love you, Ian," she said. "I'm staying to make sure you recover, then I'll go to help Mandy and Jax and prepare everything for my departure. And then I'm coming back to you —forever."

Something like a deep shock flashed through his face. "Ye love me?"

He *was* glad to hear it! A smile bloomed on Kate's face. "I love you. So much."

But his jaw tensed, his mouth curving downward. "Nae. Nae, Katie. Ye dinna love me. Ye canna love me."

"Don't tell me what I can or cannot do," Kate said playfully. "That's how I feel."

He turned and looked at the ceiling. "Ye're wrong. Ye canna stay with me forever. Ye must leave. I told ye, ye're a burden—"

She shook her head and sat up on the bed, anger burning in her veins. "No, I'm not a burden. I just saved your life, buddy. That's not a burden. Saying I'm a burden is a load of crap, and you know it."

He closed his eyes for a moment, then turned to her, resolve in his eyes.

"I canna be with ye, Kate."

She almost flinched at those words. They were like needles driven under her skin.

"And why not now?" she asked.

"Look at me. I'm a killer. A slave. A tool in the hands of powerful men."

He sounded as if he'd swallowed a toad and it was still stuck in his throat. He sighed and turned away from her. Kate's heart bled.

"You're not those things to me," she said. "I don't know a stronger man, a braver—"

"The truth is simple, Kate. After what was done to me, after what I've become, I canna give ye the love ye deserve. I even tried to kill ye in my sleep."

Kate shook her head. "I refuse to believe that. It's not true. You are already giving me more than anyone has given me in my whole life."

"Nae, sweet. There's this bottomless crack in my soul that awakes nightmares and eats me alive. And it will eat ye alive, too. Mayhap, even kill ye one night. I canna be someone who does that to ye."

Kate clenched her fists. Hope was slipping from her grasp quickly. So quickly, when it had just been within reach. "But I'm broken, too, Ian. I know what that is. I'm the same."

He nodded and turned to her. His face looking deathly. "'Tis exactly why ye must leave. Why ye canna be with me. Because together, neither of us will heal. I will never be whole again, and you have every chance in the world. Go back."

Kate reached out, but he shifted back. His gaze hardened. "Go."

The bed seemed to sway, to careen like a ship on the waves, and the whole world darkened and lost color. Twisting pain grabbed her gut, wrenching her. Bile rose in her throat. She couldn't believe this was it. He really didn't want to be with her.

"But you said you loved me—" She heard her voice crack.

"Go," he said again, louder, as if she were a stray dog.

"Ian—"

"Go!" he yelled.

Spooked, Kate backed up off the bed and stood awkwardly, almost falling. There was no longer any love in his eyes. There was only the bottomless darkness of a cruel man who took lives and survived the best way he could.

There was no place for Kate in his life.

Once again, she was unwanted, imposing, unneeded.

Except, she wasn't.

She wasn't a burden—she'd saved his life. She'd never been a burden to her sister or her nephew. She hadn't been a burden for Manning, either, despite his grumbling.

She'd helped him. She'd helped them all. And if Ian couldn't love her back, he was right. There couldn't be a future for them. She couldn't, and shouldn't, stay.

She wouldn't sacrifice her own happiness or her sister's and Jax's security for someone who didn't love her and appreciate her just as she was.

She backed towards the door and opened it. Tears blurred Ian's image in her eyes, her stomach a ragged wound, her heart a piece of torn flesh.

She threw one last glance at the man she loved and quietly exited his life forever.

CHAPTER 31

C ape Haute, New Jersey, late July 2020

FROM THE OUTSIDE, THE RESTAURANT LOOKED JUST AS IT always did. The tall windows had their sun blinds partly down, and the neon OPEN sign was lit.

But from what Kate could see of the inside, the white tables with soft faux-leather booth seating were full of diners.

The bell rang as Kate opened the door. The sound sent a tiny, familiar jolt of anxiety through her, like it did every time a customer came in. Her hands would automatically reach towards the fridge that held the patties, as she knew she would most likely need to cook a burger.

The scent of grilled meat, coffee, and freshly baked pie enveloped her as she walked in. Everything was clean and tidy. Guests she'd seen and known her whole life chatted cheerfully as they ate and drank.

Kate looked around with astonishment. She'd half expected a foreclosure sign on the doors. Not this.

Mandy burst through the kitchen doors with a plate of pancakes in one hand and a plate with a burger, fries, and a salad in the other. She didn't look tired or depressed. Actually, she'd never looked as energized and pink-cheeked before. Her hair in a pretty ponytail, her uniform clean and ironed, she moved quickly, with purpose and pleasure, like a fairy from a childhood cartoon who was about to make everything better.

She put the plates on a table in front of Barb and George Fisher and patted Barb on the shoulder.

"Enjoy!" Mandy said, and she was just about to turn and walk back into the kitchen when she saw Kate.

Her smile fell, the familiar gray-and-tired expression returned, and her shoulders slumped.

Then she plastered a smile on her face. "Kate! You're back!"

Heads turned in Kate's direction, and she got a few half-hearted greetings. Had anyone even noticed she was gone? Had Mandy even been worried that Kate had disappeared?

It didn't matter. Kate was so glad to see her sister and to be back where she belonged, where she was needed. Where she could make a difference and save the restaurant.

Kate waved to everyone back. Leaving her luggage by the door, she went to Mandy and hugged her.

"Hi, sis," she whispered. "How are you? How's Jax?"

Mandy leaned back. "We're good. We didn't expect you so early. I thought it'd take months for you to train in Scotland..."

"You weren't worried not to hear from me?"

"No, why would I? I figured you were having the time of your life, finally being able to cook all kinds of foreign dishes in that fancy program."

Kate licked her lips and looked around. It certainly didn't look like anyone had missed her or suffered without her presence.

"Come, let's talk." Kate tugged Mandy after herself into the kitchen.

There, a new cook flew between the grill and the griddle,

flipping burgers and pancakes. Pies baked in the oven. Everything looked clean and organized. But where was the cook Kate had hired to replace her?

"How have you been?" Kate asked. "I was so worried you'd have one of your episodes and wouldn't be able to manage everything alone."

Mandy waved her hand. "I was worried, too, but to be honest, I've really enjoyed managing the restaurant. I hope you don't mind, but I did put a couple of changes into practice. We went even more traditional with the menu, and people poured in. I hired Rob." She looked at the cook who grinned at her. "He's been great."

A twinge of jealousy twisted Kate's gut.

"So you've been doing great without me?"

"Well, yes, hon. We're even making more of a profit, so I repaid some of the debt. Bankruptcy isn't such an immediate threat anymore."

Kate nodded. "That's great, Mandy!"

Mandy's eyebrows rose. "Oh, hon. Please don't tell me you want to change everything back to the way it was before."

"No, no. Of course not. If the new menu has been working, we should keep it."

Mandy smiled, clenching her hands. Kate looked around awkwardly.

"What about Logan Robertson?" Mandy asked. "When are they coming?"

"I have some bad news. Logan Robertson isn't coming. I'm afraid I screwed up the program, and I'm out."

Mandy frowned. "Oh no! What happened?"

I traveled back in time, lost my memory, and met the love of my life.

"Well, he hit on me, and I stopped him."

"Oh my gosh...are you okay?"

"Yes, I'm fine. But unfortunately, the whole TV show thing isn't happening."

Mandy sighed. "Oh. Darn."

"Are you mad?"

Mandy looked around the restaurant. Every single table was occupied. Clanks of cutlery, chatter, and occasional laughter filled the room.

"No," Mandy said and hugged Kate around the shoulders with one arm. "Screw him if he wanted to do anything to you. And look, we don't even need him."

Kate's eyes blurred with tears. "You're right. We don't."

"But tell me one thing. If you weren't preparing for the show, where have you been then all this time?"

Ugh. Kate hated lying. What could she say that would be true without going into specifics? "I stayed to learn from the locals. I met someone who knows how to cook Crazy Mary."

"Excuse me!" Through the serving hatch, Kate saw one of the customers she didn't recognize wave his hand at Mandy.

"I better go," Mandy said. "You go upstairs and have a rest after your long journey, okay? I know you want to work, but don't."

She squeezed Kate's shoulder. "Rob and I got this, sis, really. Don't worry."

Kate nodded, feeling like a third wheel.

"I was expecting you'd need me to start cooking right away—but okay."

"No, no." Mandy laughed, kissed Kate, and went to see what the customer needed.

Kate hesitated a moment more, then walked out of the kitchen. She picked up her luggage and went upstairs. Even the apartment looked tidier and fresher. She went into Jax's room and kissed the top of his head. He was a handsome and smart boy with his mom's blond hair and his dad's brown eyes.

"You grew," Kate said through tears, looking at his suddenly so-grown-up face. "You're such a big boy."

Or was she tearing up because he also didn't need her anymore?

"Aunt Kate!" He giggled, evading her embrace in that shy, boyish way.

She gave him the chocolates she'd bought at the airport and chatted with him about how he and Mandy had been doing.

When she entered her bedroom, it smelled like wood and dusty blankets and old books. The scent brought the sense of anxiety back to her chest as she thought of her usual dull life, a life without Ian. She put the luggage in the corner and lay on her bed. Even her limbs felt like she didn't know what to do with them.

And inside, she couldn't help feeling like she were a splinter that had caused inflammation. When she'd gone to Scotland, the splinter had been removed, and the system had healed itself. And now she was back, trying to fit into the old wound.

But she was unnecessary. External. Harmful.

They'd been fine without her. And, surprisingly, she'd been fine without them. More than fine.

She'd been so happy there. So deliriously happy with Ian, in that world full of danger and castles and war. And medieval cooking that she enjoyed more than she could have ever imagined. There, Ian had appreciated her dishes like no one ever had. Here, she wasn't needed. In fact, under Mandy's supervision, the restaurant was doing better than it ever had under Kate's.

Why was that? Was it because Kate had always tried to implement something new, something unusual when all people wanted was traditional cooking? Was it because Kate had always thought she wasn't good enough and the feeling had created negative energy? Or maybe it was her demeanor? She'd never had a smile on her face like Mandy did. Maybe the customers had felt some distance with her, whereas they absolutely loved Mandy.

In any case, Kate couldn't imagine herself here anymore. She supposed she needed a bit more time to adjust to modern life. Her chest throbbed, her head and throat ached. It was as though she was hungry for Ian. Her hands itched to find him, to touch him, to feel his powerful presence near and around her. She longed for Dundail and Cadha and even grumpy Manning.

Over the next few days, Kate tried to adjust to her new reality. She went to work in the restaurant and was amazed to see how much smoother everything ran under Mandy's control. While Kate was cooking, Mandy managed the restaurant. She negotiated better prices with the supplier, something Kate had never been able to do. She reduced the number of dishes on the menu.

"People never ordered some dishes, so I left only the most popular ones."

That allowed Kate and Rob to precook certain things and serve dishes faster while maintaining their quality. Mandy suggested a new system of order placements that was much quicker and clearer for the waiters and the cooks.

There were more customers, higher tips, and more profit. And while she saw a big smile of satisfaction on Mandy's face as her sister directed the staff confidently and chatted to the customers, Kate felt more and more out of place.

In the beginning, it had felt like Kate was doing Mandy a favor by letting her help in Deli Luck. Now it felt like Mandy was the one doing the favor.

While it was great to be back with her family, dissatisfaction grew stronger and stronger inside Kate. What was the point of her even being in the restaurant? Rob cooked as well as Kate. Mandy had gotten the place back on its feet.

And then she realized. By not taking care of Mandy and Jax, she'd allowed them to flourish and become independent.

Was it possible they didn't need her anymore?

A week after Kate had returned, she sat in the living room one evening with Mandy and Jax. Her family, the two people she was closest to in the world. The two people she'd lived for.

Was it time she tried to live for herself? Now that the restaurant wasn't struggling, she could finally think about what she wanted.

What she wanted was for Ian to love her. For them to be together. But that wasn't possible.

So she had to do something in this century. And that something didn't lie in Cape Haute anymore.

"I'm thinking about leaving," she said.

Mandy's face fell. Jax's eyebrows rose to his hairline and he climbed onto the couch to sit next to Kate.

"Aunt Kate, don't you want to live with us anymore?"

"Well, your mom has been doing so great without me, I think I'll only be a burden."

Mandy frowned. "No, sweetie, never. It has always been the two of us against the world."

"Yes. But I don't think you need me to take care of you anymore. You've actually been doing much better on your own."

Mandy bit her lip and picked at her fingernails. "I've been enjoying running things... But it doesn't mean I don't need you. It doesn't mean I don't love you."

"I know." Kate smiled. "I love you, too, Mandy. But I've always felt out of place in Cape Haute. And you fit much better here. I think I'm going to leave and start something of my own."

"Really?"

Kate's smile broadened. Now that the words were out, lightness filled her body. It felt right, like a heavy weight had been lifted from her shoulders.

"Yeah. If you're okay with it. I'll still send money for Jax's college fund. But I don't think I can stay here anymore and be happy. You were right, I've always wanted something else. It's time to act on it."

"Kate... I don't know what to say. Are you sure?"

Kate looked into her sister's eyes. All these years, everything that Kate had become, had been because of Mandy. To provide for her, to take care of her.

A lifetime together connected them. And Kate was grateful for the time she'd had with her sister. But she saw it in Mandy's eyes, and they both knew, they'd outgrown each other. It was time for Kate to move on—but also for Mandy.

"I'll miss you, Kate," Mandy said, smiling through tears.

Jax hugged her. "And I'll miss you, Aunt Kate."

Kate's eyes burned from tears. "Me, too."

She hugged Jax back and kissed his head, inhaling the familiar homey scent of him.

"Where will you go?" Mandy wiped her eyes.

Kate wanted to say she'd go back to Ian. But Ian didn't want her. Her stomach sank at the thought, every cell of her body hurting. She shook her head. She needed to learn to live without him. A new life where she'd be independent and could finally realize her dream of creating the restaurant she wanted. A weird one. A mix. That was what she'd always imagined New York must be—a mix of everything. Surely, she'd find her customers there.

"New York," she said.

But her heart whispered that she may realize her dream in New York, but she'd never be truly happy or complete without the red-haired Highlander. The Highlander who was kinder and more powerful than anyone she knew—in this time or in the past.

The Highlander who could never love her back.

CHAPTER 32

"Nae, cousin, ye didna die."

The voice penetrated Ian's consciousness, strangely distant, as if echoing in a deep chamber. The voice sounded familiar, and Ian made an effort to open his eyes.

His eyelids felt as though they were made of iron, his body heavy and wet. At least he hadn't burned to death in that hell of high fever he'd inhabited for what felt like his whole life.

"I didna die?" Ian croaked.

He finally managed to open one eye. Owen sat by his side, his face dark against the gray sunlight filtering through the window behind him.

"Ye're alive, although ye do look like a corpse."

"Did I ask if I died?"

"Aye."

"Oh." Ian smacked his dry lips. "I hoped I were dead."

He'd hoped the misery of existence without Kate would end.

Owen brought a cup to Ian's face and held his head. Ian drank the cool water, which felt like life being poured back into him.

"Why are ye here?" Ian asked when Owen put the cup away. "Not that I'm nae glad to see ye."

"Ye've been lying in fever for days, delirious, calling fer Kate."

Her name brought a heavy weight to Ian's chest. Anguish stiffened him like a muscle cramp, painful and powerful. But there was no muscle he could move to make the ache go away. What was he going to do without her? He'd had a purpose before, to protect her. To help her get back home.

Now all that was left was emptiness. The last place she'd ever touched him was here. She'd lain in the bed with him, worried for him and so bonnie it had pained him to look at her.

She'd said she'd stay for him...

"She's gone now," Ian said. "So it doesna matter."

Owen narrowed his eyes. "Cousin. I recognize the look. I saw it on Craig when Amy was gone."

Ah, Craig's new wife. The woman who'd made Craig deliriously happy. "'Tis different."

Ian shifted to sit up, but his head spun. His wounds ached. The one on his thigh pained him the most. The ones on his chest and his arm ached and scratched—signs of healing.

"What are ye doing here?" Ian repeated the question, attempting to distract Owen from speaking of Kate...and also to think of something besides the pain.

"I came to deliver a message to Kenneth MacKenzie from the Bruce, and they told me ye were gravely wounded. I couldna leave until I saw ye were getting better."

It felt better than Ian could admit that there was someone he knew, someone from his clan who was there for him. "Aye, thank ye, Owen. How is Bruce's campaign?"

"The east and most of the Highlands are ours. We're moving to put the decisive blow to the MacDougalls and fight the scattered English troops that are coming."

"Good. What of Dundail?"

"All fine. What are ye going to do now? Join Bruce?"

Ian closed his eyes for a moment. The truth was, he had no

idea what he'd do. He'd committed himself to a life of misery for being a killer, and now he had to go through with his punishment.

"I'll go home," he said. "Protect my lands. Continue training my people to protect themselves. They are nae warriors. And they need to be, especially these days."

"Aye," Owen said. "They do."

DAYS PASSED IN DARK, TORTUROUS WAITING. WAITING TO GET better. Waiting for the pain in his soul to subside. Waiting for his head to stop spinning around Kate.

He couldn't help wondering if she was all right. If her inn worked like she wanted it to. Wishing she were here. Remembering her every word, every touch, every smile.

It must have taken him half the moon after Owen's visit to finally be able to rise and walk.

He went to the underground storeroom, the last place she'd been in his world. He searched for her presence, and thought he could smell her scent—although he knew it was impossible. He found the rock. It was just like Kate had described, the handprint and the carving right there. And next to it, the headscarf she'd worn when she'd cooked. He took it in his hands and studied it. There was a thin golden hair that glowed silver in the light of his torch. Ian stroked the strand of hair, then buried his face in the scarf, sucking in the scent of her that still remained. His whole being expanded, and everything brightened up around him.

He'd never see her again. What a fool he'd been to chase away the one thing in his life that made him feel whole. He wrapped the scarf around his wrist and tied it. He'd keep it with him always as a reminder of the woman who'd loved him without conditions.

In two sennights, he went home to Dundail. On the way, he

saw her ghost in the woods. A flicker of blond hair from behind a tree. Heard her voice calling for him. He knew he was wishing for her to be back—there were no ghosts, and she wasn't here. But even thinking of her like that brought him some small satisfaction, some sort of relief from the agonizing black hole that had taken the place of his heart.

When he arrived home, Cadha met him with an angry cackle, berating him for almost dying for the second time. Without hesitation, and without listening to him, she sent him straight up to his bedchamber. She made a fire in the fireplace and told him she'd bring him bread and cheese, and that Manning would make stew whether he wanted it or not.

Ian would normally object, but he was exhausted and still in pain and had no strength to argue with Cadha about unimportant things.

What was important was that Kate wasn't here. She'd have made a magical stew for him. Although, Manning's slop did taste better this time, surprisingly.

The next few days passed, similar to one another in their gray indifference. Under Cadha's strict supervision, Ian was regaining his health. He had created a training plan for his people, and when he felt well enough, called upon them to come and train in sword-fighting every day. He was still stiff and aching, but he made himself move and supervise the practice.

The tacksmen had come a few days after his arrival with more rent than Ian had thought he was entitled to—they had changed their ways and were no longer stealing from him. It seemed, his people were thankful for his protection and had united in spirit against the enemy.

It was a late August night, after the training, when Ian sat on the edge of the loch, mindlessly throwing pebbles into the deep waters. The loch was still, its surface a pink-and-violet reflection of the sky. Mountains on the other side were black against the sunset, looking like the backs of sleeping giants.

The English hadn't returned yet, and Ian had heard rumors

they'd been called back south by their king. But it didn't mean they wouldn't bother them again. It didn't mean the war was won.

"'Tis a lonely life," said a male voice behind him.

Ian looked over his shoulder. Manning stood there, wiping his hands on the clean apron that had become a habit for him.

"I ken what a lonely life is," he added.

Without an invitation, he sat on the shore next to Ian.

"Aye. I suppose a lonely life isna new to me, either," Ian said.

"Yer father was so lonely without yer mother. He was a different man before he lost her."

"Then 'tis in the family."

They kept silent for a moment.

"Ye're just like him now," Manning said. "After the lass left. After ye came back alone. Lifeless. Like ye lost yer heart somewhere."

Strangely, Manning had described precisely how it felt to Ian.

"'Tis what I deserve," Ian said.

A weak breeze ruffled the almost still surface of the loch, bringing the scent of fresh water and fish. Crickets chirped, unaware of the human misery. Manning's wrinkled face smoothed.

"'Tis a pile of horse shite if I ever heard one."

Ian chuckled. He'd heard Manning swear countless times, but never had his words been supportive.

Manning spat on the ground between his bent knees. "Ye dinna deserve anything like that. 'Tis enough of suffering for this family."

The old man sighed and shook his head.

"I've been in service to the Cambels my whole life. I havna marrit because of it—nae that I regret it, mind ye. I saw yer father as a lad, and then in his best years, and I saw him happy. But when God took yer mother, his misery began. Ye dinna ken yer father in his full strength and potential. But I kent him, and I ken ye."

He paused as his voice broke, and he chewed on something. His eyes reddened and watered.

"And it isna worth it, lad," his voice shook. "It isna worth it. Before ye ken it, ye're as old as I am and stink like a fart. And all ye have is yer past. And if 'tis full of misery and loneliness and regret...ye realize nothin' is worth it."

He met Ian's eyes, and Ian held his breath at the amount of pain in Manning's gaze.

"I canna do anything about it now," Manning said. "Yer father couldna do anything about yer mother in his time. But ye can do something."

Ian studied Manning, speechless. Was he going mad, or was there truth in Manning's words?

"But 'tis different for me, Manning. I let her go because I canna make her happy."

"Why nae?"

"Because I'm broken. Some wounds are too deep and never heal."

"Aye. I ken. And some people want ye nae matter what. Wounds, cracks, scars, and all."

Ian shook his head. "Nae. I canna make her happy. I dinna deserve her."

"Ye shouldna decide it for her, dinna ye think?"

Ian stiffened. Manning was right. Ian was deciding for Kate. Just like his masters in Baghdad had decided for him: who he killed; what he ate; when he went to piss. He was taking away Kate's freedom to choose because he was convinced he would never be whole. But what if he didn't need to be whole? Kate wasn't entirely happy with herself, either, yet Ian loved her more than anything in this world.

What if he'd been terribly, terribly wrong? What if God had forgiven him for all the murders he'd done? What if his way to redemption was protecting his people, which he had done and continued to do?

The dreadful feeling that he'd done something irreversibly wrong bit into him.

"Nae, I shouldna decide for her," Ian said. "But I did."

How would his life be, had he let her stay? She'd cook him dinner. He'd get fat from all the delicious food. He'd make love to her every day until she forgot who she was from sheer bliss. He'd marry her—make her his and make honoring and protecting her his life's mission.

Mayhap, that would be the best redemption for his sins that he could wish for. Making the best woman he'd ever known deliriously happy. Giving her children. Giving her her heart's desires.

Ian's eyes watered, and he pressed a thumb and index finger against his eyes to stop tears from spilling.

What had he done? Chased Kate away when she'd wanted to stay with him. When she'd said she loved him. When the happiness of a lifetime had been within his grasp and he'd just had to reach out and take it.

"I didna like the lass because she came so righteous into my kitchen," Manning said, "but I do see what she meant about cleanliness. The food tastes better, and I am nae sick as often as before. She's good for ye, Ian. Find her. Ask her to come back."

Ian nodded. "I would. But I canna. She went home. And ye ken she's from far away."

Manning hung his head. "Aye, 'tis bad, Ian. Mayhap she'll come back?"

Ian shook his head. "I'm afraid 'tis too late. After what I've said to her, she's never going to come back. So mayhap I did get my punishment from God after all. Life without the love of my life."

CHAPTER 33

New York State, late August 2020

KATE STRAIGHTENED THE GRAY MEDIEVAL DRESS SHE HAD FROM 1308 with trembling fingers. It had been so hard to put it on in the first place when she wouldn't be wearing it to go back in time to Ian. She glanced at the gatehouse of the Renaissance fair. People dressed in bright medieval costumes and in regular modern clothes entered and exited the gates, faces relaxed, cheerful.

They enjoyed pretending they were in medieval times. If she told them she'd really made the trip, would they believe her? Would they be envious? Or call 911 to commit her to a psychiatric unit?

It had been about a month since Kate had moved to New York City and worked on opening a new restaurant. This one would be medieval with a modern touch. Inspired by her experience, she wanted to bring the historic and the modern together in a mix that would be beautiful and unforgettable.

Like her and Ian. Yes, that was what the restaurant represented to her. Her and Ian. The strange mix between times that had changed her whole life.

How was Ian? She thought about him every single day, hoping, praying he was okay and alive in his own time, and that he had survived those wounds.

She couldn't be with Ian physically, but at least by cooking and working in her restaurant, she'd feel closer to him. Be able to think of him, pretend that she was cooking for him. Imagine his awestruck expression as he devoured her food.

Kate walked to the gates, checked in, and stepped into the fair. White German houses with dark-brown timber framing lined the main street. There was an inn, an apothecary, a "drinking house," a tailor, and a shoemaker. All that looked more like a fairy tale than what Kate had seen in medieval Scotland, with its low, gray stone buildings and thatched roofs.

Nevertheless, her heart thumped in her chest. Behind every corner, she was looking for Ian's tall, mighty frame, for the fire of his red hair, and her heart froze when she didn't see him.

Why was she even here?

She'd told herself it was to get inspiration for the menu and for the restaurant, but now, having come here, she wasn't sure if this modern representation would do anything but remind her of her heartbreak.

The truth was, she wanted to feel closer to Ian. She missed him so much it was hard to breathe. Her new life in the Bronx, the small apartment she shared with three roommates, her search for a place to rent and preparation of a business plan to show potential investors—all that distracted her for a short while from thinking of him. But eventually she'd have a second to herself, and her mind would flip to Ian.

Kate walked past the main street and into a market with different stalls and booths. People wandered around, drank, ate, and looked at belts, beaded necklaces, silver jewelry, dresses, tunics, knives, swords, and spices. The scent here was divine—freshly grilled meat that had been marinated in vinegar, baked goods, along with beer and wine, which were sold from giant barrels, much like the ones she'd seen in Manning's kitchen.

The thought made anguish rise in her like heartburn.

Even in this fake medieval world, she felt more at home than in New York. She didn't miss just Ian. She missed the sight of the loch and the mountains. The scent of a freshly baked bread in the open fire. The comforting feeling of honest work in the kitchen, where everything was done by hand not machines, and food was grown on the land, not bought in plastic packages from a supermarket.

Farther along, two small towers stood, not taller than two floors, and probably made of foam plastic. Kate thought of Inverlochy, its massive, impenetrable towers and walls, and chuckled to herself. There surely weren't any Pictish time traveling rocks underneath the foundation of *that* castle.

But if there were, would she go?

Just as she thought that, her eyes fell on the tall broad-shouldered figure of a man with short red hair, dressed in a tunic and the *leine croich*, the heavy quilted coat Ian wore instead of armor. He stood half turned, with his back to her, fiddling with a knife in his hands. There was a claymore in the sheath at his waist.

Kate's knees shook violently, and she locked them, but they only trembled harder. Her breath rushed in and out as though she were having an asthma attack. She walked on weak legs towards him.

She stood right next to him, still unable to see his face.

"Ian?" she said.

The man turned.

Blue eyes. Not brown.

The nose short, and he was much younger, his face rounded without Ian's strong cheekbones.

Her heart sank. Her eyes prickled from tears, and her throat convulsed in an attempt to stop them.

"I could be, my fair lady," the man said with a crooked smile. "If you give me a kiss."

He was American. No deep Scottish burr.

"Sorry." She shook her head and walked away from him.

"Your loss," he murmured in return.

Oh, how she missed Ian. Silly her, thinking he might find her here, at a Renaissance fair. Despite none of this being authentic, it had been the closest she'd felt to him since she'd left. And that alone made her want to check into the inn and live here permanently.

Her life was empty without him. All her attempts to re-create the connection she'd had with him were just that, attempts.

She'd never live a full life without love. Without happiness. Even that doppelgänger she'd met just now, had been merely a shadow of Ian—a shadow that had made her shake and tremble and almost have a heart attack.

Would she even be able to be happy *with* Ian given her issues, given that her whole life she'd been looking for ways to make herself worthy? But that wasn't what she'd been doing with him. And it wasn't what she'd been doing in New York.

She wasn't looking for external approval through her restaurant. Not even from her new friends and colleagues.

No.

She was going her own way. She had her own idea and New York City was a great environment to realize it, without begging for anyone to accept her for who she was.

The feeling was new, and yet familiar. It was how Ian had made her feel. That she was okay the way she was.

She just hadn't realized it. Now she knew she deserved to be loved and appreciated.

Kate turned and walked towards the castle, then stopped to look at a jewelry booth. A woman in a dark-green hooded cloak stood there, studying a beaded necklace in her hands. Kate couldn't see her face, but she looked familiar. Curly dark-red hair was visible from under her hood.

She looked like...

The woman looked up.

"Sìneag," Kate breathed.

Sìneag beamed. "Kate! I was hoping to find ye here."

Kate went to Sìneag and pulled her a little away from the fuss around the tent.

"What are you doing here?" Kate asked.

"I came to see how ye're doing."

"But how did you know where to find me?"

"Oh, lass." Sìneag giggled. "I ken many more things than ye think. Ye dinna think I'm just a woman, do ye?"

Kate narrowed her eyes. Had she heard the woman right? *Not just a woman?* "What do you mean?"

"Ah." Sìneag sighed. "Ye mortals. Always so skeptical. Dinna fash yerself, lass. I came to help. Ye walk around like a dead kelpie. Yer eyes are empty. Yer stride has nae lively spring. Do ye nae think 'tis enough that ye torture yerself and Ian?"

She tortured Ian? She'd wanted to stay with him. He was the one who'd told her to leave. But before she got angry, she needed to know if Ian had survived his wounds.

"Have you seen him? Is he okay? He was so badly wounded when I left."

"Aye, if ye can call that alive. He walks around in even worse shape than ye."

Kate swallowed. "What does that mean?"

"It means, he misses ye."

Kate's stomach squeezed and filled with hummingbirds.

"Did he change his mind?"

"What if he didna?"

Kate inhaled deeply, then let out a slow breath.

"I know he loves me. He has shown it to me many times. Because he loves me, he tried to protect me and send me away. He didn't think his love was good enough for me. But what he doesn't understand is that he's actually the only one who can make me happy."

A decision cemented in Kate's mind. It felt so right, like the final piece of a jigsaw puzzle settling into place.

"I want to go back," she said. "I need to see him and open his eyes. I'll make him see. I felt so much more at home back there."

"What about yer restaurant?" Sineag asked, her eyes shining slyly.

"Deli Luck is doing great. My sister does a fantastic job. And the new restaurant I had this idea for... Well, the only reason I wanted to open it is because it would make me feel closer to Ian. And what is closer to Ian than being right next to him?"

Sineag smiled, satisfied. "I do love it when you mortals come to yer senses!"

"So, how do I go back?"

"Ye ken the way, lass."

Kate hugged Sineag, her heart beating violently. She'd been wanting to go back this whole time, and now she realized she could. Her place was there. She'd see Ian very soon. She just needed to make some arrangements, give notice at the apartment, and go see Mandy and Jax to say goodbye.

Then she'd change her life forever for the second time. And go live her happily ever after with the Highlander who'd stolen her heart.

CHAPTER 34

D undail, September 1308

"DINNA JUMP BACK, FRANGEAN," IAN CRIED. "JUST STEP ASIDE and slash him from the left."

Frangean glanced back at Ian and nodded, then resumed slamming his sword against that of his combat partner.

The courtyard before Dundail was full of shouts, knocks of wood against wood, and the ringing of metal against metal. Recent rain had turned the ground into mud, and men moved their feet with difficulty, sometimes slipping and falling, but continuing to practice. It was good to train in different conditions—just like battles in real life, you never knew what the weather would be.

Ian leaned forward and rubbed his stiff, aching leg. He wasn't sure if he'd ever regain full control of the limb, but he wasn't sorry for it verra much. He'd give his leg for the chance to change the past and make Kate stay instead of chasing her away.

The training went well, and he could see the men and the boys had made significant progress since the battle for MacFilib's farm. The farm had burned to the ground, but Frangean, who was the only heir, was more interested in being a warrior than a farmer.

Ian wished the lad had chosen farming.

Still. Someone had to protect the land and the people. Such were the times.

He hoped Kate was living happily in more peaceful times. He was at more peace, as well. At least, he'd had no more nightmares of Baghdad or the ship. Not a single one. But the hunger for her presence was eating him alive. He dreamed of *her* every night. Her whispering "I love you." Her warm, soft, silky body trembling from desire and pleasure in his arms. The taste of her, the smell that drove him wild lingered in his mind long after he woke up.

He couldn't take it. Despite his wounds, he needed the relief.

The air was chilly, but he removed his tunic, letting the crisp air cool down his skin.

"Who wants the best damn practice of yer life?" Ian roared.

Men stopped fighting and looked at him.

"Three against one, who's in?" Ian continued.

Mayhap, he was a savage after all, because this brought him relief, throwing all that tension, all that misery into a direction that would be useful. Three men stepped forward, including Frangean.

"Arrrgh!" the lad cried and launched at Ian with his claymore raised high above his head.

The other two followed, and Ian took his position. Their swords at the ready, they attacked. Ian deflected them, spun, whirled, ducked. He breathed through the pain that was tearing his chest and leg apart.

Damnation. He was slower, much slower than he used to be. But he'd already fought through the wounds many times, and he knew how to spare his strength and use his body economically.

"Stop this at once!" a woman cried.

The voice was so painfully familiar it brought the immediate image of the bonnie blonde he was breathing for.

The men froze and Ian stopped as well. Panting, he turned around and almost dropped his sword.

It was *her*.

She stood by the Dundail house in a warm woolen cloak with a hood on. A big, full bag lay by her feet. Her golden hair shone under the hood. She looked thinner but just as bonnie, her blue eyes shining with anger.

Ian's heart must have stopped. He must have ceased to exist for a split moment. The ground shifted under his feet, and he stopped feeling his body.

"Kate..." he said, and it came out like a whisper, like a secret prayer.

She walked to him with broad, angry strides and stopped in front of him.

"What are you doing, Ian? Are you insane? First of all, you're clearly still recovering from your wounds." She pointed at the ugly red scar on his chest. "Second of all, it's September, for God's sake! And you're shirtless. Do you want to die of pneumonia, too? I just came back. I won't let you die on me."

She left his proximity, to Ian's disappointment, walked to where his tunic was lying forgotten in the mud, picked it up, and came back to him. She shoved it into his hands. Speechless, he put the tunic back on.

"Did ye come to berate me?" he rasped. "Had I kent 'twas how to summon ye, I'd have walked shirtless every day since ye left."

She smiled. A small, bonnie smile that she hid by pursing her lips.

"You were the one who told me to go," she said.

"Dinna listen to me. I was a fool."

She crossed her arms over her chest. "We can agree on that."

Her hand went under the cloak and produced a square sheet

of paper. On it was some sort of a drawing. Something square with letters and numbers.

"Will you build me a stove?" Kate asked.

Ian took the sheet and studied it. It was a rectangular construction of stone with an opening for a fire like in the bread oven, but flat on top and with two round plates on the surface. There was also a tube, probably for venting out the smoke.

"Whatever it is, I'll build it for ye. I'll build ye a castle if ye stay," Ian said.

"I don't need a castle. All I need is you. And a better kitchen."

She stared at him with her bottomless, sparkling eyes, and he couldn't believe his ears and eyes.

"Lord," Frangean said, "'tis where ye kiss the lass."

Kate arched one brow. Ian wrapped his arms around her, so precious and smelling like something sweet and delicious that he wanted to devour in one bite.

"I didna think I'd ever see ye again, lass," he said.

"I didn't think I'd see you, either. But here I am. And whatever you think, you can make me happy. You have enough to give. And even if you're broken, I don't need you any other way. I love you, Ian Cambel."

Something warmed and came together in his chest, and wholeness enveloped him like a soft blanket.

"I love you more than life itself, Katie. I'll spend the rest of my life cherishing you, loving you, worshiping you, and making you the happiest woman alive."

"There's one thing you can do towards that right now," she said.

"What?"

"Kiss me."

And with the broadest smile his face had ever held, he lowered his head and covered her mouth with his. As his lips brushed against hers, as his tongue met hers, fire seethed through him, melting and dissolving his latest doubts, concerns, and broken parts. Because the love of his life was in his arms, and she wanted him.

And his heart was finally whole.

EPILOGUE

D undail, October 1308

IAN TAPPED HIS FOOT AGAINST THE GROUND. HE STOOD BY the entrance to the small wooden church at Benlochy village, his heart tapping even faster than his foot.

Craig, whom Ian had asked to be his best man, stood by his side, one hand on his sword—although Ian was sure no one would disrupt the ceremony. But tradition dictated that he had a best man, meaning the best swordsman, to protect the bride and the groom.

Ian would rather die than let anything happen to Kate.

He might die soon anyway, his heart on the verge of bursting from anticipation, if she didn't appear in the next moment.

Their guests, including the whole Cambel clan, waited before the church. His uncles Neil and Dougal, Craig's wife, Amy, with a round belly, Ian's cousin Domhnall and his wife. Marjorie, Ian's cousin and Craig's sister, was on her own adventure and unable to make it to the wedding. Owen was in Inverlochy, waiting for someone important to come back, as Craig had told Ian. Owen had said that even an earthquake wouldn't make him leave the castle. Ian wondered if he'd waited for a time traveler, too. Verra few knew about the time travel. It was like a clan secret, and those who knew guarded it with their lives.

Finally, Kate appeared in a sky-blue gown of delicate wool that flowed over her curves like water. Her hair was braided into a crown around her head, with some locks descending over her shoulders to lie on her chest. Her cheeks were rosy from the cold, or mayhap from the same anticipation that trembled in his own breast. Her blue eyes shone bright as she walked. Their eyes locked, and Ian couldn't breathe. She was so lovely.

Manning accompanied Kate, his chest puffed up, his chin sticking out proudly.

Then she stood before Ian, and he had to stop himself from reaching out, enveloping her in his arms and kissing her until she softened.

The priest coughed.

"Dearly beloved," he said. "We're gathered here to join Ian Cambel and Kate Anderson in holy matrimony. Does anyone know of any reason why these two canna be together?"

Ian and Kate exchanged a glance, and Kate giggled. Ian couldn't have cared less if anyone minded him marrying Kate, but the questions were part of the church wedding ceremony that needed to be cleared before they could be marrit.

When no one said anything, the priest continued. "Are those to be wedded of age?"

"Aye," Ian said.

"Yes," Kate echoed.

In fact, they both were probably the oldest couple the priest would ever wed. Most marriages took place before the bride and groom were nineteen years old.

"As neither of ye have living parents, the parental consent isna necessary," the priest said. "Are ye nae related?"

"Nae," Ian said.

"Definitely not," Kate said.

"Aye, good. Now ye may exchange the vows."

Ian's whole body tingled as he took out the silver ring he'd ordered the day after Kate came back. His name and hers were engraved on it. His fingers shook a little as he took Kate's hand in his, the ring in front of her finger. Her hand was cool and soft, and it shook, too. She smiled at him, and everything else melted away. Just him and her.

Then the words came easily.

"I vow to lay down my life for ye, Kate. I vow to nae let a single day pass when ye dinna have the brightest smile on yer face. I vow to give ye the best kitchen ye've dreamed of nae matter how interesting yer cooking creations. Yer name shall be the only one I cry out at night, and yer eyes will be the only ones I see each morning. I vow to be yer shield and yer sword. My heart shall beat for ye until my last breath."

Her eyes watered and she smiled, and Ian swallowed a knot of emotion himself. Gently, he put the ring on her finger, and her smile bloomed, threatening to cut her face in two.

"Now yer turn, lass," the priest said.

Kate took out the ring, a simple golden band Ian assumed she had brought with her from the future. As she held it in her hand, he saw the engraving: "My heart, your heart." The words brought a surge of emotion to his chest. He felt as if physical ties extended to Kate through his hands, their bond even stronger than before.

"I vow to be your wife in every sense of the word. I vow to give you the first bite of my bread and the first sip of my wine. I vow to cherish you and spoil you every day with my cooking. And I vow to love you as long as my heart beats."

Her vows made a wave of happiness swell in him, like fresh Highlands air after the heat of a desert. Hearing her say those words out loud released the last of his doubts about his worthiness. If God had given him this woman, God must have forgiven him. Abaeze must have forgiven him.

So Ian would forgive himself.

Forgiveness and acceptance flooded his body, warm and soothing, releasing and unfolding the last of his tension and pain.

"Before God, ye are now wedded as husband and wife," the priest announced. "Ye may now kiss the bride."

Ian didn't hesitate. He pulled Kate close and took her into his arms. Then he planted the kiss he'd wanted to give her for a while. She was his, aye, had been ever since he'd first laid eyes on her. But now she was his before God, and no one could dare to say otherwise.

It was their first kiss as husband and wife.

The first kiss of them bound together.

He kissed her gently, but with the power of all the love that he had for her. Her lips opened to him like the petals of a rose in spring—soft, and warm, and tender. His tongue stroked hers, licked it, promising what he'd do to her next, to consummate the marriage. She exhaled a moan, audible only to him, and set his blood on fire with just that.

A cough brought Ian back to reality. He stopped and glanced at the priest who looked at him with reproach.

"Now I invite everyone into the church to bless the union with the sermon and the prayers," the priest said.

Their crowd of guests erupted in a cheer, and they followed the priest inside the church. During the sermon, Ian welcomed it as an opportunity to ask God personally to bless him and Kate.

After the sermon, they all went back to Dundail. The guests went in first, ceremoniously. When everyone was inside, Ian squeezed his wife's hand and they entered the great hall. Cheers and hoots burst from the small crowd of a hundred or so, and coins were thrown at them as a symbol of wealth and prosperity.

Kate and he stopped before their guests, and Ian's heart filled with warmth at the sight of his clan. They gave way to Kate and Ian, and he walked with his wife through the crowd to the table of honor.

"I must be the happiest man in the world," Ian said to Kate.

"Not as happy as I am," Kate said, leaning her head on his shoulder.

Amy Cambel came up to them, and Kate beamed, and the two women turned around and talked in English. Ian marveled at the two of them, from the future, who had both come to the past to find the happiness of their lifetime.

When Amy returned to her seat, Kate turned to Ian, giddy with excitement. "She's *really* from my country, my time. I just found a new friend," she said joyfully. "Such a wonderful woman."

"Nae as wonderful as ye are."

The servants Ian had hired for the feast brought in the dishes. Ian had to hire more cooks, too, to help Kate. But she was still in charge of the kitchen together with Manning. The Crazy Mary was brought in, emitting all kinds of delicious aromas, as well as roasted fish, game, venison, and pork. Bread and cooked vegetables were brought in, as well as more wine, ale, and uisge.

A minstrel started a Gaelic ballad, and the atmosphere grew even more cheerful. Ian had asked Manning to find the Cambel banners, and Cadha had cleaned them with pleasure. Now they hung on the walls of the great hall, just as Ian remembered from his father's early days.

Ian didn't think he'd ever been as happy as he was now.

"You're smiling," Kate whispered. "You haven't stopped smiling."

"Aye, since I saw ye by the church."

"I love it when you smile."

"'Tis because ye filled my heart. Ye mended all the cracks and found the broken pieces. Yer love healed me."

"And your love healed me."

"Do ye ken what I'd like to do now that my heart is healed?"

"What?"

"Consummate the marriage. And see if that fertility custom of holding a bairn has any powers."

Kate giggled, her cheeks blushing.

"But we have all these guests."

Ian stood up and raised his glass. "Good men and women," he announced. "'Tis customary that the marriage doesna have powers until 'tis consummated. Do ye, good people, mind if my bride and I retreat for that purpose?"

The hall erupted in cheers of approval and wolf howls. Men and women beat against the tables with their fists.

"See," he said. "The guests dinna mind."

He offered his hand to Kate and she placed her palm into his.

"Come, Katie" he said. "I canna wait to make ye my wife—as ye said, in all senses of the word."

She followed him, Ian's cock hardening in anticipation of giving her the pleasure she deserved.

But as the door of his bedchamber closed and he began undressing, the part of his body that swelled the most was his heart.

THANK YOU FOR READING HIGHLANDER'S HEART. I hope you loved Kate and Ian's story. Find out what happens next when Ian's brother Owen meets his soulmate from the future, Amber, in HIGHLANDER'S LOVE.

SHE'S ON THE RUN. HE'S DIGGING IN. WHEN THEIR DESTINIES collide in medieval Scotland, will they forge a love for the ages?

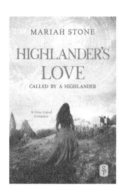

. . .

READ HIGHLANDER'S LOVE NOW >

⭐⭐⭐⭐⭐ *"A heart-stopping story that is filled with lots of twists and turns, and characters that come off the pages to pull you into their tale. I like it so much that I am forcing myself to put the book aside from time to time so that it lasts longer. lol!"*

SIGN-UP FOR MARIAH STONE'S NEWSLETTER:
http://mariahstone.com/signup

FANCY A VIKING?

And other mysterious matchmakers are sending modern-day people to the past too, also to the Viking Age. If you haven't read Holly and Einar's story yet, be sure to pick up VIKING'S DESIRE.

A captive time traveler. A Viking jarl on a mission. Will marriage be the price of her freedom?

READ VIKING'S DESIRE NOW >

⭐⭐⭐⭐⭐ *"Fabulous! What a great way to start a new series!"*

. . .

Or stay in the Highlands and keep reading for an excerpt from HIGHLANDER'S LOVE.

Mallyne Farm near Inverlochy village, 2020

Amber heard steps outside the front door and raised her head.

"Amber Ryan, stop worrying." Her aunt shook her head and took a sip of her coffee. "It's only Rob. He went to feed the cows."

Amber sighed and poked her porridge with a spoon. She'd been here for a week. She should've gotten used to Rob, Aunt Christel's son, feeding the cows and sheep first thing in the morning. And she should've started liking porridge. Where was a peanut butter and jelly sandwich when she needed it?

At least her aunt had good coffee. Her mug sat on the check-ered tablecloth steaming with a comforting aroma. The rustic kitchen was bathed in sunlight, but it was still cool, even in summer. Old Scottish farmhouses were probably never warm.

Or maybe Amber was just too used to the summer heat in Afghanistan. The thought sent a shiver through her, and she glanced at the door again. She was safe for now. No one was coming for her.

Yet.

"I should leave you guys soon," Amber said. "I need to keep moving. Sooner or later, the police or someone will come here with questions."

"Aye. Well"—Aunt Christel shook her curly red hair—"you know that neither Rob nor I will say a word."

Amber reached out and squeezed her hand. "Thank you, it means so much that you believe me."

Aunt Christel squeezed her hand back. "I knew your father,

lass. He was my cousin, and I spent every summer with him for eighteen years. And I know he didn't raise a murderer. People easily use a gentle soul like you. So, aye, I believe you were set up."

Amber released a shaky breath. It felt good to know that even though the government thought she was a murderer, she had people in her life who were on her side. Unfortunately, that wouldn't keep her from a death sentence or life in prison.

Aunt Christel took another sip and studied Amber with her soft brown eyes. "But, sweetheart, you're not a coward. You can't live on the run your whole life. What's the point? You can't have any friends. Can't marry. Can't have children. Always looking over your shoulder, seeing shadows."

Amber fingered a white porcelain flower at the base of the cup handle. She knew her aunt was right. Amber had joined the army because she wanted to see the world, fight for her country, and protect innocent people from terrorists.

She wasn't the type to cower from a fight, so why was she behaving like a coward now? Growing up, she hadn't been afraid to take the blame for her three older brothers' small sins, such as broken vases or scratches on the car. That had been her way of protecting them. But instead of appreciating her sacrifice, they'd treated her like a doormat.

"I know, Aunt Christel, you're right. My mom raised me to be a good girl. To go to church. To live an honest life. Dad is probably turning in his grave watching me hide like this and not seek justice. Everything inside is screaming at me to stand up and fight and prove I didn't commit that murder."

"Aye. So why don't you?"

Amber brought the cup to her mouth with a shaking hand, coffee threatening to spill on the tablecloth. She took a sip, her favorite drink tasteless against her tongue.

"I'd be a naive little girl if I trusted the system. Major Jackson is using me as a scapegoat. He managed to smuggle drugs from Afghanistan to America for years. So imagine how many people in the military he must have in his pocket. And now that he murdered a US officer, he'll be even more ruthless." She shook her head. "No. I cannot take him on alone."

"Perhaps nae. But why don't you ask your brothers to help? Jonathan was in the military, too. He knows people, doesn't he?"

"Right." Amber snorted. "Jonathan doesn't want anything to do with me. He sold our house after Dad died, and everyone lives their own lives."

Amber had still been a teenager when their mom had died, and the family had started to fall apart. After their dad's death two years ago, they'd stopped meeting for Thanksgiving and Christmas. Kyle was a kick-ass lawyer in New York. Daniel was in San Francisco last time Amber had heard, still trying to sell his sculptures.

"But still," Aunt Christel said, "if you ask for help... Kin is kin."

"Maybe that's how it is in Scotland. And I can't thank you enough for helping me. But if I went to Jonathan for help, he'd be the first to rat me out to the authorities."

Aunt Christel covered Amber's hand with her own, and Amber squeezed it back, her caramel skin looking even darker compared to her aunt's pasty complexion.

"Surely, nae, dear?" Aunt Christel said.

Amber sighed. "He wouldn't risk his ass for me. He has the right connections in the military, I'm sure, but he also has two kids and a wife and a beautiful house."

"But—"

"Police! Police!" Rob cried.

Everything moved in slow motion. There was the distant rustle of car tires. The front door swung wide, and Rob stood in the doorway, his silhouette black against the sun. "Police!" he shouted.

Amber jumped to her feet, jostling the table, and the coffee mugs and porridge flew off from the impact.

Aunt Christel cried, "Back door!"

Amber ran, her feet heavy, as though she were moving through a swamp. It was like she was trapped in one of those nightmares where she couldn't get away from a killer.

The hallway flashed by, and she reached the old door. Unlocked, thank God! She raced out past the barn, into a field of oats. Her ragged breathing was louder than anything in her ears. Where was she running? Where should she go?

Away. She'd hide and wait nearby for a while and then come back to Aunt Christel's to get her things. Then she'd leave. Go to the woods. Somewhere. Anywhere.

She wouldn't be punished for something she hadn't done.

Behind her, cars revved. She glanced back. They were coming right through the field after her. Amber gasped, adrenaline spiking.

Before her was a grove of trees. They wouldn't be able to get through in their vehicles. She sped up. Thank God she jogged every day and did combat training. She still wouldn't be able to win a footrace against cars.

She flew into the grove. It took her eyes a moment to adjust to the shade of the trees after being in the sunny field. She ran through the trees for a while before she had to stop and catch her breath, her lungs desperately expanding to get more air. She looked around. Thirty feet or so in front of her, an asphalt road ran from left to right, and across it, in the distance, stood a castle. Right, the ruined castle her aunt had told her about. Behind it was River Lochy.

The cars chasing her turned. They'd need to take quite a detour to get on the road.

She ran again, across the empty road, then down the ditch on its other side, almost twisting her ankle.

She made it past the trees and the bushes to a crumbling wall of the castle. The wall extended between two round towers. There was an arched gate in the middle, and through the courtyard was another small gate. If she could just get there, maybe she could hide in the bushes beyond it or swim across the river. Although it was very broad, she was a good swimmer...

She ran inside the square courtyard. On every corner was a round tower. A red-haired woman stood in the middle, and the scent of lavender and freshly cut grass hit Amber. The woman wore a long green cloak and a dark-green medieval-looking dress.

"Here, lass," he said and the woman gestured towards the entrance at one of the towers. "They'll have a hard time finding ye here."

Amber stopped and bent forward. She put her hands on her knees and panted. Her lungs ached and burned, and a piercing pain pulsated in her side.

"Who are you?" she asked.

"I'm Sìneag. I ken ye're in trouble. Trust me. Ye dinna have much time. They're coming."

Tires screeched against the asphalt. Voices.

"Arghhh!" Amber cried in desperation.

Her pulse thumped. She must be insane to trust a stranger, but there was no way she'd make it to the river in time. They could easily catch up to her on the other side anyway. "Come on! Show me."

Sìneag nodded and ran first. They raced through a doorway and into the tomb-like darkness of the tower. Sìneag went quickly down the crumbling stairs into complete blackness. Amber clutched at the wall, barely seeing anything. Rocks rolled from under her feet. Her shoes slipped, and she almost fell. Finally, she slid to a stop when the stairs reached the uneven ground. When her eyes adjusted to the darkness, she saw Sìneag's shape standing there, waiting for her.

"Come, lass, a little farther," she said.

A heavy feeling settled in Amber's stomach. She felt like Little Red Riding Hood being called deeper into the woods by the wolf. She looked up. Somewhere up there, people were looking for her, people who wanted her to be punished for a crime she didn't commit. She supposed going farther under a ruined castle to save herself didn't sound like such a bad idea compared to being caught by them.

It got darker and darker. The scent of wet stone, earth, and mold got stronger. Water dripped somewhere.

Sìneag took Amber by the hand. The woman's palm was cool and soft. "Come here. I ken this place. We'll sit here and wait. Sooner or later, they'll be gone. Then ye go out. Aye?"

She tugged Amber a few steps to her left and down. Amber put out her hand and found a cold, rough stone wall. She slid her hand down as she sat on the ground. Her breath rushed in and out quickly, and she tried to slow it down.

"How do you know this place?" Amber whispered.

"Ah, I ken it well. Have been here many times. There's a rock that interests me."

Amber almost asked about the rock, but adrenaline was pumping through her blood. Any minute, they could find her. She listened for the sound of any steps or voices, but so far, everything was quiet.

"Why did you help me?" Amber asked softly. "How do you know I didn't escape from prison or haven't stolen something? Are you not wondering why the police are after me? Did you see in my eyes that I have a heart of gold or something?"

Sìneag chuckled. "Aye. Something like that. I supposed ye canna tell me what ye're really running from?"

Amber sighed. "It's best you don't know. You may be an accomplice by hiding a criminal."

"Oh, aye?" Sìneag sounded strangely excited.

"I'm not. But the government and the army think I am."

"Poor lass. I may have an escape for ye, somewhere yer government will never reach ye."

Amber grimaced, and she was glad that Sìneag couldn't see her. This was weird. Who was this woman, and why was she trying to save a complete stranger from the police?

"I'm sorry, Sìneag. I'm grateful for your help, but don't worry about me. I'll find a way."

Sìneag was quiet for a moment. "Ye will."

Amber didn't answer. The sound of dripping water echoed off the rocky walls, disturbing the silence of the underground area. Was this what it sounded like in a grave?

The good news was that she couldn't hear the police. They weren't looking for her in the ruins. Not yet.

"Do ye want to hear a story while we wait?" Sìneag asked.

A story? It was an odd thing to do while waiting to be captured by the police, but maybe it would keep Sìneag from asking any personal questions. And it might help Amber to distract herself.

"Yes, please," Amber said.

"Well, ye canna see it, but we're sitting right by that ancient rock I mentioned."

As she said that, something began glowing to Amber's left, and she jerked away.

Sìneag laughed. "Aye, that's it. Do ye see the carving glowing?"

Amber watched in disbelief as the glow grew brighter. It was a picture resembling a child's drawing—a circle made of three waves and a thick line. Next to the lines was a handprint etched right into the rock.

"What the hell is that?" Amber asked.

"Ye wilna believe me. None of ye mortals do at first. But 'tis ancient Pictish magic. It opens a tunnel through time."

Amber didn't know whether to laugh or run. "A what?"

"A tunnel through time. Those who go through the tunnel meet the person they're destined to be with."

The hell?

"And there's someone for ye, too, Amber."

Amber frowned. "How do you know my name?"

"If I told ye I'm a Highland faerie who loves matchmaking, even if the couple is separated by time, would ye believe me?"

This was sounding more and more ridiculous. "No."

She laughed. "'Tis what I thought. But there is a man ye're

destined to be happy with, and he lives more than seven hundred years in the past."

Feet pounded outside and neared the entrance. Cold crept down Amber's spine.

Sìneag turned to her and took her hands. With the glow from the rock, Amber could distinguish her face. Sìneag's eyes were wide and worried.

"Just remember, ye need to look for Owen Cambel."

Someone was coming down the stairs. A man swore, something heavy fell, and more f-bombs followed.

"Go through the tunnel, Amber," Sìneag insisted. "It's either that or prison."

Go through a tunnel in time to seven hundred years in the past?

A flashlight beam jumped across the wall.

"Don't move!" a man called. "Police!"

Amber's heart beat violently against her ribs.

"Put yer hand in the print, and think of Owen," Sìneag said.

A gun clicked. "I'm armed. Do not move."

I must be crazy.

But this was it. Either she would be taken now, or she could try this one last thing. It was completely loony, but what could it hurt? Maybe it would open a revolving door or lead into a secret room.

She turned and placed her palm in the handprint.

Owen, she thought, feeling foolish. *Owen.*

A vibration went through her, similar to the buzz of a hair clipper. Her hand fell through the rock as though it were empty air. Her body followed. She tumbled, headfirst, her body spinning. Her stomach flipped, bile rising. She waved her arms, trying to grab on to something.

She screamed as she fell into darkness.

And then it consumed her...

Keep reading HIGHLANDER'S LOVE.

GET A FREE MARIAH STONE BOOK!

Join Mariah's mailing list to be the first to know of new releases, free books, special prices, and other author giveaways.

freehistoricalromancebooks.com

SCOTTISH SLANG

aye – yes
> **bairn** - baby
> **bastart** - bastard
> **bonnie** - pretty, beautiful.
> **canna**- can not
> **couldna** – couldn't
> **didna**- didn't ("Ah didna do that!")
> **dinna**- don't ("Dinna do that!")
> **doesna** – doesn't
> **fash** - fuss, worry ("Dinna fash yerself.")
> **feck** - fuck
> **hasna** – has not
> **havna** - have not
> **hadna** – had not
> **innit?** - Isn't it?
> **isna**- Is not
> **ken** - to know
> **kent** - knew
> **lad** - boy
> **lass** - girl
> **marrit** – married

nae – no or not

shite - faeces

the morn - tomorrow

the morn's morn - tomorrow morning

uisge-beatha (uisge for short) – Scottish Gaelic for water or life / aquavitae, the distilled drink, predecessor of whiskey

verra – very

wasna - was not

wee - small

wilna - will not

wouldna - would not

ye - you

yer – your (also yerself)

ACKNOWLEDGMENTS

Highlander's Heart is the labor of love. I had the idea for Ian already while writing the Viking series but had to set it aside as there seemed to be no story for his character that would have fit well. The idea for amnesia for Kate seemed exciting in the beginning, but I discovered that it's not the easiest one to write well. Thank goodness for my editor **Laura Barth** who helped me made this story as amazing as I had envisioned it.

My proofreader, **Laura LaTulipe**, again did a fantastic and thorough job also with checking the timeline of the series which keeps getting more and more complex with each book.

My readers who make it possible for me to not live the life of a business consultant and spend my life in hotels and airports, but to do what I love and be with my family every day.

Thank you!

Mariah

ENJOY THE BOOK? YOU CAN MAKE A DIFFERENCE!

Please, leave your honest review for the book.
As much as I'd love to, I don't have financial capacity like New York publishers to run ads in the newspaper or put posters in subway.

But I have something much, much more powerful!

Committed and loyal readers

If you enjoyed the book, I'd be so grateful if you could spend five minutes leaving a review on the book's Amazon page.

Thank you very much!

NOTES

CHAPTER 19

1. Adapted from Alexander Carmichael, *Carmina Gadelica*, vol.1, 1900, https://sacred-texts.com/neu/celt/cg1/cg1052.htm

CHAPTER 27

1. Adapted from Alexander Carmichael, *Carmina Gadelica*, vol. 1. https://sacred-texts.com/neu/celt/cg1/cg1025.htm

ABOUT MARIAH STONE

Mariah Stone is a bestselling author of time travel romance novels, including her popular Called by a Highlander series and her hot Viking, Pirate, and Regency novels. With nearly one million books sold, Mariah writes about strong modern-day women falling in love with their soulmates across time. Her books are available worldwide in multiple languages in e-book, print, and audio.

Subscribe to Mariah's newsletter for a free time travel book today at mariahstone.com!

facebook.com/mariahstoneauthor

instagram.com/mariahstoneauthor

bookbub.com/authors/mariah-stone

pinterest.com/mariahstoneauthor

amazon.com/Mariah-Stone/e/B07JVW28PJ

Made in United States
Cleveland, OH
18 March 2025

15276217R00148